NEW VOICES IN
CHINESE SCIENCE FICTION

NEW VOICES IN

CHINESE
SCIENCE
FICTION

EDITED BY NEIL CLARKE,
XIA JIA, AND REGINA KANYU WANG

CLARKESWORLD BOOKS
An Imprint of Wyrm Publishing
clarkesworldbooks.com / wyrmpublishing.com

Published in cooperation with Storycom.

ISBN: 978-1-64236-110-0 (ebook)
ISBN: 978-1-64236-111-7 (trade paperback)
ISBN: 978-1-64236-112-4 (hardcover)

With appreciation to the many people that supported this project.

Contents

Introduction
XIA JIA

In early 2019, the Kickstarter campaign for my first English science fiction collection *A Summer Beyond Your Reach* was launched by Neil Clarke. Around that time, my friend Regina Kanyu Wang—also one of the project planners—and I were invited to attend an art festival in Norway. Good news kept coming during our journey. In Tromso, we recorded a short video at the gate of Artic Cathedral, giving thanks to the enthusiastic backers, as well as announcing the third stretch goal of our project: to publish an anthology of writers who were previously unpublished in English. Our goal was to help more Chinese authors gain recognition from a broader international readership.

Being among the small group of Chinese science fiction writers to have seen their works published overseas, both Regina and I know well how such opportunities could impact a writer's career. We also understand that beyond the quality of our work, luck and timing played an important role—the simple state of being acquainted with translators, editors, publishers and reviewers who appreciated our stories. The seeds of their kindness and generosity have generated beautiful flowers and sweet fruits in our hands. The best way to repay that kindness is to pass it on to those brilliant, though perhaps not as lucky writers, and wait for another turn to blossom.

The process of compiling this anthology was a little more challenging than we initially expected. We started from making a list of emerging new writers in recent years. From there we screened out "authors who have never been published in English before" and asked them for the stories they were most proud of. At that point, we narrowed it down by choosing our favorites while making sure we maintained a balance of lengths, subjects, and other factors. Regina and I made a table to list the summary and the comment of each story in English, with which Neil could provide his thoughts. Sometimes Neil had to use machine translation to fill in the gaps and better participate in the discussion. We cooperated by these means and eventually came up with a consensus on eight stories from eight authors, eight new voices that you might not have heard before.

Congyun "Mu Ming" Gu and Shuang Chimu are two of the most remarkable new authors—they are my age, but just embarked on science fiction writing in recent years. They are female authors—I feel like I have to emphasize their gender every time I introduce them, with a clear awareness that such modifier unavoidably implies the stereotype of female writing as exception, but it is as essential to understanding their works from that edge as to understanding Ursula K. Le Guin or Octavia E. Butler. They're both scholarly writers. Mu Ming works in artificial intelligence, while Shuang Chimu has a PhD in philosophy. They explore and reflect on technological issues in academic approaches, while hold a much more inclusive vision which I tend to name as an "anthropological imagination." They are the future masters of Chinese SF in the post-Liu Cixin era. They write more in the vein of Lem, Ted Chiang, and Ken Liu than of the Golden Age masters. Their most outstanding works are too long for this anthology, so that neither of the two stories included here can fully show their ambition and power. The story of "By Those Hands" takes place in Sichuan, while "My Family and Other Evolving Animals" in a space station named Shangri-La. Both involve with local cuisine, family ties, and "craftsmanship" of ordinary people; both explore what I personally appreciate and focus on—imagining alternative technological approaches, seriously yet with the beauty of "lightness."

I have known Liao Shubo for a long time. As a college student, in the spring of 2010, she attended the first SF writing workshop I organized in Beijing. She's called me "Teacher Eggplant" ever since. Her Exupérian stories, with airships, stars, visible and invisible planets, all organized in fantastic logic, have fans in contemporary Chinese SF community, but don't receive the serious attention they deserve. That's why Regina and I were determined to include one of her stories. My initial option was "The 2D Life," about a girl who had to be transformed into 2D existence, lived a bitter and lonely life. Regina preferred "The Postman," which for me is a metafiction about writing and reading. Liao Shubo is fond of whales, after which the postman who always listened and cared about the tiniest voices is named. Perhaps most writers can find a sense of identification with these big, quiet, beautiful, mysterious creatures and their secret communications.

Liang Qingsan and I have known each other even longer. He also attended my SF writing workshop in Beijing and joyfully told me afterwards, that the only and best lesson he had learned was how all the storytelling techniques I shared could not help him in any way with what he wanted to write. Since then, he has been writing in his own way and has published several novels. His writing isn't part of the mainstream of contemporary Chinese SF, but has found its niche after all. His novels are mostly alternative history set in the late Qing, with rich and solid historical materials seamlessly woven with whimsical technological ideas—such as generating electricity by rubbing cats. "The Kite of Jinan" is a factually fictional history of technology, the kind of "fictional nonfiction" which I personally have interested in. The protagonist of the story is more or less a copy of the author himself: a "flaneur" who is wandering outside the literary circle and the academic system, climbing through old papers day by day for his very own interests.

Hui Hu, Yang Wanqing, Shi Heiyao, and Liu Xiao, are among the writers who have emerged via a variety of SF competitions in recent years. As a jury member, I was tremendously impressed by their works and have since become acquainted with them personally.

Shi Heiyao is talented in creating bizarre SF imagery embedded in seemingly normal everyday life and ordinary people. His writing, with a rich sense of allegory, is in the vein of Kafka, Philip K. Dick, and Han Song. "Pixiu" describes an artificial creature with the name of an ancient Chinese mythical creature, as well as an industry and a family associated with it. The fate of the people and that of Pixiu are intertwined in a speechlessly bitter tone.

Yang Wanqing is a skilled and prolific storyteller. We finally picked "Tombstone," a typical dystopian tale, from the fourteen stories he provided. Though Regina had some issues with its slightly stereotypical characterization (the lonely, sexually repressed hero, the uninhibited heroine as the enlightener, the rescuer as well as the sexual fantasies of the hero), I was struck by the eventually revealed dark secrets of the city, which is a horribly impressive SF image for the common dilemmas we have no way to escape from in this age.

Liu Xiao's "The Bridge" stands out with its fascinating and vivid world building. The bridge jumper hops on the Canted Bridge sweeping across the town and rushes to another world named Magna Luna, such scenes find a delicate balance between the ethereality of the fairy tale and the gravity of reality. You can't help but be attracted by the world of the bridge jumpers and feel empathy for them.

Hui Hu's "PTSD" shows the entanglement between the three protagonists in the virtual as in the physical world. With VR helmets, aircraft, tele-presence robots, and mechanical exoskeletons, they are embedded into various agencies and carry out complex interactions and confrontations. They are traumatized human beings with physical and mental defects; they are cyborg monsters with infinite possibilities as well. I can't say whether I fear, pity, or envy them, but I'm looking forward to seeing more of them.

So much has changed in the three years since 2019. It is to be congratulated that some of the authors have had works translated into English during this period and it is a testament to the quality of their work. I recently reread these stories in Chinese and English, feeling alienated and familiar all the same. In any case, I am wholeheartedly gratified that I have participated in such a meaningful project. Many thanks to the eight authors for believing in us, and may your voices be heard worldwide. Thanks to the brilliant translators. Thanks to Regina, Neil, and other editors. Thanks to all the backers of the project. This book, these stories, must be the best reward for all your kindness. I hope you enjoy reading them as much as I did when I first met them.

March, 2022
In Xi'an

我的家人和其他进化中的动物们

My Family and Other Evolving Animals

SHUANG CHIMU

双翅目

TRANSLATED BY CARMEN YILING YAN

It all started with my mom.

The previous Spring Festival, she'd brought an extra twenty pounds of fish mint aboard, planning ahead for the next year's big dinners. In the twelfth month, she'd quietly taken a bag of the rhizomes out of cold storage, proud of her own cleverness. Unfortunately, the night before New Year's Eve, my older sister got a craving and snuck into the pantry. The swarm of fruit flies flew right into her face. Three minutes later, they'd vanished without a trace. Dispersing in a rapid and orderly fashion, they smoothly established themselves throughout the two-million-inhabitant sealed space. After that, Mom was truly infamous throughout the Shangri-La Space Station.

What kind of insect would eat fish mint? It had evolved its pungency for the sole purpose of deterring pests. Thousands of species of fruit flies, across millions of years of evolution, had failed to eat fish mint. Yet my ol' mom had gotten them to change their ways.

They'd evolved.

The animal center looked into the business, and decided it wasn't a big deal. The space station council levied some fines and called it a day. So Mom regarded the matter with pride instead of shame, declaring that delicious fish mint *should* be enjoyed by insects as well as humans. We had a few words for her attitude, but we did like that pungent fishy flavor. The first New Year's Eve dinner we held in the space station was unusually abundant; the feasting drove all other thoughts out of the heads of our family of five. But no one could have guessed that it was none other than my mom who set off the evolutionary journey of the species of Yunnan Province.

I was proud.

Because my dream was to become a naturalist.

I should start from the beginning.

"The future is just not evenly distributed. It's impossible for technology to spread time flat on every geological layer. In some areas the concentration is high; in others the concentration is low. Humans pass in between them. Shangri-La Space Station is naturally a high-concentration zone."
—Wang Chang, Summer 2119, from Beijing

My mom wasn't my birth mother. My dad wasn't my birth father either. My older brother and sister were their biological children. All of them were from northern China.

Not me and my little sister. I was the only Yunnanese born and bred, born on the border between China and Burma, while Dad passed away before he got used to the rice noodles. He'd bought my little sister out from the hands of a human trafficker out of desperation. Mom thought she was also from somewhere in the southwest—Yunnan, Guizhou, or Sichuan Province. My dad uploaded her genetic data, but three years passed, and we never got a ping. So my mother officially declared: she's my daughter now. My origins weren't that mysterious; the last several dozen generations of my family had lived in the same district. Apparently, when my birth father had been younger, drug traffickers had coerced him into running goods at gunpoint. My family wound up dying unnatural deaths. Back then, my father was working with a program to bring education to the rural areas on the border. Long-distance learning might be effective, but it still required some number of educators to go to the villages and calibrate the hologram equipment, help out the local teachers, gather detailed research data, and ultimately deliver feedback to the central command for high-level adjustments to the educational framework. Dad was sent from Beijing to Yunnan and stayed. Two years later, Mom came with my older brother and sister to stay in Kunming. Dad always said that Mom was no education expert like him: she might be an elementary school teacher, but her heart was in food and gardening. Yunnan suited her. I thought Dad was wrong. Mom enjoyed rearing us as much as anything, cluck-cluck-clucking and shielding us under her wings. For years, Dad spent his time out in the villages away from home, but she took it all in stride. If Dad hadn't overworked himself and died so young of cancer, he would've brought home more children in need and expanded Mom's husbandry operations. It's fortunate that Mom found an entirely new set of rearing goals. Ol' Dad's spirit in heaven would find comfort in that for sure.

My love for animals and plants came from a set of books titled *My Family and Other Animals*, also known as the Corfu trilogy. The author was a famous English naturalist from the century before the last, named Gerald Durrell, and he'd had a family that was at once endearing and exasperating. Dad would read it to me as soon as he came home, as a bedtime story. By the time he'd finished the first book bit by bit, I'd learned my characters and no longer needed him, and I read the second and third books on my own. Only after he'd passed did I realize that I'd left him a little crestfallen. He hadn't wanted me to grow up so quickly; he'd wanted to continue reading for me. Afterward, he adopted my little sister, but unfortunately she didn't enjoy listening to his mutterings. She preferred my mother's singing.

I'll never forget my father reading the preface: "A world without birds, without forests, without animals of every shape and size, would be one that I, personally, would not care to live in . . . "

"People from the borderlands of Yunnan, Guizhou, and Sichuan have a distinct borderlander personality, and those who chose voluntarily to

live in the borderlands even more so. The task of selecting residents for
Shangri-La is not a difficult one. Some people are inclined by nature to
leave Earth and make their homes in the outer solar system."
—Wang Chang, Winter 2120,
from Banna Autonomous Prefecture, Yunnan

Durrell wrote of Greece and the Mediterranean. I'm more fortunate
than him; Yunnan is more interesting. Mom would take me to the
enormous museum run by the Kunming Institute of Zoology and take
me to explore the natural world of Yunnan. To the south was tropical
Banna, to the west were the Hengduan Mountains, to the north was the
Jinsha River, to the east were dense primeval forests. During summer
vacations our whole family would go to pester Dad, spending the first
month in the rainforest eating steamed egg with moss, the next month
drinking thermos after thermos of yak milk tea.

That was why, when Mom announced that we were leaving Yunnan,
leaving China, leaving Earth, to settle in the neighborhood of Titan,
I tried to obstruct her in every way I could think of, until the whole
family had no peace. I dreaded the dreariness of a space station and
the over-disinfected inside of a spaceship. Ultimately, my older brother
finished reading the detailed rules and premises of Shangri-La Space
Station and told me that the space station was jointly designed and
managed by the Institute of Zoology and the Tourism Office. The goal
was to create a space base containing every ecological niche in the
province; once it reached the orbit of Saturn, it would operate there
for the long-term.

He pushed up his thin-rimmed glasses. "—Which means, Shangri-
La will be able to grow banyans as well as fir trees and raise elephants
and Tibetan antelopes at the same time."

I asked, "When do we head out?"

My mom whirled into action.

My brother thought my mom wanted to move house in order to leave
a place she now associated with grief. My older sister said, be real, she
couldn't afford to raise the four of us on Earth. The space station would
have top-notch educational facilities, and it needed young people to
live and multiply in it. Voluntary relocation was a win-win.

My little sister was more on the nose. She hugged her beloved macaw and said in her childish voice, "Mom isn't one to stay in place."

"The composition of the personnel is a problem. We need not just experts, but more people who can become experts. Ideally, they wouldn't be experts in anything at this time. Without those blinkers on their mindsets, they'll be able to occupy multiple roles in the future."
—Wang Chang, Spring 2121, from Kunming, Yunnan

On the last round of the space station assessments, everyone was called in for the interview. The gaze of the man in charge, Director Wang, swept from my mom to my little sister, taking in my older sister's tattoos, my brother's tablet, and my little sister's macaw, before affixing itself to my jam jar.

"What's that?" he asked.

"Caterpillar." I lifted the jar.

My brother shook his head. My mother looked somewhat stressed.

"You like bugs?"

"That's right. Out of all the squishy bugs, my favorites are still the fuzzy caterpillars from Kunming. When my dad took me to Beijing, the dangly ones there were all green and bald. They were super ugly, and really tiny too. Jiangxi was okay. I saw a moth caterpillar that had bright blue and orange patterns all over. It looked really weird, but it couldn't scare *me* away. Caterpillars are *sooo* cute."

My older sister put an arm over my shoulders and lifted her chin, looking down her nose at Director Wang.

"I'm guessing your mother picked out that glass jam jar for you. And she must have made the air holes in the lid for you too."

"That's right."

"And she helps you feed the bugs?"

"I feed the bugs all by myself." I emphasized, "I'm the one who finds all the leaves."

Director Wang said to Mom, "Ms. Zhou, I'll adjust your access level. Once we reach the orbit of Saturn, you'll still be employed full time in elementary school education for the Saturn living communities. But at the moment, the educational duties in Shangri-La Space Station are light, and by my observation, you also have considerable talent for animal husbandry. It just so happens that Professor Fang of the Zoology Institute is short on staff. You can report there to start."

"Animal husbandry?" my brother couldn't resist asking.

"It's written in the records that you two are biological children, while the two of them are adopted."

"Just what are you getting at?" My older sister's temper rose.

"Miss, don't get the wrong idea. I, for one, am not a nurturing man. Just bringing up one single daughter drove me to exhaustion. Looking at people who can rear cats and dogs and flowers and plants gives me a headache. At first, I couldn't understand how anyone could raise a whole brood of children. With age, people want peace and quiet. Then I went into the Institute of Zoology, and after twenty years, I've reevaluated that opinion. People's hearts come in different volume capacities. I can fit in a daughter and a cat, and that's it. Others have room for a pile of children and a pile of grandchildren, and often they can raise mammals, reptiles, and amphibians with just as much innate understanding. Your mother is a broad-hearted woman. In an enclosed space station, raising you few wouldn't nearly satisfy her capacity."

The macaw loudly squawked his approval, "That's right! That's right!"

"Life originates like blossoms on the same tree, dispersed by the wind, some caressing the hanging curtains and falling upon the bed, others running into fences and dropping into the dung pit."
—Wang Chang, Spring 2122, from Tengchong, Yunnan

Auntie Fang worked in fruit fly molecular biology and genetics. Tall, boisterous, and plump, she made a striking contrast with Mom. They became bosom buddies at first sight.

Auntie Fang's son and husband had already gone ahead to Titan. She hadn't seen them for three years, and she'd have to wait another six to see them again. Nevertheless, she was full of vim and vigor. The first time Mom went on an outing with Auntie Fang, to learn to collect live fruit flies for use on the space station, they brought me along. I saw

Auntie Fang lift a corner of her shirt and inject a shot of insulin into her belly, all the while glued to her screen and furiously messaging a friend group.

"My son liked my post!" she whooped. Her son worked as a laborer in outer space, frequently outside the range of civilian communications. Compared to holing up in a laboratory, Auntie Fang preferred the outdoors. She'd read the Corfu trilogy too; her dream had also been to become a naturalist. Sadly, Earth had no opportunities left for discovering new species. She'd chosen Yunnan and fruit flies.

"This area was fairly isolated during the Ice Age, serving as a refuge for many ancient species, and it has some very complex ecosystems. Just be patient, and you'll always find some exciting little critters." The first time we'd met, she'd taken out a white object the size of the box for a deck of cards. She ran her finger along the bottom, and it quickly unfolded. A round frame sprang from the opening, from which hung a thin white nanofiber cotton mesh. The box shell quickly contracted into a cylindrical handle. A high-tech bug net.

She then took me to the insect capture location where she'd planted bait beforehand. Yunnan summers were broiling in the middle of the day, but we still wore protective leather boots and leg wrappings. She used the net to scout ahead, shooing away small critters and snakes. When we arrived in the damp, cool habitat, she stomped amongst the leaves to startle insects, making them fly up, before scooping around with the net, folding it, and closing up the opening with her hand. The small flying insects were thus trapped inside.

"See," she said, crouching down. "These are fruit flies."

In the eyes of others, fruit flies were no better than miniature houseflies. In my eyes, they were lively and adorable.

Auntie Fang took a glass straw from who knew where. One end of the straw was fitted with rubber tubing, with a piece of mesh in between, and on the other end of the rubber tubing was a glass mouthpiece. She held the glass mouthpiece between her lips and poked the straw into the gathered opening of the net, sucking the fruit flies she'd identified into the straw one by one. Then she shook out the net, blew the fruit flies gathered against the gauze into a test tube, and capped it with a sponge plug, her sequence of movements well-practiced and fluid. She stuck on a label: *Shangri-La Space Station*.

She asked me if I wanted to try. In my excitement, I stepped on a snake that hadn't gotten out of the way in time. It wrapped around my calf and bit me.

Fortunately my leg wrappings were tough, and the snake was small. Its teeth couldn't find purchase. Auntie Fang seized it speedily at the seven-inch weak spot and dropped it into the transparent lunch box that we'd thoroughly cleared out earlier.

I goggled at her, thinking that not even a wizard could be more impressive. And she imparted her arcane wisdom, saying, space stations could use snake wine too. I told her, my mother knows how to make it. And then I asked her, when we went to space, could I be her student? We struck palms to seal the promise. That year I was ten.

"—I don't know whether you, who are reading this, have read any of my other books, but if you have, or if you have only read this one with pleasure, it is the animals that have made it enjoyable for you." Thank you, Professor Fang, for gifting me this book. Durrell will be a companion to pass the time and remember Earth with."

—Wang Chang, Winter 2123 by Earth reckoning, from Shangri-La

A month before boarding, we passed our last New Year's Eve on Earth. Auntie Fang, slightly tipsy, announced that Director Wang, who was in charge of Shangri-La's biosphere, had agreed: she could deliver forty jars of snake wine into the heavens. My mother had also chosen her allotted portion of vegetables and fungi for human and animal consumption: pea shoots, Yunnan zucchini, taro, macrolepiota mushroom, fish mint. What she didn't say was that she was bringing an extra twenty pounds of fish mint and thirty pounds of macrolepiota packed in oil. She'd secretly shaved off a little from the Napa cabbage cultivation and used the room for pea shoots. By the time she was discovered, it was too late. We'd already passed the orbit of the moon.

It was ten years from Shangri-La Space Station powering up to taking off. When my mom signed up, the ship was already built, and the ecology adjustments inside were reaching their end. We moved out from Kunming one year ahead of time, staying inside the space station, moored near Tengchong, to get used to the environment inside. The closer we came to the launch date, the longer our periods of stay. When we left Earth, I only felt a little sense of loss. My older sister called it being slow boiled like a frog. She and my brother were the few to grieve. Most of the migrants were too busy with the schedule and the hardships of breaking new ground to sigh at the parting. That went for me too.

As Auntie Fang's apprentice, I took over the feeding work that should've been Mom's, while she focused on raising plants. I quickly grew familiar with the ecology setup in the space station. Shangri-La had arranged everything based on the distance to the engine and the temperature of the compartment, the propulsion method and level of centrifugal force of each zone. The area close to the engine was designated as rainforest, while the outer centrifugal area was high-altitude plateau climate. Everything else was laid out in steps in between, keeping the species and ecological niches widely spaced apart. It really was like a gigantic sealed terrarium. Other than nuclear and solar power, no energy entered the system, and very little waste was released. Under ideal conditions, it would form a complete suite of Yunnan's ecology. Inorganic material, organic material, plants, animals—they'd form a closed cycle of creation and consumption.

Like a work of art, like a crystal sphere drifting through outer space, like Shambhala.

Yet in less than three months, Auntie Fang's snake wine grew bugs. My older brother was right at the age for songwriting and poetry, and his latest creation-in-progress had him craving wine. He'd been eying Auntie Fang's stash from the beginning; he couldn't resist stooping to theft. He went to the distillery, threading his way past the fermentation and distillation equipment and into the darkness of the wine cellar. Too guilty to bring a light, he tripped over a jar, and a flock of fruit flies billowed up. Terrified, he'd pulled the alarm. He didn't know that fruit flies also drank snake wine.

Auntie Fang was equally alarmed when she rushed onto the scene. She'd expected to attract insects, but not this soon, or this many.

She talked things over with Director Wang, and they reached the decision to let Shangri-La's ecology self-adjust on its own, without human interference. I helped her capture quite a few live specimens;

my lips hurt from all the sucking on the glass mouthpiece. As for my brother, the experience scarred him for life. He never drank again.

"Low-probability events happen with inevitable frequency. In outer space, we must carefully remember this law."
—Wang Chang, Spring 2124 by Earth reckoning, from Shangri-La

The fish mint fruit flies appeared on the first Spring Festival on Shangri-La Space Station. Their Latin name was a pain to say; only my mom and little sister could pronounce it with a cadence that made it sound lovely.

Auntie Fang was careful; she spent two weeks confirming that it was a new species before naming it: fish mint fruit fly. From its genetics and morphology, she determined that they'd mutated from the snake wine fruit flies.

Mom grew even prouder. She'd brewed the snake wine. She'd picked out the fish mint. My older brother thought that Director Wang's prediction had come true. Mom was more than just animal husbandry staff—she'd spurred the arrival of new species of animals.

The fish mint fruit flies quickly accustomed themselves to the ecology of the space station. They made themselves at home on the veins of the fish mint in the farms, laying eggs and reproducing, doing no real harm to the food chain. The Shangri-La Institute of Zoology couldn't make heads nor tails of it. There were nearly a hundred space megastations in the solar system, and countless medium- and small-scale ecosystems. Few new species had been developed, and even fewer had spontaneously arisen. The fish mint fruit flies were a rare exception. A few months later, Auntie Fang's paper appeared in *eLife* magazine. She summed up the various factors, such as space radiation, the space station environment, and the gene pool of Yunnan wildlife, which implied the logical possibility of a new species arising. My name was listed on the paper. I felt like I'd become a real naturalist.

A new species had appeared due to uncertain factors—to prevent further surprises, the space station began a series of investigations and contingency plans that, after much hassle, didn't go anywhere. Ultimately,

Director Wang made his peace. He announced, "As long as I don't have to take care of them, the more new species, the better. The plans of men and machines don't amount to much next to the plans of Heaven. Mother Nature has the broadest of hearts, the greatest capacity for tolerance. You can't go wrong with following nature's example."

"Often one must be free of wants to observe the deepest mysteries."
—Wang Chang, Spring 2126 by Earth reckoning, from Shangri-La

With the second Spring Festival on Shangri-La Space Station, several new species flew in on the pea shoots Mom had so carefully nurtured. The oyster mushrooms and cordyceps had also nurtured new bugs. Auntie Fang had her hands full. I started helping her perform lab tests, dissections, and gene analysis. The pea shoot fruit flies had mutated from the snake wine fruit flies. The cordyceps fruit flies had mutated from the high-altitude graminivorous fruit flies. They didn't eat the fruiting body part of the cordyceps—they ate the bug part it grew parasitically out of. I considered them carnivorous insects. The oyster mushroom fruit flies were even more complicated. Auntie Fang had to contact the nematode research team to confirm that the nematodes in the soil had mutated earlier than the fruit flies. Afterward, the mutated population had gotten caught and embedded in the mycelium of the oyster mushrooms, which absorbed their nitrogen compounds. As a result, the oyster mushrooms had begun to secrete new chemicals, attracting a fruit fly population that was previously fond of eucalyptus secretions.

"The entire ecosystem may end up mutating top to bottom," Auntie Fang warned Director Wang, not without a hint of delight.

Director Wang was a lot more even keeled. "That's perfectly fine. Species have gone extinct because of human pollution. Today, nature is evolving to make up for past losses. We'll go with the flow, go with the flow."

The ecological policy of Shangri-La Space Station was thus decided without a ripple.

I was there that day, carrying a pot containing a small taro plant just starting to flower. I was so fixated on the taro flower that I'd forgotten all about Director Wang and Auntie Fang. I wanted to tell my older sister and brother right away: the taro bud fruit flies and the taro flower fruit flies were mating.

My brother liked reading and literature, loved everything ancient. In Shangri-La, under the supervision of specialists, he'd turned to learning the languages and mythology of minority ethnic groups. My older sister was the opposite. She liked video games, tinkering with machinery, loved everything modern. Upon entering high school, she'd fast-tracked into studying engineering while taking a role at the maintenance department. Due to the tidal wave of mutations among the insects, Mom's animal husbandry work had become increasingly complicated, and my brother and sister were roped in to help. My brother took care of text classification and recording observations while my sister upgraded the cultivation equipment. They participated profoundly in the evolution of species.

The taro flower fruit flies were a common point of contention. The petals and stamens of the taro nourished one kind of fruit fly; the buds and calyx secretions nourished another. Not only were the two kinds reproductively isolated, but they also looked pretty different. Like Shangri-La's ecosystems, my brother said. BS, my older sister said, it was just that their reproductive organs didn't fit together. At that point, my brother would start talking about cultural constructs, my older sister would start talking about natural morphology, I'd be squeezed in between them talking rubbish, my mom would carry my little sister off to somewhere else to eat. She understood us, she said. Confined in the space station, we needed weird topics of conversation to relieve the psychological pressure.

I maintained a strict scientific attitude; I didn't immediately tell Auntie Fang about the historical moment I'd so briefly witnessed alone. I carried the pot home. I couldn't find my brother or older sister, only Mom. I told her to grow a few extra plants of the same kind of taro, so I could observe, document, and study the next generation's inheritance. Mom refused. I only had Auntie Fang's access level and wasn't authorized to do experiments in the cultivation area. "This is scientific discovery!" I yelled. "The sort of discovery that can make it into *Science Magazine*."

Mom naturally didn't believe me, but she gave it some serious thought. "Can you borrow some petri dishes from Auntie Fang?" I told her yes. She said, "Then how about you do the observations at home? I'll make some taro nutrient medium that the fruit flies can eat." Mom separately ground up the stamens and buds, creating two types of nutrient medium. I reared the two kinds of fruit fly separately, waited for them to produce offspring, and then, when the offspring were mature, placed the males and females of different species together, had them mate, and placed the larvae into different nutrient media. Something interesting happened. Not only could they mate, but they could also produce fertile offspring. The offspring's food preferences were determined by the species of the mother. I wrote up a report and turned it in to Auntie Fang. Seeing her surprise and delight was the best reward in Shangri-La. A year later, the paper came out in *Nature* magazine. Auntie Fang listed me as one of the authors.

But we didn't have time to celebrate. A meteor in the asteroid belt hit Shangri-La.

"We imposed excessively strict standards on the internal environment of Shangri-La but overlooked the potential for catastrophic disaster coming from the great universe. I should reevaluate my understanding of human adaptability. We must exhibit more tolerance toward the companions around us if we want to venture far into deep space, to adapt ourselves to the universe."
    —Wang Chang, Winter 2127 by Earth reckoning, from Shangri-La

At that time, we were about to welcome our fourth Spring Festival on Shangri-La. We'd received ample resupply at Mars; a new ring of storage compartments surrounded the exterior of the space station. My mom's cultivation center produced continuous bumper crops, greatly improving the diets of animals and humans alike.

It was as we approached what would've been the twelfth month on Earth. Just as people arrived at their posts, something shook the entire station. Every light went out in the living and research areas.

My little sister was trapped in the avian rearing house for two full hours, crying until she was hoarse. By the time my older brother pulled her out, she was shaking all over. I had a bad fright myself, clinging to

Auntie Fang. My older sister immediately rushed to the repair frontlines. My mom rerouted the cultivation center's temperature maintenance resources to make up for the heating shortfall in the living area. By the time normal function was restored, eighty-five percent of the edible plants had been frostbitten into mush.

The hard core of the meteorite had punctured multiple protective layers, obstructing the engine transmission. The one blessing among all the misfortunes was that the ship's engine core had survived undamaged. Many were injured, though no one died.

After forty-eight hours of repair and inspection, the initial determination was that Shangri-La could still make it to Jupiter for repairs and resupply, then travel to Saturn to resume its role as a space station. The most urgent matter was the lack of food. The emergency rations could barely feed the humans, let alone the animals. This could be the end of Shangri-La's food web. Our whole family holed up in the living room. What worried me the most wasn't the fate of the household, but my dreams of becoming a naturalist.

At the all-hands meeting, my mom asked to speak. After two days of discussion with Auntie Fang, with input from my older brother and sister, she'd produced a letter of apology and an emergency food supply report.

At the meeting, Mom unabashedly finished reading out the letter of apology. Silence reigned beneath the stage. The gist of it was, after the last Spring Festival, she'd picked up ecological modeling, and discovered that the cultivation center had more plants and insects than the humans and larger animals could consume. She hadn't followed proper warehousing procedures; she hadn't wanted to put in any preservatives or additives.

The Mars resupply had provided several empty bulk storage containers, hanging off the outer rim of the space station. She'd taken all the feed that could've been processed into ration reserves and made them into nutrient medium. She'd even registered them as a project, claiming them to be experimental samples for improving nutrient medium. At this time, all this "food" remained completely untouched, in cold storage at the edges of the ecological zones.

Director Wang asked, "What kind of nutrient medium?"

"Mostly for feeding insects, such as fish mint nutrient medium, pea shoot nutrient medium, and taro bud and calyx medium. They're all edible for humans too. There's also meat culture medium. Toward the end of last year, our looper caterpillars evolved into something like the ones on Hawaii—they can extend their mouthparts and eat other insects—so I started feeding them meat. Anyway, all of this is edible. I didn't add preservatives, but I did add yeast, agar, some corn meal, and potato starch. They've got proteins and vegetables, all the amino acids. There's enough to feed everyone until we reach Jupiter. We won't even need other ships to give us emergency resupply."

Director Wang asked a further question: "So, for the next half year, we'll all have to eat nutrient medium?"

Auntie Fang answered that question. "No, we'll also have to eat the compressed emergency rations. To tell the truth, the defrosted nutrient medium is too good to give it all to humans to eat. We've made a plan to input certain portions of the nutrient medium into the various ecosystems all over the space station, to ensure the animals have enough to eat until the plants mature and do what we can for the continued growth of the ecosystems. We had an accident; we can't just ask for help from the outside world the moment we run into an accident. It goes against the founding principles of the Shangri-La ecosphere."

Everyone nodded. Auntie Fang's plan passed unanimously.

So, on New Year's Eve, the dining table was covered in petri dishes large and small, tall and squat, alternately flat and skinny. We took up ice cream scoops, dipped them into the petri dishes, and dug up nutrient medium of various colors to eat. We'd been eating three weeks of compressed rations and nutrient medium, so we all knew that the nutrient medium tasted better. This was probably the last meal of entirely nutrient medium we were going to have this half year.

After the new year, I discovered several bluebottle butterflies with wings turning from brown to blue on their upper surfaces. An expert from the lepidopteran team confirmed that the wings of butterflies and moths were all turning increasingly colorful and splendid.

In August, we arrived in the orbit of Jupiter. The Jupiter Space Research System placed great importance on Shangri-La's ecosystems and gave us considerable help. My mom was summoned by the center to take a concentration in animal nutrition. My older brother completed college, receiving his diploma at the Europa Institute. My older sister received her advanced skilled worker certification without having yet graduated. While everyone was gone, and Auntie Fang was busy with the rendezvous, I took my little sister wandering around Shangri-La. For the first time, my sister displayed her incredible talent. She tugged at me, saying, "The birds' singing changed. They found better things to eat."

I took her to the ornithology lab. Everyone working there recognized my sister. They told me she'd discovered the change in the birds' behavior early on. After the incident with the meteorite, plants were short, whereas more insects could feed on the nutrient medium. The green pigeons and weaver finches had therefore begun to turn carnivorous in their diet. Nowadays, the plants were recovering in the ecosystems, but the birds had gained a fondness for new tastes, developing a series of cries to communicate how to catch insects.

The next day, I found Auntie Fang and told her that the birds were mutating. Her eyes left the microscope; her hands set down the dissection pins. She was silent for a moment, then said, "I thought before that yeast, looper caterpillars, and fruit flies evolve quickly because they go through generations quickly, while larger animals would be slower. Looks like things aren't that simple. Adaptability is a wonderful thing. Maybe it won't take future generations for mammals to change."

"Will we change too?" I asked.

"After this year, you'll be taller than your mother."

"—The great voiceless and voteless majority who can only survive with our help." I wish Durrell could've lived longer and built his zoo in space. His later years would have been happier that way. Without them, we couldn't live. In space, not only do they have a vote, but they are also the leaders of nature, while we are only the marginal electorate."

—Wang Chang, Spring 2129 by Earth reckoning, Shangri-La

The fifth Spring Festival on Shangri-La Space Station went off without a hitch. Director Wang gave a speech: it had been a difficult year, he said; may our ecosystem return to the way it used to be by the next Spring Festival. After his speech, he came down from the stage, but then went back up to add, "Correction, our ecosystem won't return to the way it used to be. We need to take more care. The meteorite went through the ventilation and contaminated the ecological niches on multiple levels. We need to mentally fortify ourselves in preparation for more complex mutations and evolutions."

Director Wang was once again prophetic. Fifteen days later, when my older sister went to the zero-gravity area for equipment testing, she discovered two small insects. She recognized them as vine-eating fruit flies. The equipment area wasn't sterile, but organisms rarely showed up there. By the time she returned to the living area, it was late at night. She stole my bug net and suction equipment, picked up two spare vials, and returned to the zero-gravity area. Early the next morning, she tossed the occupied vials onto the sofa, flopped down, and fell right asleep.

My little sister got up first. She saw the fruit flies, mindlessly banging around and struggling to fly, but couldn't wake up my older sister or me. Mom happened to be out. She woke up my brother. He saw the label—zero-gravity equipment area—and, taking only my little sister, headed out for the zero-gravity recreational park.

She released the fruit flies from one vial, then removed the sponge plug from the other vial, telling my brother, "See, they look much better when they're flying, like birds doing a mating dance." After many years of osmosis, my brother had at last gained some instinct for animal evolution. He forced back the sponge plug and hurriedly used his glasses to scan and record the scattered flight trails of the fruit flies in the zero-gravity environment. Auntie Fang once again received a firsthand report.

In April, springtime on Earth, she made a special trip to our home to perform a 3D holographic presentation. "Insects are divided into three segments, the head, thorax, and abdomen. Adult insects generally have two pairs of wings and six legs. Fruit flies belong to the order Diptera; the hind wings have dwindled to club-like halteres, which normally don't serve any purpose. But look at the way they move in zero gravity. The halteres are visibly rotating, because in the absence of gravity, or when the direction of gravity is unstable, they need a stronger sense of space and location. Their halteres have evolved. When they fly, their body and limbs rotate with the halteres. I tested every type of fruit fly in the space station—all of their halteres have evolved. We already had the zero-gravity public park, and after the incident with the meteorite, the divides between the zero-gravity zone, the reduced-gravity zone, and the Earth-gravity zone have weakened. The evolution of the fruit flies wasn't interrupted by the damage the meteorite did to the ecosystems; actually, we sped up the timeline. I have a thought to submit a proposal to Director Wang.

"I trust you all. These five years, you've known my work and supported me better than those two in my family—you're all like my family. I need your advice—"

"Just a sec!" My mom straightened and patted my brother on his slouching back. She had us all sit up tall. "All right. Go ahead."

"I want to eliminate the sharp divides in gravity between areas and turn the entire space station into a gradient of gravity, similar to how it would be to traverse latitude and altitude, from the Banna Basin to the Tibetan Plateau, only with a much steeper range of change. Right now, in order to imitate the different ecosystems on Earth, the divisions between ecological niches are too fixed and unnatural, or, in other words, unbefitting the environment of outer space, the 'natural' state of the space station. I believe that only a smooth transition of gravity can create a space that allows everything organic and inorganic to freely exchange resources, grow, and evolve."

Having spoken, she seemed apprehensive.

We expressed our approval raucously.

Auntie Fang's proposal gave Director Wang a terrible shock. For several days he shrank away, before recognizing that an individual's policy decision was wholly unable to resist nature's demonstrated history of radicalism. He surrendered. He forwarded the proposal to his higher-ups and received enthusiastic approval. After the meteorite incident and the evolution of the animals on board, the higher-ups already considered Shangri-La an enormous experimental ecosphere. The Zoology Institute and the Engineering Department spent half a year completing the gravity gradient demonstration.

On the first day of the year, by lunar calendar reckoning, the gravitational sluices of Shangri-La were to open. The entire station was full of restlessness and excitement. The engineering department dismantled the barrier that separated the outer area of the southwest wing from the inner area, converting it into an enormous rectangular open space. Director Wang pressed two buttons, dark blue and dark green.

The entire station sank into silence. Everyone was watching the numerical distributions change, the black-to-white range of different gravitational zones ticking constantly until the once-clear demarcations between them blurred away.

Thirty minutes later, the insects began to find their bearings and migrate. Mom pointed at the banyan trees in the low-gravity areas. The supple aerial prop roots, which had yet to plant themselves into the soil and become sturdy, woody trunks, started to drift in all directions. "They'll become lighter and airier," Mom muttered to herself, beginning to consider her new workload. The others eagerly went to explore the gravitational transition areas between floating and falling.

My brother summed it up: "Really, it's humans who are the most adaptable of all."

In the next two years, the ecological systems of Shangri-La experienced unprecedented growth. The incident with the meteorite had accelerated the renewal, thinning the messy tangle of existing ecological relationships, so that afterward, as flora and fauna sought survival, they developed behaviors to adapt to the steep-gravitational-gradient environment.

"At night, Saturn comes, and holds out its hand."
—Wang Chang, Winter 2132 by Earth reckoning,
Spring by Saturn reckoning, from Shangri-La

In the twelfth month of the eighth year, we finally arrived at Saturn.

The space station gradually entered orbit. The enormous gas giant cast a long shadow, shading ring after orbiting ring. Right then, I suddenly remembered Dad, and a story he'd read to me. The explorer in the story had lived during the twentieth century. Arriving at the North Pole, he'd sat on the just-melting broken ice of late spring to early summer: the sea stretched as far as the eye could see, covered all over in broken ice. He said he'd thought of the rings of Saturn.

The rings of Saturn were also made of icy debris, several kilometers broad. If you sat on the broken ice and gazed as far as you could, beside the endless dark vault of space above your head and below your feet, the brightest source of light would be that line of endless broken ice. Dad had said that, out of all the solar system, he'd most wanted to go to Saturn. After eight years, I finally discovered what my father had wished for.

When the space station followed its trajectory to graze past the rings of Saturn, I had the fortune of seeing the astronomical-scale ice glide past in front of my eyes, while behind me, the plants and animals of Shangri-La grew riotously. Vines freely extended tendrils. Long-armed apes clung on to the vines, swinging upward, and upward again.

In that moment, I knew that I would venture deeper into the universe.

That was my ninth Spring Festival on Shangri-La.

The space station didn't immediately merge with Saturn's ecological assembly. Due to the evolution and changes in animal behavior inside the station, we underwent strict quarantine. Saturn central command specially built a small-scale space station as a point of interaction.

Auntie Fang was part of the first batch there; she'd gained a sweetly smiling little granddaughter. They spoke to each other through a glass wall through the intercom. Our family was the last batch to leave the space station. The five of us pressed against the glass, looking at the bustling Saturn natives on the other side.

Mom said, "We're finally here."

My thoughts had drifted elsewhere.

She noticed. She had to lift her arm to reach my hair.

She went on tiptoes and gave my hair a ruffle. Quietly, she said, "If you leave ahead of time toward Pluto, you'll be spared most of the quarantine procedure here."

"—It is up to everyone to try to prevent the awful desecration of the world we live in, which is now taking place, and everybody can help in this in however a humble capacity. I am doing what I can in the only way that I know, and I would like your support." The Zhous' youngest son is preparing to leave the solar system. He's been a fan of Durrell since he was a kid. I believe the voyage of Shangri-La simultaneously served as a reminder to him and me. To bring nature to other corners of the universe, to live and multiply, is another way to resist the desecration. I'm grateful for his continued support."

—Wang Chang, Spring 2133 by Earth reckoning,
Spring by Saturn reckoning, from Shangri-La

Five years later, in spring by Earth reckoning, I arrived at the Kuiper belt. I opened up a frozen, meticulously concocted nutrient medium feast, celebrating the first Spring Festival I would spend alone. After defrosting, a little fruit fly came crawling beside the fish mint nutrient medium, wagging its halteres. I decided to share my meal with it.

I received a video message. My brother wrote the script, my older sister filmed, my younger sister provided a rich symphony of birdsong, and my mother gave a rambling account of their New Year celebration. The Shangri-La Gravity Gradient Ecological Park had officially opened. Director Wang had come over to be the park manager. He continued to emphasize the narrowness of his heart; he only knew how to govern through inaction, while Auntie Fang was the real executive power. She'd made it a real grand opening. Flocks of birds flew from high gravity to low gravity, their flying posture and paths of motion fluidly changing. Golden-banded and silver-banded kraits snaked and swayed their bodies in zero gravity, forming helixes like DNA chains. Herds of elephants lightly came out of the bush; a baby elephant trumpeted water into the air, playing with the spheres of water with its nose. The Yunnan snub-nosed monkeys' radiantly golden-furred offspring had already learned to somersault backward. A South China tiger leaped into the air, waving its tail like a rudder to balance itself. It slid its scapulae, extending its torso like flowing water, returning from the weightless zone back to its kingdom of gravity. It was truly beautiful.

My younger sister had just graduated and gone straight into the Ornithology Foundation. My mother had become the park's mammal-feeding manager. In my brother's words, she'd finished the work of rearing humans, and gone on to the grand project of rearing animals. He, in the end, had inherited Dad's work, becoming an educator. My older sister had already arrived on Uranus to help build a new ecology base.

"I want to go too," Mom said at the end. "That planet rotates on its side, so you see the ring flat on, like a halo around it. By the time you're back, that place is going to be a lot more interesting."

A glistening tree frog hopped onto her shoulder, extended its tongue, and ate the giant firebug she'd helped Auntie Fang culture.

"It evolved again!" she complained.

I held back a laugh.

The transmission ended. Once again, I faced the dark universe on my own.

But I still had my little companion.

The animals would continue to evolve. One might travel far, but home was where the heart was. I would be forever grateful to the family and animals that nature had bequeathed me.

Originally published in Chinese in *Non-exist*, February 15th, 2019 as part of the "2019 Science Fiction Spring Festival Gala."

桥

The Bridge

LIU XIAO
刘啸

TRANSLATED BY ANDY DUDAK

Old Ji is the only stall vendor in Summit Town unwilling to go to the
sunny side of Canted Bridge. His used goods stall is in the lowest,
most desolate nook, not far from the bridge shade. The greasy orange
entrance curtain is raised, indicating he still has occasional customers.
His son, Little Ji, is a manual laborer who sometimes lugs goods a fair
distance, and at the start of today's journey, Old Ji rushes out, bent at
the waist, poking his finger in the shadow of Canted Bridge, nostrils
flaring with anger.

"I climbed the bridge!" he shouts. "That's a lot further than you're
going!"

The small town's denizens look upon Old Ji with mockery, but this
doesn't bother him. He straightens his back and kicks the empty oil drum
by his shop, as if to display his vigor. Not that this impresses anyone as
to his bravery. All it provokes is laughter, amid which a neighboring
vendor, Old Noodle, asks:

"You've really climbed up to Magna Luna? Level with me Old Ji. Are
the rumors true? Is it all treasure up there?"

Old Ji looks up toward the crescent of light at the sky's zenith, then glances at the long tower of the bridge at his side. He snorts, as if it's beneath him to answer.

"Well then, why aren't you rich?"

This is a sore spot for Old Ji. Stung, he glares resolutely at Old Noodle, who only grins and presses on:

"Old Ji, if you don't get rich, you'll never command that son of yours. I heard Little Ji tested over ninety. All four subject examiners gave him three ticks. How does that sit with you?"

"Pfft. Little bastard." Old Ji spits indignantly. "Underhanded ways. Restless . . . he doesn't learn. He never learns."

"I heard that new toy is fast indeed." Old Noodle gets closer and lowers his voice. "Old Ji, excuse me for saying so. In the old days you were a renowned bridge jumper, but a dozen days up there and you only come back with the one basket on your back . . . enough to provide for how many people? Isn't it better to . . . "

"Underhanded ways! He'll never learn!"

Old Ji's sudden vehemence and volume startles Old Noodle, whose head recoils on a shrinking neck, and he forgets what else he was going to say. Old Ji takes the opportunity to loom large, and snort again, and in his victor's posture sweep his gaze about. In that pose, he seems like he might, at any moment, step across the vast gulf between Earth and Magna Luna and bid farewell to his current poverty.

Old Ji wasn't so poverty-stricken when he was younger. As a first-rate bridge jumper in Summit Town, his prospects might even have been described as limitless. Back then, the Canted Bridge that led straight to Magna Luna was still making its circuits, every eighteen days sweeping over the mountaintop town standing aloof from worldly strife. On market days, when the bulky, craggy mass of the bridge approached, bustling peddlers and buyers would grow quiet and gather to watch, unable to look away. The optimal place for bridge jumpers was a strip of land about a hundred zhang long.

And one day, there was Old Ji—not so old then, waist bundled in white cloth, forehead bound in an orange scarf—and a dozen or more competing jumpers with their baskets strapped to their backs, standing majestically on the precipice, facing the direction they would fling themselves in the hopes of grabbing onto the bridge base. Magna Luna moved slowly overhead. At an altitude that long-winged falcons had difficulty ascending to, the bridge structure grew dimly visible in the thick fog and suddenly loomed. As it got closer, a mighty tide of wind, seemingly capable of moving heaven and earth, preceded it, rushing over the mountaintop, and leaving onlookers breathless. When the floating bridge base got close enough, people shrieked and scattered, but Old Ji stood his ground. The remaining competitors broke into runs, striving to keep up as the mass of the bridge moved by, looking for the right moment to jump, to get a handhold and start climbing.

But years of gale force winds had polished the rocky mass of the bridge to a smooth gloss. Bridge jumpers slid and scrabbled and fell, some of them en masse.

The ironlike bulk of the bridge approached a cool and detached Old Ji. A collision seemed imminent. He took several steps back with sudden force, ducked, and the bridge base cruised just over his head. Then his hands were out, reaching for a long-familiar cranny. He grabbed, held firm, brought both feet up, and then he was airborne. A dozen seconds later, the bridge base having streaked across the hundred-zhang running ground, Old Ji alone was flying away from the mountaintop and vanishing toward the horizon.

On the next market day eighteen days later, Canted Bridge once more drew near Summit Town, and Old Ji leaped down to envious gazes. He was thin and unshaven. He carried a bundle on his back, and his orange headscarf fluttered half-loose in the wind, like a flame. With long strides he passed through the public square and entered the purchasing station. There he unbound himself from his white cloth bundle and emptied it on the counter. Chunks of crystalline ore, large and small, glimmered under the admiring gaze of a pooling crowd.

"First rate . . . two and half tael, one tael, seven-tenths of a tael," said the station keeper, blinking through bifocal lenses. "Second rate . . . seven tael, four and six-tenths tael. Third rate . . . one and a half catty. Eh, worm-eaten and rat-nibbled, a bag of broken stones and shattered tiles. It's as high as I'll go."

The spectators were immediately abuzz with excitement, shouting and cheering. The young, deferential shop assistant handed over a roll of banknotes. Old Ji took it between two fingers and, without counting it, stuffed it in a waist pocket. The assistant then proffered the remainder in coins, which Old Ji casually scattered over the heads of the crowd. The change came down like rain, tinkling on the floor. Amid the scrambling, riotous chaos that followed, Old Ji flung his bindle over his shoulder and strode out, head held high.

Using a skill passed down from his ancestors, he traveled between Summit Town and Magna Luna, making a nice profit over the years, enough to buy property and get married and create a well-off, influential, dignified small-town family. His only headache was his son. Although Little Ji was always looking up at Magna Luna with longing, he had no interest in the skill that was his birthright—never mind climbing the Canted Bridge himself.

"I think you've seen how everyone in town envies us," Old Ji said once in the dead of night, intent on revealing the family secret. "Quiet now, we mustn't wake your mother."

"What is it?" Little Ji was at a curious age, always ready for a new mystery.

"The secret to successful bridge jumping. What else?" Old Ji opened the bottom of the chest and rummaged softly through the contents, finally extracting a piece of paper. "Your old man uses it to make serious money."

"How do you make money, Dad?"

Old Ji began lecturing on bridge jumping, relating the defeats of other climbers and his own successes ascending the bridge, and finally the secret of that success:

"The sides are impossible to get a handhold on. You must change that thinking. You see, this is a topographical map of the bridge's base. If you grab on here . . . and at this point here . . . and step up here, you'll get yourself onto the bridge. No one else knows this."

"I thought only big, grand places needed maps." Little Ji couldn't comprehend the misery of moving in the less than half a meter between bridge base and ground, and so felt a dozen zhang space didn't merit a topographical map.

"No, not just big places." Old Ji sensed his son's pleasant surprise, then a feeling of disappointment, of loss, filled his heart, and he couldn't help seizing the opportunity to ask:

"Well, then, someday . . . how about I teach you to bridge jump?"

"No fun. No thanks. I want to play with cars."

Subjected to this and other unfilial attacks, Old Ji couldn't avoid falling into dejection. As he aged, growing hunchbacked and feeble-legged, his skill flagging, his son lost to pleasure-seeking and lack of ambition, he couldn't help feeling more depressed. At least his son wasn't the only one. Many young people of Summit Town spent their days singing and galivanting. Not one was practicing to be a bridge jumper. Old Ji's status was assured, at least for the moment. He didn't have to worry about immediate pretenders to his throne.

The same year that Little Ji rejected the special skill of his ancestors, opting instead to be young and carefree, visitors came up the mountain.

Summit Town wasn't cut off from the outside world as such, but its high elevation, along with many generations of sloth, had long ago rendered most denizens uninterested in communication. Canted Bridge was like a great, precise pendulum, delineating everyone's rhythm, habituating them to lives beginning and ending on the mountaintop, even making them forget there were people down the mountain just like them. However, when two strangers on cross-country four-wheelers came up the mountain, the rare novelty of it set Summit Town abuzz. The mayor, face wrinkled like a time-creased bellows, came forward to receive the guests, as if to reengrave the long-faded word "hospitality" on the human heart. When the feasting began, places of honor were accorded to Summit Town's law clerk, who was in charge of all kinds of procedures, and the old blind couple who'd been teachers here for so long—and Old Ji, recruited to help entertain the guests.

They seemed to only want to talk about Magna Luna and Canted Bridge.

"Miraculous really," said the bearded guest. "So close . . . almost a direct connection. Truly miraculous. Mayor, has anyone in your town here gone up to Magna Luna?"

The mayor assumed an air of self-satisfaction. He downed a cup of spirits, then lifted his chin, aiming it at Old Ji: "You're at the right table. This one here is our town's most renown bridge jumper. May I present Old Ji . . . "

The visitor stared in amazement, making Old Ji a bit uneasy, but he managed a courteous nod and some modesty: "I'm old now. Can't climb so well anymore."

"Please excuse my lack of manners," the bearded man said. "I've heard that there's crystalline ore up there. Perhaps a lot of it? Or no?"

To Old Ji, this sounded like an inquiry into his family's property and resources. He felt it prudent to neither confirm nor deny. "There's some, there's some."

Fortunately, Whiskers didn't pursue this line of questioning any further. He spoke with someone else in a low voice for a while. Old Ji heard "double star system," "rarefied atmosphere," "low gravity region," and a few other things he didn't understand. Something deep and indescribable in him recoiled, as if warm light had found its way into a dark ice cave through a small hole.

Half a year later, more four-wheelers made the ascent. The visitors established themselves as downland representatives in Summit Town, and the leader, as before, was Whiskers. They looked on as Old Ji gave them a bridge jumping demonstration, and they cheered loudly. Old Ji, flustered and panicked, nearly slipped from his purchase. When he returned to the mountaintop eighteen days later, he felt some indescribable change had taken place. His son was still running wild, but now apt to run toward Whiskers. The downland leader seemed all too welcoming of the town's young people into his sphere, seemingly with an eye toward some advantage, something to do with his intentions in this remote place. One day he even fired up the largest four-wheeler and drove the town elites—the mayor and his family, and the old blind couple—for three circuits of the public square.

"Wow!" gasped an admiring Old Noodle, squatting on his heels at the front of the crowd.

Old Ji, farther back, couldn't help craning his neck to see. The vehicle halted by lucky coincidence, and Whiskers spotted him.

"Old Ji! Come on. Come, come."

He hadn't expected this invitation. After a dumbfounded moment, he waved his hand in refusal. "Uh, no. Out of the question. No."

Whiskers seemed to think this a mere pleasantry. He got out and pulled Old Ji toward the vehicle, then guided him into the passenger seat. Then the machine was off again, embarking on a figure eight. Dizzy, Old Ji watched the crowd on his side fall away, and he realized he was hurtling forward. The old mayor in the back seat stroked his mustache and laughed.

"Old Ji! This is amazing, isn't it? Why don't you give it a try?"

"Uh . . ."

Old Ji recoiled in his seat, slack-jawed and nearly drooling, breathless. An enthusiastic Whiskers said, "Indeed, our vehicle here is easy to drive. I'm sure someone as brave and capable as yourself, Old Ji, won't even need lessons. You'll master it at a glance. Come on, give it a try!"

The vehicle had just completed a circuit. Whiskers helped the old mayor and the others out, then put a stupefied Old Ji in the driver's seat. He taught Old Ji to grip the steering wheel, and then to pedal the gas, and the machine crept forward. Prideful Old Ji didn't want people to see his timidity. He gripped the wheel with the firmness of a bridge jumper clinging to the base. But he hadn't gone fifty meters when—the lively crowd again swinging into view with their multitudinous gazes and judgments—his arms cramped, and he panicked, and a lamppost loomed, and he crashed.

The collision thoroughly undid Old Ji's bridge jumper prestige. Thereafter the townsfolk spoke of him with ridicule, proclaiming his stature vanished into thin air. After a few days, people noticed he was looking older and thinner. He stopped acknowledging Old Noodle's greetings. All he seemed to do was bend at the waist and berate Little Ji:

"Running around all day like mad! I don't even have the words! As . . . " He paused to cough. " . . . as long as you're under my roof, you're forbidden to behave in such unruly ways!"

"But . . . " Little Ji said, aggrieved and defensive.

Serenity gradually returned to Summit Town. Whiskers, perhaps feeling sorry for Old Ji, led his downlanders in a regretful departure from town. The day they left, everybody but Old Ji saw them off. The vehicles crawled in procession down the mountainside, slowly getting farther away, until they were submerged downland and gone.

Time flew and more than ten years passed. Summit Town, as always, was bustling and peaceful as an anthill. If the fated change of scene hadn't come, the town might have gone on as before, tranquil until a critical mass of human-made boredom had accrued and forced change. One night, a violent quaking woke everyone. Panic spread through the town, but no one knew what was going on. The shaking seemed to come from underground depths and continued for a long time. There was no daylight the next morning. The town was enveloped in inky blackness, as on the eve of an approaching tempest. Another four days passed, and the dense dust cloud continued to blot out sky and sun. Windblown grit stung people's faces. Most hid in their houses and didn't dare emerge, but the obstinate and blind old teacher ventured out, tapping and listening his way along as he always had. After he'd been gone a while, his wife opened the door and wailed into the murk. Several daring fellows, noses and mouths covered in burlap masks, organized a fumbling search. It was some time before they returned with the limp, half-dead form of the teacher.

"There was a ghost!" he said when he woke. "It crashed into me! It crashed into me!"

These words brought fear to many townsfolk. Another half-month passed, and the windblown dust began to abate. Some visibility returned. People discovered, to their shock, that Magna Luna's Canted Bridge was in the process of coming to rest over Summit Town. It was still half a meter above the ground, but no longer sweeping past on its fixed route. Instead, it swayed in the vicinity, sometimes colliding with the mountaintop, ploughing soil then turning to go—sometimes seeming to stop short, hesitating, hovering, then returning, pushing its way through township land, caving in unlucky walls. Obviously, the old teacher had been knocked down by Canted Bridge that night.

The townsfolk had no choice but to set aside a big plot of land for Canted Bridge's havoc-wreaking. They had no other plan apart from this. But matters soon evolved beyond anyone's expectations, when a dozen or so iron birds—bigger than long-winged falcons—came soaring toward the mountain. They drew near and began circling the bridge.

"What are they doing?" Old Noodle wondered, squinting upward. "Looking to nest?"

"Those are flying vehicles." The law clerk had listened to more downland rumors than most. "I don't know for sure, but there might be people in them."

Old Ji gazed with astonishment at Canted Bridge, which had, once upon a time, been his livelihood. It seemed to him that everyone wanted to halt the bridge and seize his bridge jumper title. As he tried to calculate what the new circumstances meant to the bridge jumping profession in terms of difficulty, he glanced about, seeking potential rivals, but no one seemed to be taking things seriously. The aircraft lingered in the sky for days, more and more of them ascending to higher elevations and out of sight. The mass of the bridge gradually slowed amid the dust haze. Occasionally it seemed to bend, exhibiting a faint curve, like a willow branch caught in a quagmire. The people of Summit Town were surprised beyond words. Could it be that Canted Bridge, climbed for so many years, was actually soft? Pliable? Even more unexpected was the next two months of aircraft slowly bringing the massive bridge to a fixed position over the mountaintop, then very slowly easing it down.

It finally touched the ground one evening, raising a small cloud of dust.

Old Ji watched, dumbfounded, facial tics alive. Suddenly it was like he'd been deserted. His deep-set eyes moistened. He lifted his head, rubbed his nose, and gave a hateful snort.

Old Ji rose late the next day. When he opened the door, he saw a crowd gathered outside his shop, which had long been closed for business. At the center of the crowd was that downland visitor, Whiskers, his hair whiter than before, his voice louder:

"Yes, very lucky, most auspicious. A real heaven-sent opportunity. Who could've imagined Canted Bridge would come to a halt? We thought it was an earthquake at first, but after a few days we saw several meteorites had crashed down. Meteorites . . . do you all understand? Down below, our observation station discovered them. And so I spoke with my leaders, and we saw a great opportunity, a once-in-a-lifetime chance. The leadership dispatched me, and now Canted Bridge has come down. From now on, you will all climb up there. All of you!"

Old Ji listened to the rumors coming from the crowd: Whiskers was the government-appointed chief of the arrested Canted Bridge. The townsfolk nodded to each other, watching him with admiration and respect. The law clerk was organizing a celebratory feast, while another group was setting to work at the bridge base, pouring a foundation and driving the piles that would fix the bridge permanently. Old Ji stood in his doorway, reckoning the cost of the feast would fall to Summit Town's households. If he didn't go and eat his fill, it would amount to a big loss. But he couldn't seem to put one foot in front of the other. Little Ji, on the other hand, didn't hesitate to venture into the crowd. He was a young man now. Old Ji called after him to no avail.

He'd grown up rather thin, yet strong. Normally he did manual labor at his father's shop, the heavy lifting, and like his contemporaries he had a rebellious streak. For instance, he was always secretly turning on a light to read by at night, provoking complaints from Old Ji about the cost of electricity:

"Earning money isn't easy, boy. You have to save if you can save. You must behave with integrity and play the hand you're dealt. Running wild all day . . . what? Are you up to some master plan? I order you not to waste your time, but you just won't listen. Dammit, if before you had just . . . "

Old Ji sighed at his greatly diminished authority. He half-heartedly watched Whiskers inciting the crowd. Since Canted Bridge had halted, many people were climbing it. Even Old Noodle had ascended, in grandiose style, to enjoy the scenery. Old Ji hated Old Noodle's unprofessional climbing from the bottom of his heart, but he said nothing.

"Dad, I want to study to be driver," Little Ji said, returning to the shop.

"What?" This was no trivial matter. Old Ji doubted his ears. "Drive vehicles, son? You?"

"I really want to." Little Ji's eyes were bright, stubborn, unyielding. "Our financial circumstances are getting worse year by year. I can't grow old here eating free meals. What's wrong with learning a new trade?"

"A trade like running wild?" Old Ji wanted to strike something, but nothing was on hand. "Work for me and behave yourself. I can't permit anything else!"

Thus, via conflict, ended father and son's first exchange on future prospects, but Little Ji's behavior didn't improve. Instead, he became even more "unfilial." After the reinforcement of Canted Bridge was complete, material began to arrive from the base of the mountain: tall, slender, sparkling things allegedly called "rail tracks." Amid the clanging racket of excavation, Little Ji and some other young people watched a group of safety-helmeted workers use simple cranes to get the rails erect and placed on Canted Bridge.

"The track will eventually go all the way up," Whiskers explained to Little Ji and others, pointing at a partially dust-obscured Magna Luna. "All that good stuff up there can be freighted down. A round trip will only take two or three days. Maybe even just one day."

"Freighted?" Little Ji asked in amazement. "By what?"

"Freight cars, of course, drawn by electric engines. You folks don't understand that yet." Whiskers seemed to recall something. "Hey, after the rail is completed, Canted Bridge will need drivers. It'll be just like driving a car. Little Ji, I seem to recall you enrolled . . . "

"My old man won't allow it." Little Ji was a bit anxious. He straightened his back and squared his shoulders. "But you know what, it doesn't matter."

In the end, probably thanks to Whiskers' prestige on the ground, Little Ji's vehicular education launched smoothly. As the track was laid higher and higher, the iron birds came and went more frequently, and Whiskers often rode them into the sky, sometimes not touching ground for days at a time. And suddenly, bafflingly, there was more work to do in the shop. Little Ji had no choice but to work through the night, until his back ached, and still find energy for his studies. Fortunately, after three days, the workload returned to normal. Little Ji stole glances at his father, who always remained cool and composed.

Little Ji passed the final test of his driver's curriculum and concealed it from his father, and he actually did quite well. The news spread through town. The examiners were pleased with Little Ji's skills, and his opportunity to eat government grain was just around the corner. Old Ji's expression was obvious to everyone watching in excitement and anticipation, waiting for father and son's final blowout. It only took the slightest noise from within Old Ji's shop for ears to perk up.

Old Ji's shop business had been in steady decline for years. Half a year before, he'd been strapped enough to move from his decent original property to the remote nook. It didn't help that Old Noodle, whom he'd always disdained, was now his neighbor—and he grew even more sullen. He wondered apprehensively how his son had become so unfilial, how the world had become so unrecognizable so fast, and how, in this motionless bridge era, he had no prospects.

"Old Ji!"

It was dusk, long after Little Ji had finished his course, and Whiskers was loudly calling at the shop entrance. Old Ji poked his head out, startled. Whiskers was covered head to toe in rock fragments and dust, but he looked full of vigor. It seemed he was just back from above, once again.

"I won't come in and sit," Whiskers said. "I just wanted to let you know that the work above is just about complete. I've received notice that next month the railway will be open to traffic. There's to be a ceremony. Will you come? Little Ji is one of the driving masters, so congratulations are in order! Everyone will be there, Old Ji. Everyone!"

"What?"

For the second time in his life, Old Ji was surprised beyond words. Whiskers, having delivered his message, felt free to go. Old Ji came to his senses and rushed several steps out of his shop, meaning to pull Whiskers to a halt, but his hand didn't reach.

"This, this . . . "

"What now?"

"For something like this . . . I mean, poor folks like us aren't suitable, are we?"

"Poor folks? Old Ji, your thinking is all wrong. Why do you think we've repaired the road if not to get rich? You know how resource-rich Magna Luna is. You saw it all when you were younger, in grand style. Let me tell you, Little Ji is very clever. He can do anything he sets his mind to. You really are blessed."

"Clever? Even compared with downland driving masters?"

"It's cost effective, Old Ji, and localization, adapting to a local environment, also creates employment. You wouldn't understand." Whiskers seemed unwilling to explain more. He glanced sidelong at the house, inside which Little Ji was listening. "You must come to the ceremony."

After Whiskers had gone, Old Ji limped weakly back to his shop. Little Ji was shouldering two sacks of lime plaster out the door. His thin torso glistened with sweat in the light of sunset. Old Ji's brow furrowed as he unconsciously shook his head and heaved a quiet sigh.

THE BRIDGE

• • •

Opening day for the railway comes in the blink of an eye. Early in the morning, Old Ji listens to the sounds of Little Ji getting dressed in the neighboring room. The lad leaves without eating breakfast. Silence descends on the shop. Old Ji lies in bed staring, wide-eyed. He tosses and turns, but it's useless trying to sleep after waking in the morning, so he gets up. Outside, the street is full of bustling activity, people squeezing by, all headed for Canted Bridge.

That afternoon, Old Ji partially raises his shop curtain and prepares to receive customers, but pedestrians spare him no more than glances. Nobody stops. Old Ji gives up on business for the day, closes the curtain, and gropes about in the gloom of the shop. He paces, growing unhappy and hungry, and finally limps out through the side entrance.

It's chilly and sunny outside. The clamor of gongs and drums emanates from the direction of Canted Bridge, spreading rumor of the ceremony, drawing layer upon layer of crowd. Old Ji doesn't want to be seen heading in that direction, so he detours, taking a roundabout approach. The bridge's sun-exposed face gradually comes into view. Several lines shine bright and silver on the impossibly long mass of the bridge, plunging straight into the zenith of the sky. At some point, objects known as "carriages" have been hung on the silvery rails. Each is adorned with a red silk ribbon like a burning flame. Several important-looking personages sit on a platform before the carriages, and Whiskers stands off to one side. The resonant sound of speech comes to Old Ji on the wind. He doesn't get closer to hear what's being said, but he casts his gaze about. He spots a row of young people wearing red flowers on their chests, his son among them. Old Ji smiles, surprising himself—and still smiling, he can't help feeling some resentment.

The long-winded speech isn't over until dusk. Then a group representing the townsfolk raises an inscribed stone stele. The law clerk has been racking his brains for months to come up with the prose poem to be engraved. Now he faces the stele and recites and sings, punctuating the performance with traditional syllable-breaks. This time Old Ji understands a little. The lyrics look back at the construction history, but also seem to gaze into the future. Canted Bridge will be a vital link between the ground and Magna Luna. There will be plenty of work in transport and immigration both.

Is it possible a driver has good prospects? Old Ji wonders, scratching his head.

The dim light of evening gradually prevails. The platform lights come on, contrasting sharply with the outer dark. When the traditional chant is complete, the law clerk and Whiskers exit stage left and right, and someone pulls one end of a silk ribbon. Applause wells up, but soon there is silence again. Someone else goes to center stage and stands there for several seconds, and the silk ribbon snaps and floats down toward either side.

Old Ji takes this for a bad omen, but the audience cheers.

Little Ji and the other young people walk onto stage. The head of the procession speaks briefly and thankfully, then each opens and gets into a rail carriage. Their headlights come on, piercing the dark night sky. Flashing red lights appear along both sides of the railway, like stars in military formation leading to the heavens. When Little Ji threw his hat in the ring, Old Ji peevishly avoided looking at the bridge or looking up. But now he can't help himself. This is a spectacle like none he's ever seen. He can't take his eyes off it. A muffled roar of awe comes from the crowd. The carriages tremble lightly, then begin to slowly rise. People watch in amazement, eyes wide and mouths agape, their admiring expressions like those that once greeted an honored bridge jumper.

Suddenly, one of the carriages halts only three or four meters off the ground, the screeching of the rails stabbing Old Ji's eardrums like iron. Alarmed, he immediately runs for the bridge. He's only gone a hundred meters when he sees one of the distant carriages open and Little Ji's head emerge. The young driving master makes a simple gesture at Whiskers, then shuts the door. The carriage begins once more to slowly rise, then accelerate, soaring higher and higher.

"Little bastard," Old Ji mutters, panting. "You almost made your old man sprain an ankle."

He takes the opportunity to turn and limp off in a different direction. He makes his sluggish way to a cliff near the edge of town and squats. Feeling wronged and impetuous, he has his back to Canted Bridge, but he can still hear the cheering, the unceasing acclaim. He can't help turning his head and looking up. The red rail lights are like a heavenly path hanging down from Magna Luna, spanning the vast night sky. His son's carriage and the others are like a string of sparkling meteors, slowly climbing toward that high, remote place.

"All grown up, are you? Ready to spread your wings and fly? Not a second thought for your dad? No matter how disobedient, aren't you still my son?"

Although Old Ji feels depressed, he realizes his son is, in the end, climbing to Magna Luna. He is following in his father's footsteps. This brings Old Ji a gradual sense of relief. He turns back around, gazes down upon the night-shrouded lowlands. Distant lights sparkle here and there, like lanterns floating on an underworld river.

It's getting late, and the air is turning cold. Old Ji shivers. People are dispersing from the bridge, so he prepares to depart. He has just stood when he recalls something. He fishes a piece of paper from his pocket. He tears it into pieces, sighs, and releases them to scatter on the wind like so many white butterflies. Soon they have all floated away into the night sky.

First Prize: 7th Lightyear Award for Best Micro-Fiction (2018).

Originally published in Chinese in *Tadpole Stave*, February 18th, 2019.

墓碑

Tombstone
YANG WANQING
杨晚晴

TRANSLATED BY ANDY DUDAK

Imagine a tombstone. The entire mass of it is black, towering high enough to pierce clouds, like an old scar on the city's skyline. Imagine when the clouds roll in dense and dark, and this tombstone is plugged into the cloud layer like a syringe, pouring the heroin of human souls into the tear glands of nature. Imagine when the sky is clear and boundless. The tombstone's shadow sweeps across half of New Anchorage, turning this vast, ash-gray city into a great sundial.

As if to demonstrate the human soul's immortality, the depth of time measured is hard to fathom: from ancient, cannibalistic times, when primitive humans devoured raw meat, to the modern burning of floral and faunal remains interred for hundreds of millions of years, to yesterday's destruction of homelands by the mysterious power of the atom. And now, gazing up at that tower, we believe we've arrived at last: life without bloodshed, a guarantee of longevity, like that promised to Heaven and Earth.

But now you know that tower only measures the infinite void of death. It is just a tombstone, towering over the piled skeletons of humanity.

A tombstone towering over civilization.

"They won't let me see his body."

She lowers her eyes as she speaks, straightening the gold pendant hanging from her neck. After a moment, she adds, "But I can imagine."

She leans forward, putting a striped straw in her mouth. She grinds her teeth, preoccupied, the straw bending, like acute pain escaping her mouth.

I grip her ice-cold hand.

The deceased was her respected teacher Lloyd Hariri, a paragon who worked with her on the Minos Field. Officially it's being called a suicide, but the rumor is Hariri used his masterful abilities and preeminent imagination to achieve a death of great spectacle and ceremony.

Milling machine. Lathe. Homemade gunpowder. Molten steel sprayed everywhere. Hariri's corpse lies in a small-scale weapons workshop that produced a large-caliber, homemade pistol with no rifling.

The bullet entered his temple at close range.

I can also imagine, but I can't reconcile that tableau with my impressions of Hariri: the bald head, the deep-set, heavily lidded eyes, the dimples when he smiled. And yet he staged a lavish fireworks show on his skull.

He isn't the only scientist to die recently, but he's certainly the most attention grabbing. His story stands out from the madly swarming forum posts of Augmented Vision. I'm at a loss amid the diverse and muddled death scene reconstruction sims. This excessive witnessing of death limits my imagination, rather than aiding it.

She gazes out the window. "He chose true death." She seems to be staring at something far off and blurred. "Why?"

I follow her gaze, as if she might have found an answer out there. In a gray curtain of rain, the vehicle lights are a blood red river. Looming over that is the black tower.

No answers there. Just finality, true death.

Don't be foolish, I chide myself. Roi asked why but didn't expect an answer. No one can give her the answer she seeks.

She turns to face me. "The first time I saw you it was raining just like this. I still remember . . . " She notes my skeptical look.

"Remember what?"

She shakes her head, her smile dispelled. Softly shouted classic rock fills the pub.

I look around at the curling smoke and the few human shapes, dubiously lit, quietly chatting. Cluck cluck, coo coo. I reckon that in such times, the mere existence of a pub like this, a place that allows people to get together, is a kind of miracle. How did Roi find it? My gaze meets that of the waiter behind the bar. He's cleaning cups. A cold shiver runs through me. I don't like his expression, a familiar one. He's seen my black and purple uniform.

"Xiaofan," Roi says, "did you know Hariri often came here?"

I shake my head.

Biting her straw, she continues to gaze at the rain.

"We . . ." She closes her mouth on the next syllable, as if her thoughts are locked in struggle with her speech. She stands. "Let's go."

We rent a small flat, one of those standard modules with no Seismic Cancelation System. It's compact but has everything we need: living room, bedroom, kitchen, and bathroom. There's seldom much sunlight to speak of in our bustling, out-of-the-way alley, so the white walls maximally reflect artificial light, allowing several clusters of sickly green plants to persist like invalids. When we turn off the artificial windows, we can always see that immense black tower floating on the mist of New Anchorage, like a mast in the ocean.

Roi and I go to that mast, and return from it, every day. We follow the same route, but for different occupations.

"Xiaofan." Roi is curled up on our double bed, which nearly fills the bedroom. "I think I've got a cold."

I go in and feel her forehead. "What was it? Yesterday's downpour?"

She smiles tenderly. "Babe, it's just a cold, not a fever."

That's my love, through and through. Her logic pathways are always unobstructed. She'll correct your mistakes without a sense of superiority.

"I've requested a day off from my supervisor. Be careful out there."

I hesitate in the doorway.

"Relax, okay?" She blows me a kiss. "I have Ann to keep me company."

On the tram to Osiris Tower, people's expressions are blank. They're lost in retinal implant communications and entertainment. Outside my porthole, high-speed motion smooths out the details of buildings, making for a vague, ashen scene. Only Osiris Tower, sufficiently distant, sufficiently tall, remains distinct to my eyes. It is steady, sharp edged. As the tram gets closer, its obsidian-like form occludes more and more of the sky.

I watch it but think of Roi. We are both in the service of death. Other than that, we have nothing in common.

I remember moving through the staff canteen toward her. It felt like such a long distance at the time. The adventure began with a bet and getting to her wasn't easy. I felt those looks on my back, gazes awaiting my humiliation. Every step broke the record for the shortest distance between us. I could see her in profile: brown skin, pointy nose, black frame glasses, curly hair bundled at the back of her head. My knee hit a stainless steel bench en route. The pain was excruciating. Cold sweat oozed from my pores. *Okay, relax*, I told myself. *At least she's alone at her dining table.* I came around it to sit opposite her. My weak legs surrendered precipitously to gravity. I crashed into the seat.

She looked up, light flashing on her glasses.

"Eh, hello. I'm Li Xiaofan. I . . . I'm in Area Two."

Area Two. A blunt opener, to say the least. Blunt and not a little momentous, an Area Two guy making conversation with a scientist. If Roi had left at that moment, I would've felt relieved of a great burden.

But she didn't. She stayed, just like a certain someone had guaranteed she would.

"Well hello, and how are you?" Her smile revealed perfect canines. "Roi Lei."

Roi Lei. The name rolled off the tip of her tongue. Thinking of it now conjures sensations, dim mental associations, her pliant yet tough voice, the mild shampoo fragrance that suffused her. She wore an orange uniform and struck me as a lovely tulip. I remember being in love with her from the moment she opened her mouth. It was a compelling directive, implanted deep within my logic layers. Being without her wasn't an option. I had to keep going.

Whoever is lonely at this moment, is lonely forever.

"Hi. I, uh, wanted to consult you." My voice trembled. There was an immense question in my heart, a questioned fanned to burning by a lack of detailed explanation from official sources, and I flung this question at her, nearly forgetting my true purpose.

"Well," she said, wrinkling her delicate nose.

That's it, Li Xiaofan, your good luck has come to an end, as has this dialogue. I felt dizzy under bright white lights, in danger of floating away. I struggled to focus. Then came her voice: "The answer is complex. Let's take it slow, shall we?"

Shall we? I bit my lip. Those two words would've been enough to make that group of guys piss themselves in terror, but I didn't think this at the time.

I nodded.

"So," she said, gathering up her hair. "This work of ours . . . we change a human consciousness into Osiris particles. You know that much, I think? Osiris particles can perfectly imitate a neural network, in structure and function. An Osiris particle network as a whole is decoherent. It can interact with the domain of larger-scale physics, while its individual particles, by means of their spin states, can act as neurons doing impulse-suppression. Then, via Hermes messenger particles, states can be propagated. Of course, this is an extremely simplified explanation." She paused. "Did I go too fast?"

I shook my head. I was quite stupid, hence Area Two material, one of numerous Charons on the River Styx. As far as a Charon was concerned, prying into the secrets of death was a sin.

"We give people souls," I summarized, with not a little affectation.

"Souls." She closed her eyes. "Material ones."

"But if Osiris particles duplicate a consciousness, doesn't the original self die with its brain?"

"Good question." She gave a mischievous wink. "'Duplicate' isn't the best word. Let's call it 'peeling away.' That's a better way to understand it. You've heard the story of the Ship of Theseus? The principle's the same. The 'peeling away' process involves repeated substitution: neurons are replaced by Osiris particles one by one. You're still you as it happens. After about thirty billion replacements, your consciousness has been peeled away from your mortal body. Continuity of self is preserved. You're still you."

I listened, only partly understanding. There was a kind of assurance in her eyes and bearing. "I" would not perish. We Charons were not executioners.

I stood up. "Thank you."

"You're quite welcome." She extended her hand. "It was so nice to meet you, Li Xiaofan."

I took her hand, and there were trains screaming through my blood vessels, and Roi was their only passenger.

"Nice to meet you too."

The tram arrives. Passing beneath the underground station's vast transparent dome, you can see the honeycomb-like interior structure covered by Osiris Tower's black polycarbon façade. The occasional blue flash illuminates these cells. Roi said they have something to do with electrical capacity and energy storage. You could perhaps gaze up along the tower's commanding height, but I wouldn't suggest it. So close to the base, even if you didn't injure your cervical vertebra, you couldn't possibly see all the way up to the summit.

Thus, in a kind of autohypnosis, I see Osiris Tower descending from the heavens. It's a great ladder to God's paradise. And soon I will enter it, and change into my black and purple uniform, and go to the River Styx.

Before that, I must do something for my love.

Roi has been acting a bit strange for the past two days. I think it has to do with Hariri's death.

I send a silent message into the void.

The fried steak is burned. There's too much dressing on the salad. For dessert there's mousse and a small cake, passable, because we got them from a Western-style pastry shop a few days before and kept them in the fridge. Roi watches me apologetically. "I had time today, so I just . . . didn't ask for Ann's help."

Ann is our AI. She's currently projected against the far wall of the living room, playing her zither. This simulated young lady's hair is done up in a bun, and she wears a traditional Han Chinese dress. Roi customized her thusly.

"Roi was quite diligent and careful. I can attest to that." Ann's voice emanates down from the ceiling. The two of them seem like sisters sometimes, speaking in whispers, keeping secrets. I put down my fork and knife and caress Roi's hand. "Babe, when I was little, a spread like this would've been a sumptuous feast."

Her brows knit. *When I was little.* I said it. If you're always detouring around certain words and phrases, like avoiding open sewage, then you've likely got taboo vocab on your hands.

Roi knows, of course.

But today I went ahead and said, "When I was little." In passing, to be sure, but the despair and humiliation is here now, regardless. It's a kind of conditioned reflex that can run through a lifetime. Every time I say it, it's like my heart pumps salt into my blood vessels. This time I grit my teeth and forge ahead. I tell her of a time before the Great Scattering, when my family was destitute. Of running a maritime blockade and how the boat capsized. Of my father and little sister freezing to death in the Arctic Ocean. Of my mother trading her body for food, and early one dismal morning, opening her wrists.

"Babe, I'm so . . . " Roi's eyes redden. "I'm so sorry."

My throat burns. "If it wasn't for the Tower, it would be everyone's fate."

The muscles at the corners of her mouth tighten.

Those painful memories were just foreshadowing. What I really want to say is next:

"Roi, I know some scientists are skeptical of Osiris Tower's operations. After all, the way it gets energy is so clean, so efficient. For post-Scattering humanity, it seems like cheating. But you know how I see it? The Tower . . . " I watch her eyes intently. " . . . the Tower gave me dignity. The dignity people have when their bellies are full. When they're warm. When they don't have to fear the long night. Human dignity."

She can't meet my gaze. "Xiaofan, why did you bring this up?"

I sigh heavily. "That place we went yesterday, Roi . . . do you know what it is?"

Some people say New Anchorage is human civilization's last redoubt. You can see where they're coming from, what with the city's population and organization, its advanced and flourishing society.

And in view of its inexhaustible fountainhead.

Open up a ninth grade history text, and you'll see how the city's technocratic government uses natural science to model history: cities germinating on grain surpluses and the need for division of labor, cities gathering population (with the negative side of things, like the resultant plagues, omitted), population spurring demand, demand spurring innovation, writing, the wheel, metal smelting, and probably taxation, and the nation state, the progress of science and technology and organization and the resultant manufacturing surplus, and population growth in turn, and so on.

This is human civilization's fundamental model—of course, this is an extremely simplified explanation—with production surplus as its beginning, and population as its inner motive force.

In the eyes of New Anchoragers, surplus and population alone have made the city outstanding, and unrivaled. But I must add a third element: the Great Scattering.

The mid-twenty-second century's Great Scattering was an apocalypse for human civilization. Many elements in superposition, strengthening each other, brought it about:

Global warming led to rising sea levels. Humanity's dry territory was reduced and broken up.

Temperate zones were no longer suitable for agriculture or habitation. Humanity migrated to the northern hemisphere's high-latitude expanses of dry land.

This mass migration led to the collapse of existing political and administrative subdivisions. City-states emerged in the northern hemisphere's high-latitude regions.

Energy shortages and political instability made large-scale trade and distribution difficult. Most city-states, after springing up rapidly, capitulated to famine and riots. Populations scattered again, this time without direction.

This was the so-called Great Scattering.

Forgive some presumptuous conjecture, but those lucky enough to scatter to Alaska, to New Anchorage, must have marveled, fresh off the boat and thinking they'd arrived in paradise. The climate was pleasant. The people were genteel, courteous, well fed, and clothed. The streets overflowed with an optimistic mood unrivaled in this era. The city had the feel of a super-metropolis. It would have been shocking to stumble upon a place so rich, secure, and healthy in these times of energy shortage. How did it exist? If you put this question to a citizen of New Anchorage, they might respond with a tolerant laugh, then raise their hand and point toward the black scar on the heavens.

Osiris Tower.

• • •

Roi and I haven't been getting along for the past couple days. I wonder if it has something to do with Hariri's death.

Death itself means nothing. The profound meaning lies behind death, in what it can bring about. In what it ends, and what it leads to.

I don't understand.

Let me put it this way: death ended Hariri's service to us. And death led to doubt.

I understand the first part. But doubt? What doubt?

Think about Hariri and Lei's work. If they don't think they're "helping the souls of the dead transcend suffering," if they believe they're committing murder . . .

But that's preposterous!

Calm down, Li Xiaofan. Answer me this . . . yesterday afternoon, before going home, where did you and Lei go?

A pub on Liberty Street.

The Blackbird Pub, right?

Right.

Did you notice anything . . . peculiar?

Like what?

Never mind. All you need to know is that the Blackbird Pub is a meeting place for dissident elements. For you and I, and of course still for Lei, it's a dangerous place.

Dissident elements?

From a mathematical perspective, if a group is big enough, there will almost certainly be some "heterogeneity." This paradise of ours is no exception. There will always be people dissatisfied with the status quo. There will always be those who take subversion as their duty. There are people like this, now, harboring a stubborn prejudice against the Tower, a prejudice handed down from barbarous times of scarcity, and they're preparing to turn this prejudice into action. There are indications that Hariri was a dissident element. His suicide was a kind of statement.

But Roi is no dissident! I vouch for her. Chief Executive, I—

Guarantees can't change anything. Li Xiaofan, don't forget why you're at Lei's side.

I . . . won't forget.

Very good.

• • •

Here is the River Styx, the intermediate zone between birth and death. My place of work. If you get the chance to enter it (I guarantee the chance is minimal), you will find "River Styx" to be quite a romantic formulation.

It is an immense, transparent, ring-shaped tunnel divided into thirty-six areas, enclosing the Tower's core, the Minos Field, like gelatin encasing meat. Due to an unceasing influx of souls, the Minos Field fluoresces blue. Washed in this light, and pure white lamplight, and console light reflected off white floor tiles and white airlocks, we Charon workers seem lost in a strange, hazy world.

Like being under water.

An Area Two worker conversant in classical myth noted the connection between our work space and river of life and death. We naturally became Charon from that legend, the ferryman between life and death. We place the dead on transfer platforms. We handle bodies with brain tissue not yet completely inactive. I press a button and the near-side of an airlock opens. It closes, and the other side opens, and the deceased is reborn. Behind me, outside the tunnel, friends and family of the deceased bid farewell. Through layered plexiglass they see a steel-blue mist clear. It is the deceased's consciousness, transformed into Osiris particles. A soul made corporeal, in other words. A soul has no inherent color. You see it because of the Minos Field.

Life and liberty. But life's liberty comes at a cost. As a soul, you must be seized by the Minos Field.

You must serve.

People hate us—not our work, but what we represent. It's a taboo of the inauspicious, a taboo from the age of barbarism. That's what Roi told me. I didn't really understand what she meant. I merely serve. I perform my role, and that service is practically built on the despoiling of my own life. There's no hard evidence but being near those transformations day in and day out is sufficient to hasten you toward doom: among thirty-six Charons in their primes, three or four must be replaced every year. Parkinson's, Alzheimer's, schizophrenia, aphasia, amnesia, cerebral cancer . . . There's a tacit understanding among us regarding the Minos Field's effect on the brain.

Aken, Slim, Friedrich—of these so-called friends who bet Roi wouldn't say more than three sentences to me, only one remains. People take our misfortune for a curse. Even we think so. So, the fate or chance that brought Roi and I together was inconceivable. I took it for God opening a new door for me, even though my colleagues never got so lucky.

"Theoretically speaking," Roi once said, "I'm a Brahmin. Priests, clerics, these are my ancestors, servants of death. In this way, you and I are no different."

Then we kissed for the first time. I remember how she passed her breath into my mouth, like God pouring spirit into a pottery figurine. Ah, Roi.

Facing today's deceased, I think of that first kiss. It's a kind of blasphemy. I size up the dead person before me:

Male. Caucasian. About twenty years old. Face serene. My Augmented Vision gives me the maximum conversion time of fifteen minutes. I close my eyes. Breathe deep. Open my eyes. Lightly touch the button. Then comes the electrical machine buzz. Forty-five seconds later, my "ferry passenger" enters the Land of the Dead. A dizzying, nauseating, low-frequency sound announces him. The Osiris particle transformation begins. First, the blue fog seeps from the top of the head like fast-growing hair. Slowly, the quivering blue miasma begins to disengage. It still maintains the self's soft tissue form. A few seconds later, the blue vapor breaks away from the head and rises tentatively into the air, as if it can't believe its sudden liberty. After this brief hesitation, its volume suddenly expands, and it rises heavenward like a Daoist Immortal, rapidly leaving my field of view.

At this stage, transformation is complete.

The corpse comes back out, seemingly no different from minutes before, pallid and shriveled like a wax figure. Behind me in the "leave-taking" room, some of the deceased's loved ones cry. Others smile, and still others move awkwardly between both.

This is quite normal for people facing death and this fixed, final settling place.

Ashes to ashes, dust to dust. I stand in silent recollection. The mortal flesh will leave for Area Three, where those colleagues will handle it. One more transformation, resulting in nothingness. But none of this merits grief. As you know, the young soul, humanity's most precious resource, bringer of material wealth, will enter the Tower's Honeycomb and begin its service.

A modest toll that must be paid on the road to eternal life.

"Li," Aken says, his tray clattering on the table. "How many have you processed today?"

I strike an exaggerated thinking pose to express my distaste for the word "processed," a distaste I've communicated to Aken many times.

He seems unconcerned. "Five for me." He sips his drink. We occupy a four-person table in this bustling canteen, sitting diagonally opposite each other. The empty seats belonged to Slim and Friedrich. Like anyone who's been working in the system long term, we observe certain rituals. For instance, the seating arrangements at this table have never changed: Slim, Aken, Friedrich, and myself, counterclockwise. Previously full of complaints, longings, harmless bets, and dirty jokes, now those two empty seats are like circuit breakers, cutting off the cheer, cold and desolate. Perhaps eating in melancholy silence has Aken feeling out of sorts. "Let's talk about something else," he suggests. "Just now I processed someone who'd been hit by a car."

That gets my attention, and I look up from my lunch. "A car?"

Immensely pleased with himself, Aken goes on: "The impact lacerated a coronary artery. Extreme blood loss was the cause of death. But guess what? No one came to say goodbye to this character."

"Huh . . . "

He chews a brown protein stick, his jaw working vigorously. "That gang of freak scientists from the Transportation Department did the calculation, didn't they? If the driverless dispatch and pedestrian discrimination and evasion systems haven't frozen over a large area, then the probability of an accident like this is equivalent to standing somewhere random in the Sahara Desert and getting struck by a meteorite within twenty-four hours."

I lick my lips. "But it could still be a coincidence."

"Coincidence?" Aken shakes his head. What's that in his gray eyes? Pity? Ridicule? I don't know. When everyone close to you goes away in the end, your frame of reference in this world can become indistinct. Sometimes I can't even tell if it's me who's crazily spinning, or the whole world around me. In my muddled skull, everyone is complex, difficult to fathom. Everyone is without reason. Like Aken. Even Roi.

Ah, Roi.

"Stop lying to yourself," Aken says.

My fist hammers the table. "What the fuck is that supposed to mean?"

Aken remains calm, seeming to enjoy my anger. "Death by vehicle. Nobody saying goodbye. Either the deceased had no loved ones, or they didn't know he was being processed. If your brain isn't broken, you know what I'm saying."

I watch him through a daze, teeth grinding. "Suicides aren't transformed."

Everyone knows this, but I feel it needs deploying against Aken's crafty logic. I recall a middle school teacher taking the time to carefully explain this provision: "New Anchorage's prosperity comes from ingenuity spurred by vigorous need. The foundation of all this is population. There are actually many people with a death wish." Her gaze swept over the classroom, finally settling on me. "Past trauma, deformity, psychological illness, and so on, all of these can lead to suicide. Now add a promised afterlife, and that can make people even more apt to rashly abandon life. Meaningless expenditure of life would damage the foundation of our success. So, in order restrain this type of behavior, suicides are disqualified from transformation."

Why was she looking at me as she said this? Was it some kind of hint? Did she perceive something hidden in my heart, like a cancer cell, that would sooner or later devour me? Under her gaze my heart ached. I felt sick. Like the first time I saw the corpse of a city smashed and scattered by revolution.

She was compelling me to gaze into the heart of that corpse.

Many years later, that middle school teacher's prophecy came true, to some degree: at twenty-two, I chose a vocation that could rapidly consume my life force. I didn't know if she'd be gratified or regretful that her words turned out prophetic.

"Suicides aren't transformed," Aken repeats. "But when you need a piece of firewood for the furnace, do you really care where the wood comes from?"

I grip my fork. The teeth reflect ice-cold light.

"Of course, my analysis hasn't been rigorous enough. There is another possibility." The provocateur eyes me. "The driverless dispatch system was undermined by human action. The guy was murdered."

"You . . . "

"Li," he says, leaning over to put a hand on my shoulder. "Come on. You've never had your doubts?"

I shrug out of his grasp, glaring.

"You know they didn't transform Slim." Aken's voice is knife-edge cold. "But do you know the reason? Insufficient neuron connection pattern recognition. Fucking insufficient recognition! We've been doing their dirty work a long time, Li. You and I both know how high the compatibility rate is with transformation. Or are you still unclear on that? Here's why they didn't transform Slim . . . because Slim had Alzheimer's. Because a senile Slim couldn't work for them in the afterlife! That's how it goes, I guess. Those who deserve transformation don't get it, and the undeserving do. This is a bit different from the story we've always been told."

I gape at him, thousands of refutations going through my mind. I can't give them voice. His malicious, fanatical gaze oppresses me, somehow ending the argument. I grab my tray and stand.

Aken follows suit. "You should listen to other versions of the story, now and then. Go ask your genius girlfriend, or poke around in AugViz." He taps his temple. "How do I put this? Form your own opinion."

Osiris Tower is one thousand three hundred and thirty-one meters tall. Packed into those meters are a hundred thousand heat differential electrical generators, the so-called Honeycomb. This development toward high elevation comes down to two things: first of all, "souls" have a tendency to rise, like heat, and the Minos Field needs layer upon layer of capturing capacity to maximize the harvest; secondly, the Tower is an open declaration of this city's wild ambition.

Reaching heavenward, an obelisk of human civilization.

That's not cheap, of course. To attain such unprecedented height, Osiris Tower is filled with Seismic Cancelation Systems. Setting aside the construction cost of these, there are transport and maintenance costs. The massive energy requirement of the computing units, master control units, and fine-tuning units is almost too much for a postmodern city-state to bear.

Only New Anchorage can afford such extravagant waste, and it is entirely dependent on its efficient energy source. The output of Osiris Tower's hundred-thousand Honeycomb cells meets the needs of the tower itself, and to spare. Transportation, communications, lighting, farming, entertainment, comfortable rooms neglected after human civilization's total collapse, have been refurbished thanks to the diligent souls in the Honeycomb.

Of course, Xiaofan, we all understand that one day we will be those souls. Their duty will be ours. As our New Anchorage educators take great pains to inculcate in us, that duty can be described with just two words: To serve.

I hear her footsteps, soft, halting. I send a tracks-covering order to Ann, quickly returning to a public channel of AugViz. The lock pops, the door is pushed open.

"Babe," Roi says distractedly. "Why are you back so early today?"

"I think it's you who's late." I throw up a flashing exclamation clock.

"Work was busy?"

"Mm hm." Head bowed, her gaze lingers on the man in the holograph display. "What's he on about?"

"The state of public security." I dial up the volume. "The Chief Executive says New Anchorage is in crisis. Illegal assembly. Subversive activity. Strange deaths . . . "

She snorts. "So the Chief Exec is starting to pay attention to strange deaths? I think all he cares about in the end is getting fuel to the furnace."

My pulse quickens. "What do you mean? What fuel? What furnace? I don't understand."

Roi waves a hand, smiling exhaustedly. "Never mind, Xiaofan. Let me ask you something. Do you really believe him?"

Him. She can only mean the figure in the hologram, the apex personage in this city of ours.

"I believe," I reply, after less than a second's hesitation.

Karl Schlich—discoverer of the Osiris particle, father of transformation theory, the Chief Executive—is not just an abstract idea to me, like he is to most people.

I met him in person.

At that time, I was still just an admirer of Roi. I was sipping coffee in the Tower entrance hall when a high-level text intruded upon my AugViz:

Go to Area Zero, Room 11104. The route will show in your AugViz. Don't say anything, and don't ask anyone about this. K.S.

I took it for a practical joke at first. Area Zero is the Tower's administrative space. Among the Tower's thirty-five thousand staff members, about three hundred have access privileges to Area Zero. A thirteen-person committee is elected from these three hundred. These thirteen scientists are called consuls. They're in charge of Osiris Tower, and thus in charge of the whole city.

It's as well to think of Osiris Tower as Mount Olympus, and Area Zero as the abode of gods and demigods on the summit.

So, at that time, a petty and low-ranking Charon stood up, and was guided by AugViz to that place. He'd hesitated only briefly. The message was so terse, brooking no dispute. It didn't feel like a practical joke. He passed through corridor after white-lit corridor, growing mesmerized. At first, his soles dragged on the white floor tiles, screeching like a vigorously worked two-handed saw. Gradually his pace quickened as he consumed the distance between himself and this mystery. Everyone turned a blind eye to his transgressive passage: busy scientists in orange uniforms, admins in blue, logistics officers in green. Doors opened silently before him, as if they'd been awaiting his arrival, and he was able to follow this path beyond the usual limits of his privilege. He entered a lift and soared upward, hovered briefly, then continued ascending. There were no transfers as the lift made slight course corrections. Ten minutes later, he gently decelerated to his destination. Trying to guess how far he'd come, he reckoned he was near the top of the Tower.

Area Zero, Room 11104.

The door opened. Before him there was only sky. Below, the lively, bustling city. Quaking with fear, he advanced a step. The electrochromic glass went from transparent to white before his foot. He was quietly grateful to whatever conjurers had been put to such good use.

A wheelchair floated silently toward him.

"Li Xiaofan." It was he of the outstanding talents, hoary-bearded, old but alert. "Welcome."

K.S. Karl Schlich. "Karl—" I was dripping with cold sweat. "Chief Executive, Your Excellency . . . "

In textbooks he'd been just a portrait. We'd never been told the father of New Anchorage needed a wheelchair, nor that his head leaned like an old tree branch to connect with a brain wave translator for voice synthesis.

The wheelchair's loudspeaker commanded me to sit.

I eased into a floating chair. The old man drifted off a few meters. Against the light, the white-uniformed figure of K.S. became a black silhouette. The glass under him remained transparent. From my angle, he seemed a mountain looming over New Anchorage.

A bent, narrow mountain.

"You work in Area Two."

I swallowed saliva. "Yes, Chief Executive."

The silhouette seemed to nod its head. "Well done, lad."

I had gained an audience with the King of the Gods. I'd obtained his praise. I should have had many ideas at that moment, and in fact I did, too many, a thunderous roar in my mind, from which I couldn't distinguish any one thought. So, I had to fall back on instinct to respond. I fabricated an ugly smile.

The silhouette was silent a while. I thought this happy encounter was coming to an end, but then came that wizened, synthetic voice: "Roi Lei. Do you know this person?"

After a dazed moment, I nodded.

"Do you want to be her boyfriend?"

My legs were shaking. Someone once told me Osiris Tower is a tree climbing toward the kingdom of heaven. In the eyes of its leaders, every branch and every leaf has its place. We who depend on the tree can only keep from publicly breaking with the order of things.

"I do," I said.

"Very good." The old man moved out of the backlit area, and there seemed to be a silver halo on his bald pate. "Approach her. Get close to her. Comply with my instructions as they come, and you will have what you desire."

I was silent a moment. "But, Chief Executive, why—"

"Don't ask that." He floated toward me. "I need something done, and you are a suitable candidate. Scientists are New Anchorage's most precious assets, especially those involved in the theory and mathematics of Minos Field efficacy improvement. Roi is one of these. Scientists are very intelligent, of course, but they are certainly not invulnerable. Sometimes sensitive, sometimes weak, sometimes immoderate or stubborn." His synthetic voice was like flowing mercury. "They can be used by people with ulterior motives. They can be troubled by inner voices. They can prophecy great things from the slightest signs or fail to see the forest for the trees. I need you to watch over this girl, Li Xiaofan. Don't think of it as monitoring, but as protecting."

He didn't have to spell it out. It was obvious he meant my inherent traits—loyalty, unconditional belief, even stupidity—to counteract Roi's dangerous tendencies.

I felt overwhelmed by this great man's favor, and in awe of his majesty.

"As you know, the scientists have drawn up a stringent anti-surveillance and control bill, in order to protect their small psychic domain. But there are always ways to bypass unnecessary and overelaborate formalities. Li Xiaofan, I need you to report to me regularly on her activities. If something out of the ordinary happens, it should be reported to me in a timely manner. Remember, this is for her own good. You'll be protecting her and protecting this city."

That's what I've been doing for the past three years: monitoring my love, ostensibly in the name of love.

Just before I turned to leave, the Chief Executive said, "Li Xiaofan, why did you choose to work in the Tower?"

"New Anchorage saved me," I said, gravely serious. "I want to serve it."

"Very good." The old one smiled drily. "And in return I'll give you Roi. She will be your well-deserved recompense."

The foundation of New Anchorage's success is clearly its population and source of energy. These two elements are not locked in a zero-sum game, but in a positive feedback loop that drives the city's development and maturation.

People flock to New Anchorage for what the city promises: a secure life, and an afterlife, both guaranteed by science. On average, two hundred and forty-one people die every day in this city of twenty million, for this or that reason. Subtracting those deceased who can't be transformed—due to serious brain trauma, late delivery, or violation of Committee regulations—about seventy percent of citizens end up in Osiris Tower.

In other words, Osiris Tower ingests one hundred and sixty-eight souls per day on average, or sixty-one thousand three hundred and twenty per year. One hundred thousand Honeycomb cells provide electricity to the city and maintain a full load state, so each soul's service term is 1.63 years on average. That's quite brief in the context of eternal life. During its tenure, a soul, free of all manner of macroscopic limits once imposed by the brain, can perceive the high-speed, chaotic microscopic world, and interact with it. The soul is required to do what Maxwell's Demon did. In its Honeycomb cell, it divides fast-moving atmospheric molecules from slow-moving ones. With the system's total energy unchanging, a heat differential is manufactured. This differential is converted into electrical energy.

This is the most efficient way to generate power. As the textbooks taught us, the process' economy is astounding. Apart from what the Minos Field and transformation process consumes—an insignificant amount—the wastage of heat differential generation can practically be disregarded. A megacity gets power, and the dead get souls. In less than two years, they are released from service, and off they go. Where? To paradise? The afterlife? Somewhere in the ocean of stars? Death has been a mystery throughout the ages. New Anchorage's scientists have decided to leave this ultimate question to our imaginations.

They merely promise liberation from mortality. This is why twenty million people crawl and strive in the Tower's shadow. Osiris Tower is their religion, and the Chief Executive, far removed from the masses and reality, is thus the high pontiff.

It seems religion has finally prevailed in its centuries-long struggle with science. It resorted to a trick most shrewd, most deadly: it used science for its own ends. Even a lowly Charon's basic science literacy is sufficient to think it through:

Hundreds of years after humanity demonstrated the impossibility of a perpetual motion machine, after the vanguards of civilization retreated in disarray, have we really defeated the laws of physics? Are we really exploiting an inexhaustible energy source? Have we really replaced God, even become God itself?

Xiaofan, do you really believe?

Li Xiaofan, are you suspicious of Roi?
Chief Executive . . . what do you mean?

I mean Dissident Element L. I think you've heard the moniker?

I . . .

You needn't be circumspect. Dissident Element L's subversive views are a kind of treacherous virus . . . efficiently disseminated, highly infectious, impossible to completely eradicate. With such political views going around, I needn't remind you, dissident organizations are beginning to exhibit unusual behavior. I believe this is very dangerous.

Chief Executive, you can't think—

From the few clues we have, we know Dissident Element L understands Tower operations very well, though they distort this knowledge. We believe they're a member of the scientist core. Dissident Element L is quite cunning. They have concealed themselves for a long time. But my hunting dogs picked up traces, and I can tell you, as a result of the tech department's tracking, this person's access point is near your residence.

But it doesn't mean for certain that—

Not for certain, no. AugViz is a muddled, confusing space. Anything's possible in there. That L could stand for Roi Lei, or Li Xiaofan, or even Lloyd Hariri. Cleaving to the principle of scientific rigor, we mustn't lightly decide someone is a saboteur. So, I need your help.

If . . . I do mean if, Roi really is Dissident Element L . . .

We treasure every scientist. This is why we haven't launched a formal investigation. When it comes to subversive activity, we like to carry out rectification measures. Li Xiaofan, I believe you are devoted to New Anchorage. Remember, the fate of twenty million might rest on your choices.

May I presume to ask a question? What did you mean by rectification measures?

That question is beyond the scope of your authority.

The journey home has never seemed so long. My heart feels hung and suspended, like the tram I ride. Black clouds swarm on the horizon, dousing everything in gloom—glass curtain walls, streets, alleys, ant-like streams of people—as if meaning to seize all the world in darkness and silence.

Only the Tower stands tall and upright.

The tram passes over Liberty Street, decelerates, stops at the station. I see a steepled, three-story, redbrick structure amid a motley and precipitous cluster of buildings. There is a kind of bustling liveliness among the people passing in and out of the place, different from before. I remember that indescribable afternoon, Roi and I sitting amid the anonymous crowd.

The Blackbird Pub. Dissident elements. Subversive activity. Lloyd Hariri.

Roi.

I think the answer is already there, in my heart. I just don't want to face it. I return home. Roi's not there. My burning, chapped lips open as I call out for Ann. She appears, a fine gauze in the air.

"Ann, tell me everything Roi did that day I wasn't here."

That day, after I left, she got out of bed and opened an encrypted email Lloyd Hariri sent before he committed suicide. The message left her silent and perplexed. She was in a trance all day, until she realized I was about to get off work. She rushed into the kitchen.

A few days later, she took up the mantle of Hariri's Dissident Element L identity. She published essay after essay in AugViz. Soon afterward, she accepted two invitations to the Blackbird Pub. The essays are just there for me to find. Her tracks aren't hidden. She could have set up high-level privacy privileges, but she didn't. She's been waiting for me to discover her. Me, her fool.

"Roi . . . "

She stands in the doorway, and I fix my eyes on hers. Deep wells, so innocent, innocence to make your heart burst with love. "Roi, what did he say in that message?"

"The truth." She returns my gaze. "A truth we have chosen to over-look."

"A truth that you choose to believe!" I roar, my desperation ignit-ing. "Who do you think you are? Do you think you're cleverer than the greats?"

She closes her eyes and slowly shakes her head. She seems resigned, as if to execution. "Why did Lloyd want the atonement of true death? Why does Schlich remain consigned to his frail human body? Could it be he'd rather endure humiliation and agonizing medical treatments than the next life, supposedly so gentle and attractive? Xiaofan, think about it. Have you ever in your trade transformed someone from Area Zero? Why are the higher-ups so afraid of the political views on

AugViz? Surely you've heard this one . . . 'Your staunchest opponent is whoever most believes you're right.'"

Oh Roi. Now I'm your staunchest opponent.

I take her hand, not too light, fearing that she might slip away here and now, and not too tightly, fearing she might become a dream, a mist, and dissipate between my fingers. "Roi, I—"

"Hush." She puts a finger to my lips, takes hold of my face. There's a resolution in her I've never seen before, as if one word from the talk we're postponing could tear open the space-time between us. I shiver, drawn to her lips. She kisses me deeply. She blows her breath into my mouth, like God pouring spirit into a funereal pottery figure.

My broken heart is again glued together, bringing a distant pain.

Tonight, we again become one. We are cautious and solemn, like we're sacrificing ourselves. From darkness we charge into the light, from bliss we rush toward extreme loss. In love, we charge toward death. After what seems years of gasping for breath in silence, Roi gently bites my earlobe.

"My favorite part of you."

I force a laugh. A tear sits poised in the corner of my eye. I'm back on guard, at the ready. "Roi, let's leave this place."

She gets up on an elbow, fixing me with those eyes again, those deep wells shining. "Leave?"

I nod. I want to tell her I could abandon a stable and worry-free life. I could throw myself into the unknown, into an opaque future. I could peel off the safe gauze of security, ignorance, blind faith, confront the old black scar on my heart. I could do all that if we are together. But I just nod, because I know she already knows.

Roi lies her head on my chest, and we're quiet again. Her breath is regular and moist. I'm starting to think she's asleep when she says against my skin, "I just have one last thing to do, tomorrow."

My neck hairs go erect. "At the Blackbird Pub?"

She says nothing.

Something dark and viscous stirs in my heart. I pull her closer. "Roi, please don't go there. I have a bad feeling about it."

She covers my mouth. "That's bad luck."

That's my Roi through and through. She knows when to deploy logic and when to leave it behind. This spontaneous end of the conversation is her vow, her determination. She's a Brahmin who means to challenge her god. She cannot be dissuaded. What can I do but hold her in my arms?

As the rain patters out there in the night.

I spend the day in great agitation. I send four people to rebirth, taking longer than usual with each of them. My hand shakes en route to the Execute button. The closer it gets, the more violently it shakes. I try to convince myself it's not the secret I keep, but the beginnings of Parkinson's.

Li Xiaofan, please confirm the identity of Dissident Element L.

I say nothing.

Li Xiaofan, please confirm the identity of Dissident Element L.

I choose silence in the face of the Chief Executive's demand, just as my conscience has always done in the face of knowledge. I should warn Roi, but she's not in the canteen. I text her, but she doesn't reply. For the rest of the workday, I'm a pot of soup coming slowly to boil.

The tram glides through a fine rain, Heaven and Earth overcast.

This is your city.

In the gloom and wake of swaying vehicles, light converges into a red, turbid stream.

How many dirty secrets hide under this city's abundance? These people, facing life's sunset, take solace in the afterlife to come. They follow blindly. They are selectively blind and deaf. Including you, Li Xiaofan.

I close my eyes. It's Roi's voice in my ears now, saying to me what she never could before.

You can turn a blind eye to the darkness. That's your choice. You can even choose to become part of it, the darkness. Or you can draw your sword. Or climb up to a high place and scream your loathing of past, present, and future to the bustling masses.

I have to admit that compared with Roi, I'm a coward.

A sudden change comes over the tram car. People are whispering. I open my eyes and immediately I'm staring, gaping. An intangible hand clutches my heart. Blackbird. The tram pulls into the station. I rush out of the car and stagger into a stream of people, and then it's like I'm drowning, desperate for oxygen. Dissident elements. I'm running along Liberty Street. The gentle rain has become something insidious, harboring evil designs, like insect stings on my face. Wailing. Cursing. The clamor of an ambulance. Dilapidated, ruined walls shelter fire from the rain. Smoke billows upward, waving in the wind. I stop amid the scattering crowd, and there it is before me, the charred corpse of the redbrick structure.

A fire blossoming in the rain.

Rectification measures.

I feel nauseous, short of breath. It seems there's not enough oxygen. I'm gulping air, the smell of burning, that almost sweet smell of incineration, redolent of the countless times I smelled burned bodies. The smell of my last bit of faith going up in flames.

I kneel and vomit.

Xiaofan.

My ears buzz. It's a voice message from Roi.

Xiaofan, I'm behind you.

I turn. On the other side of the street, there stands my love, like an orange tulip in the gray downpour. I get up and pass through the rain and tears enveloping the world. She's coming toward me.

"Roi—"

My shout is engulfed by shrieking, the cacophony of impact and destruction. The orange tulip in the rain, swept away by a cruel black mass. Where she stood, a break light's red contrail dissipates and descends in the curtain of rain.

Roi.

It all seems like a dream:

The Blackbird conflagration, the out of control truck on Liberty Street. Accompanying Roi's dying mortal flesh to Osiris Tower. Replacing the Charon on shift (he understands clearly this is a violation, but he doesn't hesitate). At her side, watching the countdown to rebirth, second by second toward zero. Locking the electric door. Canceling the transformation. Commands, threats, insults from the guards outside. Laser cutters burning through the door. Pointed boots ferociously kicking my ribs, police truncheons splitting my scalp. Being thrown into a stinking, ice-cold cell.

But it's not a dream. It's all real. And the pain is real and deserved. Roi, I gave you true death. It's all I could give you.

When it's time to say goodbye, Aken is red-eyed. His beard makes him seem ten years older. We don't speak. We just embrace in silence. Then he returns to the River Styx. I am tainted, forever banished. Banished by the Tower.

I curl up fetal on Roi's love seat, where our hands and feet would entwine. I shiver with something like a fever. My tears won't come. A hollow cooing issues from my throat.

"Xiaofan." It's Ann's voice, as if having crossed gulfs of time. "Roi set some things aside for you."

I rise, hugging myself.

"Roi . . . for me?"

"An encrypted email, offline. Shall I read it for you?"

I nod.

My Darling Fan:

When you read this message, I will be dead. I want you to know this isn't the outcome I hoped for. I wanted to go far with you, Xiaofan. I wanted us to throw ourselves into a more difficult life, free of hypocrisy. I wanted to be with you that way, Xiaofan. I really did.

But I have a responsibility to this world, an unfinished task. Tomorrow I will publish my discoveries, along with Lloyd's message. I have a connection at Blackbird Pub . . . I know this will be the most dangerous and difficult journey of my life. The Chief Exec has already begun to suspect me, via your eyes. Do I guess right, Xiaofan?

Suddenly I'm choking on tears, trembling, like it's possible to shake off all the blotches on my conscience.

Xiaofan, I know you love this city with all your heart. I know you love the Tower, and I understand your love. But sometimes intense love is like sunlight. It can cast shadows over everything. You've chosen to turn a blind eye to what's in the shadows. All those willing victims serving some grand cause, a righteous goal concealing despicable methods. You and I are well aware of this city's unspeakable matter. It is not my place to criticize you, because I was once a monitor like you. I monitored Lloyd, and there's no denying I'm to blame for his suicide. But you need not blame yourself, my love. In the end, we all find our own way to atonement, don't we?

I stare dazedly at the sequence of words on the display.

I have a secret. It's not a dark secret. On the contrary, it's beautiful. Once upon a time it sustained me through a gloomy life.

You asked me how I could possibly like you. Admittedly, our situation is an uncommon one. With our status gap, the probability of us as a couple ought to be vanishingly low. When you asked me that time, I said your work was not essentially different from mine. Maybe that was even true, but I had a more important reason I didn't share.

I'll never forget the first time I saw you. It was a misty evening, there was a gentle rain. It was on Liberty Street, on the sidewalk, in the evening crowd. An old man fell down. I wanted to help, but somebody beat me to it, a figure in purple and black. He knelt over the old man and searched for a pulse. He attempted CPR and did mouth-to-mouth. The crowd was indifferent, detouring around the whole scene, like water flowing around a stone. I don't know how long you tried, but you finally gave up. You stood. Your head was bowed. You were like a grim statue, soaking wet, standing guard over the body.

I was under the eaves of a shop, watching you. I remember your face.

The ambulance was slow to arrive. The old man's death was confirmed. They loaded him up and sped off toward the Tower. You turned around and left. I saw your face. I saw loneliness there, and pain, and something rare in these times of ours . . . you respected death. You respected people.

I remember your face. I had been thinking long and hard about how to approach you, and then you came to me.

Whoever is lonely at this moment, is lonely forever.

My consciousness is like stagnant, lifeless water for a long time. Finally, there are a few ripples. I understand now. I understand what brought Roi and I together: death. Respect for death. Maybe there was a ubiquitous pair of eyes, and it saw me, and it saw Roi, and saw how I looked at Roi, and how she looked at me. And it knew how to exploit such gazes.

And so it summoned a petty and low Charon. It promised him the sweet fruit of romantic love.

I wipe away my tears and keep reading.

Three days later, Dissident Element L reappears in AugViz. The committee does its best to quash things, but doubt in the afterlife, and in the Tower, is spreading like a wildfire.

And I will stand here, in the flaming remnants of Roi's life, burning hotter, until I'm a white-hot incandescent lamp wick, using my light and my pain to scatter that once insufferably arrogant darkness around me.

I will turn the words you set aside for me into a declaration of war. I'm sure this is what you meant for me to do.

Roi.

A tirelessly working demon reducing the entropy of a system, without doing work, thus achieving the function of a perpetual motion machine. Xiaofan, do you really believe the cosmos would allow it? An open violation of the Second Law of Thermodynamics? Over two hundred years ago, Hungarian physicist Leo Szilard showed that Maxwell's Demon wouldn't actually violate physics with its molecular observations. It would need energy for its work, and so would by necessity produce entropy, no less than that lost to the ordering of the molecules.

In brief, there's no such thing as a free lunch. The demon would spend the order of its own consciousness to get that "heat differential."

This is the predicament of every soul in the Honeycomb. A human consciousness is the most highly ordered system in the known universe. For negligible energy input, this system gives you a stable, orderly output. Quite the worthwhile transaction for such an energy-dependent megacity!

Xiaofan, why not imagine your inevitable future? You die, you enter the Honeycomb. You begin your work. Over and over, you sort molecules by velocity. Your consciousness is in a high-speed world, and you repeat your work hundreds of millions of times. And yet, no end is in sight. You gradually forget your term of service wasn't supposed to exceed two years. In your subjective reference frame, perhaps two thousand years have already passed. Perhaps twenty thousand. Your consciousness is consumed and exhausted, bit by bit. At last your ego disintegrates. You burn down to a tiny ember. You become an automaton, going through mechanical motions.

In this purgatory of prolonged time, your consciousness is finally defeated. You've functioned as a unit of fuel. You've contributed something precious to this city, the most valuable thing a person possesses.

Your soul.

This is the coldly logical answer. I wouldn't be so sure about this truth if it weren't for the ruling municipal gods' persistent suppression, slander, and even annihilation of dissident scientists.

We—and I hope this "we" includes you—need to bring about change.
Change begins with accepting the truth.
Now, imagine a tombstone . . .

First Prize: 6th Lightyear Award for Best Short Story (2017).

Originally published in Chinese in *Double Helix: A Selection of Yang Wanqing's Science Fiction Short Stories*, 2021.

弹震症

PTSD

HUI HU
灰狐

TRANSLATED BY REBECCA KUANG

"You have one chance to do the right thing."

Han Jun reread the message twice to himself, and then hit enter.

The response was quick, concise, and blunt. "I understand. I know what I have to do."

Han Jun nodded. If things had progressed this far, then he'd already half succeeded.

He'd lurked on every major website, forum, and We-media comment section, reading posts and messages in order to find someone like the person who called himself "resolute9527."

Over a long period of observation, Han Jun had learned that resolute9527 was very busy, that his living standards were a bit below average, and that he was usually active after eleven o'clock at night. He was constantly complaining, and his mind was full of both idealism and bottomless fury. Most importantly, he had a hazy sense of ethics, and he was willing to act on behalf of ill-defined, illusory justifications.

"Making tools is a crucial distinction between humans and animals. It is one of the skills that has enabled millions of working people to support their families over thousands of years. Our society today was built from countless parts created by laborers. However, the 3D printer has upset this equilibrium. Its emergence has replaced the jobs of millions of workers. It has put tens of millions of workers out of work and on the streets. We must boycott the 3D printer. This isn't a matter of personal preference. This concerns the balance and development of society. We must salute all the workers who created our computers, our cell phones, our microwaves, our cars . . . no, our entire society. Making tools is a defining characteristic of humanity, as well as a human right. We must defend our rights!"

Han Jun bashed out this string of empty phrases. He didn't believe them, but he knew that resolute9527 would. resolute9527 wouldn't doubt a single word.

"Tomorrow morning," replied resolute9527. "10:00 a.m. in the industrial park, at New Industries Corporation."

Those who opposed the 3D printing industry had organized a protest over the Internet. As usual, they would wave banners and shout slogans. Although they all had different reasons for complaint, they were united by their fight against the 3D printer.

After learning about these protests, We-media civilian journalists had begun to stir, hoping to capture some explosive, clickbait-worthy news bits. But Han Jun had a different idea, and for that he needed a target.

"Yes," he wrote. "Be prepared."

"Understood."

"What are you going to wear?" Han Jun pretended to ask this casually. But he needed a way to find this stranger among the crowd so that he could film him. Even though he had no way of predicting what the person on the other end of the web was going to do, given resolute9527's regular words and actions, Han Jun thought he had a pretty good chance of obtaining some eye-catching news.

"I'll be wearing white and blue stripes. I'll be easy to recognize."

"Great."

Han Jun sent his last reply, then started to clean up the evidence. He deleted his account from the site, as well as all records of correspondence in his registered inbox. Now nobody would be able to find him through resolute9527.

• • •

The next day, Han Jun arrived early to Binjiang Industrial Park. He dodged past security and climbed up the side wing of Rongguang Pharmaceuticals Factory. From there, he could see the entire front entrance of New Industries Corporation.

3D printers were originally simple gadgets for civilian use, used most commonly to make cutlery or small toys. But New Industries Corporation had used its own proprietary technology to develop 3D printers to the level of industrial mass production. This had been a big blow to traditional industrial manufacturing, but it wasn't nearly as bad as the online discourse made it seem. However, as more and more voices added fuel to the fire, industrial 3D printing had practically morphed into a monstrous threat, perceived as the last straw that would destroy traditional industry and bring about total economic collapse.

The protestors had already arrived. They numbered about three to four hundred, which was more than Han Jun had anticipated. Although Han Jun had always been in contact with these kinds of people, he still had no idea where they derived their passion.

He sat leaning against the cement wall on the building's roof, put on a VR helmet, and then launched his drone.

VR technology let him inhabit the drone, a device no more than seventy centimeters wide, just as if he were a bird. The drone jumped over the parapet on the roof and dove toward the crowd.

The three hundred and sixty-degree rotating camera on the drone's underbelly sent a live feed to the VR helmet, letting Han Jun look in any direction he wanted. This video segment would be uploaded on the Internet, so that everyone with a VR system could experience being on the scene with the drone.

He followed behind the crowd, maintaining a height of seven or eight meters. From up here, nobody could hear the drone's quiet rotors. Observing the scene, he decided to wait until chaos descended before he flew in closer.

The protestors lifted their signs and marched forth in silence until they stood in front of New Industries Corporation's front doors. Then they grew more agitated. A handful of leaders stood at the front of the ranks, punching the air with their fists, rhythmically chanting their prewritten rhyming slogans. It was then that Han Jun noticed resolute9527, but . . .

That blue and white striped shirt was a school uniform.

For a moment, Han Jun was struck dumb. He hadn't anticipated that his carefully chosen target might turn out to be a child. resolute9527 looked to be about fifteen years old, and he was rather short and slender. His blonde highlights nearly covered his eyes. Though he wore a school uniform, it was clear from his posture and the expression on his face as he chanted with the crowd that he was no model student.

But he was still undoubtedly a child.

This generation's children were more impulsive; more inconsiderate of the consequences of their actions.

Secretly, Han Jun was delighted. He flew the drone closer. He had already begun to craft the boy's story in his head: he was from a poor family; his father had been fired because of the 3D printer, his mother was seriously ill, and so this kid had declared war against New Industries Corporation . . .

Several staff from New Industries Corporation came out of the building. A middle-aged man who appeared to be in charge began addressing the crowd. Han Jun filmed a close-up of his face. Contempt, disdain, loathing—all emotions that would just strengthen the opposition—were crowded on this stupid man's expression. Indeed, not a minute later, the protestors got restless and started to push forward, one after the other. New Industries Corporation's armed security guards blocked their paths with raised plexiglass shields.

The drone surveyed all this from above. The scene resembled a tidal wave crashing upon rocks.

resolute9527 joined the surging crowd. His skinny frame was jostled this way and that by the crowd, but his energy was unmatched. The young, hot-blooded teenager managed to force his way through the crowd to the front. He leaped up high, one foot trampling against a riot shield. The guard behind the shield stepped back, but another one beside him filled the gap, using his shield to knock resolute9527 to the ground. A small wave rippled through the crowd.

This was the spectacle Han Jun had been waiting for. He guided the drone to the side to get a view of the guards and the protestors standing in opposition. The camera zoomed in on resolute9527, blurring the faces of the people in the foreground and background.

Han Jun congratulated himself. *This shot composition is too perfect.*

resolute9527 once again charged at the shields. He was a Sisyphus, dauntlessly pursuing justice.

But after several more tries, he had to stop. His forehead had been wounded at some point. Dark red blood trickled down his skin, covering half of his face. He paused to wipe it off. Then, once his breathing had evened a bit, he lifted his shirt and pulled out a glass bottle. The neck was stoppered with cloth. Inside sloshed a colorless liquid.

Han Jun knew what that was—a Molotov cocktail.

He felt a sudden jolt of terror. He'd anticipated an assault. He'd even anticipated blood. But this . . . a Molotov cocktail, fuck, that was a weapon.

The boy ignited the cloth. Bright yellow flames quickly leaped into his hands. Some people realized what was happening and retreated. The only person in the view of Han Jun's camera was now resolute9527.

Everything in Han Jun's vision seemed to slow down. The glass bottle left the boy's hand. It rotated in the air, the curved bottle reflecting the morning sun's rays, before slamming against the riot shields. It bounced back, fell in front of the boy's feet, then exploded.

The flames quickly grew several times their height, tracing the spilled flammable fluid up resolute9527's body. The boy was terrified. He took two dazed steps back as the flames continued to roll and gnaw across his body. Then, at last, he seemed to register pain.

The flaring yellow figure dashed about aimlessly, creating a vacuum wherever he went. Both the guards and protestors watched him from a distance, but nobody stepped up to rescue him. The boy toppled over, smashing the other bottles concealed under his shirt. More flames burst forth.

Han Jun forgot that he was operating a drone. He flew closer and closer, observing it all in a daze. The VR helmet's transmissions made him feel like he was right there. His face burned, as if he himself were being roasted in a raging inferno. He'd turned off the audio before he started to film, but he couldn't turn off his own involuntary howls. He had started this. He had destroyed this child.

Silently, he watched as the flames danced on the teenager's body. Bright lights seared his mind, and he knew then that he would never be able to forget what he'd just seen.

• • •

"Ahh!" Han Jun gave a shout and toppled out of his chair. Around him, his colleagues didn't even pause for a second before continuing on with their work. Everyone was long-accustomed to the fact that Han Jun still suffered frights when he took his afternoon naps.

"Another nightmare?" asked Xu Qing, his desk neighbor.

Han Jun rubbed at his eyes and forced out a smile. Four years had passed since that day, but he was still plagued by the same dream. He had long accepted that this was his punishment.

"Ay, you really should go see a psychologist. These fits of yours are giving the rest of us nightmares." Xu Qing looked down at Han Jun as he leaned against his desk.

"What time is it?" Han Jun glanced at the clock on his desktop screen, then answered his own question. "I've still got twenty minutes. No, I should rest a bit more."

"Forget about your nap." Xu Qing patted Han Jun firmly on the shoulder, then leaned in closer to whisper, "Have you seen the company's newest promo video?"

"What promo video?"

"For that new project—the VR ARMOR."

"I thought the announcement wasn't for another six months. They've already shot the promo?"

"Not yet, but my buddies in the publicity department sent me some rough cuts. Want to see?"

"Why would I want to see?" Han Jun asked, puzzled.

"It's terrifying. Once you see it, those nightmares of yours won't seem scary at all."

"What are you talking about? Is this a company promo video or a horror movie?" Han Jun shot his colleague an annoyed look.

"Watch it and you'll understand." Xu Qing squeezed his way over and swiped his phone in front of Han Jun's monitor. The video began to stream.

Han Jun leaned back in his chair, arms folded over his chest as he watched the screen.

The sky-blue NETLORD logo appeared on the screen, followed by the words VR ARMOR in shining metallic italics.

VR ARMOR was the newest full-body virtual reality system that NETLORD was planning to launch. It was an exoskeleton like the kind often seen in science fiction games, but it didn't let the user walk wherever they wanted. Rather, countless sensors and force feedback devices were installed in the interior. It created more of a sealed environment than the regular VR helmet, allowing the user to fully immerse themselves in the virtual environment.

After nearly ten years of development, the technological level and expressive power of VR systems had already made it difficult for users to determine between the virtual and the real. NETLORD had risen rapidly in recent years by developing its own VR system, ROOM. As VR gradually permeated the lives of ordinary people, ROOM's market share had come to rival that of Windows. The software giant of the past had inaccurately predicted trends and spent too much effort on human body motion capture and recognition, which meant it was now struggling to regain its old spot at the top.

But NETLORD wasn't about to slow down. It wanted to make further leaps in the field of virtual experiences. VR ARMOR was part of a new generation of VR systems invented under the company's guiding philosophy of making things both "more realistic and more imaginary." Just seeing the words "VR ARMOR" gave Han Jun a surge of emotion. This product was what he, a NETLORD employee, had struggled with his colleagues for countless days and nights to achieve. This was his pride and joy.

But the next second, the image changed, and the smile congealed on Han Jun's face.

A pink, round object appeared on the screen. Its surface was rough, bumpy, and scarred, unevenly covered in darker and lighter patches. After taking a few breaths, Han Jun realized that this object was a face—the face of a burn victim. An imaginary blaze began to burn in his mind, melting away his reason and courage, leaping higher and higher as it blazed, creaking and groaning.

"Fuck, this . . . "

"His name is Zeng Ping," said the video voice-over. "Four years ago, he survived a terrible fire . . . "

The person, whose face resembled stir-fried cabbage, turned and stared straight out of the screen. A crack split the lower half of the face—that was Zeng Ping's smile.

"How about it, NETLORD?" Xu Qing scoffed. His tone was quiet, but Han Jun gave a sudden start, as if struck by a bolt of lightning. The composure he'd been trying to maintain collapsed. Just when he'd started to believe that he could regularly cope with the nightmare that haunted him, the nightmare had turned back to face him and smiled.

His legs went limp. He slid down his office chair.

"Hey, are you okay?" Xu Qing realized Han Jun had disappeared. He bent over and saw Han Jun curled up under the desk, rubbing at his face with his hands so hard it seemed as if he wanted to gouge his eyes out.

"Come out from there! Are you okay?" Xu Qing pulled Han Jun up with one arm and propped him up against the wall. Han Jun continued rubbing at his face, as if trying to wipe something away.

"It can't be. It can't be." Han Jun muttered the same words over and over like an incantation.

"What are you saying? Hey, drink some water!" As Xu Qing watched Han Jun's hysterics, he resorted to the simplest of tactics: a slap to the face.

Han Jun stopped shuddering. Obediently he took the proffered glass of water and gulped down several swallows. He felt a surge of nausea. He pushed Xu Qing and stumbled for the bathroom.

He didn't succeed. He made it only several steps before he opened his mouth and vomited on the company's shiny-enough-to-see-your-reflection microcrystalline floor tiles. Saliva, tears, and snot mixed on his face. He heard the patter of footsteps behind him. Colleagues gathered around him, but they maintained a cautious distance. Xu Qing stood by his side, careful that Han Jun's vomit didn't stain his leather shoes.

He patted Han Jun on the shoulder. "Why don't you go home and rest?"

Han Jun didn't turn around. He was still rubbing mindlessly at his face. "Put in a leave request for me, please," he said. Then he charged pitifully through the safety corridor and ran all the way down the stairs.

When he got back to his apartment, he rummaged through his drawer for the flash drive on which he'd stored all the records of that incident. Han Jun had never discussed it with anyone else, nor had he ever broadcast the video. Four years had passed, but those flames dancing on the young boy's body had kept burning in Han Jun's conscience, never going out.

After that day, Han Jun had given up on his VR We-media aspirations. He'd sent his resume out to every company he could think of in an effort to get a serious job so that he could leave his old life behind for good. He was lucky to have been hired at NETLORD. Now he had friends, colleagues, and a dream worth fighting for. He'd even found some minor success, because VR ARMOR's success was in part due to his efforts.

He inserted the USB into his desktop and moved his mouse over the video icon. He gave a bitter laugh. He'd been dreaming of that scene every day over the last four years. He could vividly remember every single lick of flame. Now he had to watch it all over again.

Then he scolded himself. He'd forgotten—he didn't have the equipment to play VR videos at home.

The power of VR systems lay in the fact that the user was in a sealed visual environment. The motion sensors inside the helmet could rotate the image along with the movements of the user's head, creating a truly immersive feeling. This also explained the rise of VR We-media. Users could experience the whirling thrill of rollercoasters or dive into the sea to admire swimming schools of fish, all from their own sofas.

Or they could watch a teenager burn to death from half a meter away.

Those realistic sensations had left a strong mark on Han Jun. He didn't dare draw close to flames anymore. Nor could he enter virtual reality.

But he wanted to see that recording again. He couldn't put his finger on why; he simply knew he needed to.

There was software available online that could convert VR videos to 2D files. Han Jun searched for a cracked version, installed it, and then started the file conversion. The file was very large. His screen indicated a conversion time of about half an hour, but Han Jun knew from experience that it would really take more like three hours.

He stood up and rubbed his stomach. He'd vomited his breakfast in the office hallway. Now it was nearly lunchtime, and his stomach had begun to protest.

If he had a VR set, he could have done what his colleagues did—go to a VR block, head to a commercial street, order food from a digital cafeteria, and then wait for the delivery boy to bring it to his home. But he didn't, so he had to go to the restaurant himself. He didn't mind.

He strolled to a mall two blocks away and ordered a bowl of beef noodles from a small shop.

It wasn't a work holiday, but there were quite a few people strolling about the mall. Although some forecasters had once predicted that the rise of the VR service industry would cause the decline of brick-and-mortar stores, after all these years, this phenomenon hadn't occurred. Humans were creatures most capable of adapting to change, but in their bones, they were still quite traditional.

The beef noodle chef was an exception. He wore a VR helmet and interactive gloves, waving his hands in the air to control a cooking machine two meters away that pulled noodles, cooked them, and poured soup.

"You could just use your hands," Han Jun said. "Why do you need the VR?"

"This is called VR Web Plus. Have you ever seen a cook wearing a suit? This is our store's specialty." The chef faced the wall, addressing Han Jun through the camera on the checkout counter.

Han Jun nodded and picked up a piece of beef. The meat juices burst in his mouth; rich and fragrant.

Reality was reality. That would never change.

Daisy Fenton took a deep breath and pushed open the laboratory door. Although she'd been here many times before, she still felt a chill every time. She felt like she was standing before a pitch-black cave, inside which lurked a wolf.

But there was no wolf inside the laboratory. Just half a person.

She strode toward the computer, wrinkling her brow as she glanced at the data on the screen. She hesitated a few seconds, and then pressed a button.

Beside the computer, a VR ARMOR-type helmet slowly opened, revealing the face of the user inside.

That face was flat, without hair, and without even a single pore. The fire had burned his skin into a waxy shell. His features were only holes in that flesh-colored ball of wax, on which his eyes gleamed from within little pits. Daisy managed not to look at the rest of his body, which was even more wretched than his face. The burned skin of his limbs had fused together, turning him into a mummy bound in his own skin. His hands and feet had withered away, consumed by the fire.

Two years ago, when NETLORD had been planning the release of the VR ARMOR full-body immersive virtual reality set, they'd needed a special spokesperson. Daisy had found the pitiable child named Zeng

Ping. Back then he'd resembled a giant spider's prey, wrapped in all sorts of tubes and wires and trapped in his narrow hospital bed. His badly injured throat emitted a keen hiss every time he breathed like a person lost in the wilderness, desperately blowing a whistle for help.

NETLORD had invested in Zeng Ping's treatment and linked his recovery to the VR ARMOR's development. Over the past two years, they had shot a series of videos about Zeng Ping. Within the virtual world, Zeng Ping could walk again! Zeng Ping could run again! Zeng Ping could even fly!

During the focus group sessions, the randomly selected potential customers, moved to tears by the carefully edited videos, had indicated they would absolutely purchase a VR ARMOR set. It wasn't the VR set they were purchasing—it was the consciences they'd long lost touch with.

The videos were crammed with positive messaging. In reality, Zeng Ping's father had sunken into alcoholism and his mother had been unable to face what her child had turned into. After accepting NET-LORD's compensation for their cooperation, they'd both disappeared, abandoning Zeng Ping to the company.

Because of Zeng Ping, Daisy had been promoted to the highest tier of company leadership. But she and Zeng Ping had been bound together ever since.

"What is it?" Zeng Ping asked.

"You've already been in there for six hours," Daisy said.

"Oh, right, good thing you reminded me. I ought to go for a run. Mind grabbing my sneakers for me?" Zeng Ping lifted his thighs, shaking the feet that weren't there.

Daisy didn't respond to Zeng Ping's sarcasm. "You can't stay inside for too long. You have to stay clearheaded while testing the system."

"You're right, I'm always getting reality and virtual reality confused. Look, in the real world I can't even walk! I sure want to stay awake!"

"You . . . " Daisy shook her head, silently cursing herself for being dragged into this situation again. Zeng Ping was like a black hole of gloom and dissatisfaction, and he could suck people's minds in there with him. Speaking with him for too long always induced thoughts of suicide.

Whenever he woke up, Zeng Ping would make requests to NETLORD, but he could only communicate with Daisy, which meant Daisy had adopted the second job of nanny.

"How was this R-ARMOR update?"

"It's fine, but ... "

Zeng Ping was an asshole, but his observations about virtual reality systems were very accurate. From time to time, he'd come up with wild yet feasible ideas, and based on the facts, his opinions were often correct. He proceeded to list eleven such thoughts, which Daisy jotted down. She'd hand those off to the programmer later.

"Wait!" Zeng Ping called.

"What?"

"That thing I mentioned ... "

"You're only seventeen," said Daisy. "We aren't giving you access to the sexual activity apps."

As the date of VR ARMOR's release announcement drew closer, the company's office was swamped with clips of Zeng Ping. Han Jun spent that time hiding at home. But his fifteen days of leave quickly passed, which gave him two choices: quit or return to work.

Trembling with anxiety, he returned to the office. His colleagues seemed to have tacitly agreed not to say anything about his vomiting in the hallway. Perhaps they were looking out for Han Jun's feelings, or perhaps they just didn't care. That was the nice thing about being a programmer—everyone was a bit odd, and nobody had to waste much time on human interaction.

The key to curing a disease was to face the root of the problem. As he watched the clips of Zeng Ping daily "improvement," his feelings, a complicated mix of guilt and regret, slowly began to recede. The burning nightmare continued to plague him, but he could no longer hear Zeng Ping's wretched screams in his sleep. Once, he even dreamed that Zeng Ping was smiling at him from within the flames, the same way he smiled in the clips.

VR ARMOR's release was a massive success. Using Zeng Ping as a spokesperson made people realize that VR ARMOR was not just an enhancement of the VR helmet, but an entirely new lifestyle. That, on top of NETLORD's remarkable design and perfectionist craftmanship, gave even the pickiest of critics no grounds for complaint.

The company gave all the employees generous bonuses and also organized a vacation abroad for the development team. But most of the programmers complained that they didn't want to travel. They would rather stay at home playing video games instead. But in their private VR environments, they still chose the outdoors option. All of their virtual avatars started wearing fishing shorts, sunglasses, and broad-brimmed hats.

NETLORD's stock price climbed higher and higher. Their production line was booked up with orders that would keep them busy for two years. This high tide lasted for a week.

"Why does everyone look so gloomy today?" Han Jun realized that the atmosphere was off the moment he walked into the office. Nobody even raised their eyes to look at him. Everyone sat at their desks, sullen and silent.

"Someone uploaded a video on the Internet," Xu Qing said. "It was a huge attack on our company."

"What video? Send it to me."

Xu Qing glanced at Han Jun, his mouth pressed in a thin line, and then passed him the VR VISION on his desk.

Han Jun held up the milky white VR helmet and hesitated.

"There's only this version," said Xu Qing. "Hurry up and watch, it's shocking."

"I . . ."

"Your face is all pale." Xu Qing furrowed his brows. "Are you okay?"

Han Jun shook his head. He examined the helmet in his hands and then, gritting his teeth, fit it over his head. After several years of updates, the VR helmet felt completely different from the helmet he had last worn four years ago. It was lighter, and it felt neither too soft nor too hard where it came in contact with his skin. It wrapped firmly around his head, letting no light leak in. It was quite comfortable.

When he was sure he wouldn't start hyperventilating, Han Jun raised his head and gave Xu Qing a thumbs up, indicating that he could hit play.

The screen went from black to blue. A red light appeared gradually in the distance. Then, in a flash, Han Jun returned to the morning of that day. He was hovering seven or eight meters in the air, overlooking the crowd of protestors slowly and resolutely marching toward the offices of New Industries Corporation.

Flames, a spinning Molotov cocktail, and Zeng Ping's face. All resurfaced in his mind.

An icy hand squeezed at Han Jun's heart, and the cold spread from his chest through his limbs. He yanked the helmet off. "What is this?"

"Keep watching and you'll see." Xu Qing spread his hands. "Our spokesperson used to be an anti-3D printing protestor. In a whole crowd of demonstrators, that kid was the fiercest. He threw a firebomb at the security guards and got burned as a result. All of our VR ARMOR is 3D printed, and we found that kid to be our spokesperson. Do you see what a joke we've become?"

"No! I mean, who uploaded this video?"

"We don't know. But a lot of customers who placed sympathy orders have cancelled them. Our stock price just tumbled seventeen percent. Hey! Han Jun, where are you going?"

Xu Qing was talking to himself. Han Jun had already left the office.

What was going on? Who had uploaded that video? How had they gotten that file?

Han Jun's mind swam with questions as he made his way back to his apartment. He booted up his PC and ran the security code he'd compiled himself. He stared as lines of code raced through the self-diagnostic window, but he couldn't find anything suspicious. He ran the code again. Then he started rummaging through his home. There were no signs of forced entry on the doors or windows. His combination lock registered no incorrect attempts. None of his possessions were missing.

Everything was normal—except the USB inside his drawer was gone.

"There's no need to keep looking. I took it."

Just as Han Jun's anxiety was peaking, a clear, crisp female voice sounded at his side.

Han Jun jumped so hard he nearly flipped the desk on its side. He steadied himself and looked around, but he couldn't see anyone.

"Who—?" Han Jun swallowed hard, then asked in a hoarse voice.

A small hexacopter drone flew out from the corner of his room and floated in front of his face. "It's me." The drone paused for a moment. "I'm sorry I had to resort to special methods to retrieve your things."

"Special?" Han Jun shouted. He stepped toward the drone, which quickly retreated, as if trying to maintain a safe distance. "This is called stealing!"

"Apologies." The drone spoke in such a timid, reproachful tone that Han Jun found himself relenting.

He took a careful look at the drone. It was only a dozen or so centimeters in diameter; so small it could easily have sat on top of his hand. Its six tiny rotors spun constantly, creating six circles of white light, though they were utterly silent. The aircraft's outer casing looked simple and crude. It wasn't decorated, and it didn't bear any manufacturer's particular style; which meant it must have been self-designed and 3D printed. But for an aircraft this small to have four cameras, a pickup microphone, a speaker, and a high-power engine . . . whoever had designed this craft wasn't crude or simple at all.

Han Jun waved his hand at the drone, but it deftly dodged aside. Although it relied on the camera's depth perception and collision avoidance programming, the drone could also avoid him using precise algorithms. However, based on his many years' experience flying a drone, Han Jun sensed someone was controlling this craft in real time.

That meant the driver was nearby.

"Why did you want to upload that video?" he asked. He began to pace around the room, slowing when he neared the window. The street outside was quiet and empty; the leaves of the parasol trees had already turned yellow. There was also a person jogging down the road, but he saw nothing suspicious.

"It's very important. I must halt the expansion of VR ARMOR." The aircraft hovered at Han Jun's shoulder, as if they were walking side by side.

"Why?" Han Jun paused and carefully regarded the drone.

"Because." The droned enunciated the words one at a time. "There cannot be any more victims."

"What does that mean? What victims?"

"How long was it between when VR was first released to when it fully penetrated the market? Only a few years? Has it gone through safety testing? The past two generations of VR helmets were half-finished products. Back then, the screen resolution wasn't stable and there weren't even any apps, but they still hastily sold six million units. They were basically using their customers as experiments. There have been reports of panic attacks and epileptic seizures. This is wildly irresponsible. The VR system hasn't been fully developed, yet now they want to push out the VR ARMOR. I support this kind of new equipment, but not now. It needs perhaps another thirty years." The contradiction of these righteous words coming from this rather childish girl's voice out of a miniature drone made it hard for Han Jun to accept what it was saying.

He shook his head. "What you're saying is too biased."

"How is this biased? When humans used leaded gasoline, how much harm did it cause? There's a thirty-five hundred-kilometer-wide hole over the South Pole created by large-scale freon use eighty years ago. Not to mention nuclear power plants, genetic modification, and even the pedometer in your watch. Science and technology are moving too quickly. We use new innovations on a massive scale before their safety is guaranteed, but the consequences get pushed to the next generation."

Han Jun smiled. These words were too much like those he used to brainwash people with online. "My goodness, how old are you?"

"Why do you care?"

"You should pay less attention to Internet stars and their videos. They'll do anything for more views. The electricity you're using now was produced by a nuclear power plant. Genetically modified food has been eaten by two generations; what's the problem with that?"

"Not enough time has passed. We have to be careful."

"Enough. I'm the one who developed VR ARMOR," Han Jun declared proudly, intentionally leaving out the words "one of." "We've gone through hundreds of thousands of tests, and there are absolutely no problems."

"Then you tell me, how long has it been since you've worn a VR helmet?"

"This . . . I have a special condition." Han Jun hemmed and hawed for a moment. "That doesn't prove anything."

"I have other forms of proof."

"What forms of proof?"

"Me," said the drone. "I'm a victim of VR."

"What happened to you?"

"I can't tell the difference between virtual reality and the real world." The drone gave a hollow laugh. "They say I'm ill, but they still don't have a name for it."

Then Han Jun knew who was flying the drone. He turned and ran out of the apartment.

• • •

The R-ARMOR helmet opened. Zeng Ping took a moment for his eyes to refocus, then glared at Daisy. "Hey! Haven't we talked about this? You can't just yank me out like this. A second ago I was walking on Mars; the next second I'm looking at you standing there."

Daisy didn't speak. She just watched him, her expression uncertain. "Whatever it is, just say it. I'm busy."

"Our project has been put on hold," she said.

"On hold? Why? Isn't it going very well? So is the R-ARMOR project. Why do we have to put it on hold? The company has invested billions in this; are you guys idiots?"

"How do you know how much the company has invested?"

A crack split open in the ball of flesh, revealing jagged, uneven white teeth. "I get around pretty well in there."

Daisy shrugged. "If you were really any good, you'd know what I'm talking about."

"What do you . . . " Zeng Ping abruptly trailed off, then retreated back into the R-ARMOR.

"I'll wait ten minutes," Daisy said. Zeng Ping was about to learn everything, and suddenly she couldn't help but feel a burst of malicious glee.

"Why don't you come in too?" Zeng Ping asked.

"I prefer reality."

Daisy watched as the R-ARMOR slowly closed, swallowing Zeng Ping inside. She relaxed a bit. Because of the video of the protest, the upper management had abruptly changed their attitude toward Zeng Ping. Their cooperative relationship was terminated. This was in fact Zeng Ping's last day at NETLORD. After this, he'd be sent back to his bleak, ruined home. Out of their humanitarian spirit, NETLORD would donate a sum of money which, if he lived within his means, would be enough to let Zeng Ping to enjoy five years of basic medical and recuperative treatment. But it wouldn't be easy for him to encounter virtual reality anymore.

That was real life; the truth of reality.

After VR ARMOR's development had been completed, Daisy had felt that they should let Zeng Ping stay entirely inside the virtual world. So she'd suggested Reality Armor, which combined virtual reality technology with the capabilities of an exoskeleton. It resembled a robot. It could be either worn or remote-controlled, and it was integrated with most of the functions of VR ARMOR. This R-ARMOR suit was the sole prototype, but Zeng Ping seemed to have completely lost interest in the outside world, and he spent his days engrossed in the virtual world instead.

This project, born of selfish motives, could no longer survive.

Daisy walked around the R-ARMOR suit, then found a chair to sit down in. She very much wanted a glass of wine, but apart from a set of equipment connected to the R-ARMOR suit, there was only Zeng Ping's hospital bed in the corner, in which he had not slept for a long time. A layer of dust had settled over the equipment meant for emergency medical treatment. Because of Zeng Ping's appearance, and more importantly because of his twisted personality, nobody wanted to be with him. So this room, which was called the high-tech equipment laboratory, had been set up in the lonely northern wing of the building. The northern wing had originally been the 3D printing facility. When testing VR ARMOR, all of the components could be printed and tested at their convenience. Now that VR ARMOR had entered the mass production stage, the 3D printing lab was temporarily shut down. Sometimes, Zeng Ping would impulsively let Daisy create two prosthetic legs for him, but he would always quickly lose interest in reality and return to the virtual world.

Only after walking through the long corridor and returning to her own office could Daisy have a sip of single malt whisky. Otherwise, she'd just had to bear it.

She didn't know what would happen to her after Zeng Ping was sent home. Perhaps she'd have to say goodbye to her large office and her whisky. Yet after the first time she'd met Zeng Ping, she'd chosen to stay here. Perhaps she was suffering from Stockholm Syndrome.

A faint noise came from within the R-ARMOR. Daisy realized that she'd dozed off. She stood up and walked next to the exoskeleton suit. Zeng Ping looked at her, and the blaze in his pitch-black eyes made her shudder.

"Who uploaded this?"

"We don't know."

"Even NETLORD can't find out?"

"The video has already spread all over the Internet. It doesn't matter who uploaded it, what matters is how to recoup our losses."

"Right! They're slandering me and my reputation. Should I accuse them of libel?"

"No!" Daisy raised her voice, startling Zeng Ping. "I'm talking about the company's losses. Your image conflicts with the image we've so carefully curated. This hurts NETLORD's public reputation. The company is thinking of ways to fix it."

"Fix it how . . . " Zeng Ping's eyes brightened, but then immediately dimmed. "Ah . . . by separating themselves from me."

Daisy nodded. This wasn't playing out as pleasantly as she had imagined. On the contrary, she felt somewhat guilty.

"If I were in charge, I'd do the same," Zeng Ping said calmly.

"I'll do my best to fight for some . . . " Daisy blurted, but Zeng Ping cut her off.

"No need. Is there anything else?"

"No."

"How much longer do I have?"

Though she already knew the answer, Daisy still glanced at her smartwatch. "Until tomorrow afternoon."

"Alright. Let me stay in here a little longer then, to calm down," said Zeng Ping. "If there's anything else I'll call from you from inside the VR."

"That . . . " Daisy opened her mouth, but couldn't think of anything else to say.

The R-ARMOR closed once again. Daisy walked out of the lab room, strode through the long hallway, and headed to her office.

She could finally have that glass of whisky.

She took two steps, then heard a separate set of footsteps echoing behind her in the empty hallway.

She turned around. The R-ARMOR was following her.

"Zeng Ping, what are you—"

The R-ARMOR raised its hand, curled its fingers into a fist, and punched Daisy in the forehead. She collapsed to the ground.

"I've calmed down," said the R-ARMOR. "Now, I'm about to get angry."

"Who are you looking for?" A middle-aged man opened the door. He was shorter than Han Jun but seemed about twice as heavy.

"Um, that . . . " Han Jun glanced at the thin hair on the man's balding head, unsure of how to begin. "There's a girl in this home, right?"

The man furrowed his brows. Before he could start cursing, Han Jun hastily continued, "Please let me meet with her for a moment—I have something to discuss with her."

"Fuck you—"

"Dad, let him in." The man was halfway done with his curse when the hexacopter drone stopped by Han Jun's shoulder and spoke.

The man shrugged, then turned to let Han Jun in. Han Jun squeezed between his gut and the doorframe to enter the room.

The drone led Han Jun through the living room into a bedroom.

A small, slight woman sat leaning against the bed. She wore a VR VISION helmet. Her face was completely hidden; only the curve of her chin was visible.

"How did you know it was me?" she asked.

"Whenever I'm riding the elevator, the old auntie next door always tells me about a strange girl on this floor who never goes outside. She says she seems to be sick with something." Han Jun glanced at the girl, then at the drone, unsure of which he should address. "Besides, a drone this size can't be remote-controlled from over three hundred meters away. And in a building like ours, any signals past a hundred and twenty meters would be too weak to work."

The girl nodded. "You are quite correct."

"Did you design the drone yourself?"

"Yes."

"It's really quite elegant." Han Jun craned his neck, examining the device. "It's better than that of many aircrafts on the market."

"Um . . . that . . . could you please not get too close?"

Han Jun turned to look at the girl, who was two meters away. The bit of her chin visible under the helmet had blushed red. He realized that she was talking about the drone.

"Oh, sorry." He took a step back.

"For my own convenience, I designed a lot of . . . what should I call them? Bodies that I can possess. But most of them can't be printed by my small personal 3D printer."

Han Jun thought for a moment. "You can't tell the difference between the real world and virtual reality, so you've made a series of devices to help you perceive reality in the virtual world?"

"You're making it sound too complicated, but that's more or less it."

"Interesting."

The drone alighted on the top of the girl's head. She stood up. "Apologies, my name is Lu Qi."

"Han Jun. But you've known that for a while."

"Yes."

"So you've been watching me all this time?"

The aircraft left the top of Lu Qi's head and wound around Han Jun's side. "Yes. As a matter of fact, I've been watching everyone in this building . . . "

"That's pretty unethical."

"Well, given how I am, I can't go outside, I can only . . . "

"I don't want to hear your excuses," Han Jun interrupted. "There are some things that you can't do, no matter what the reason."

The reprimanded Lu Qi took a breath, then let out a sound like a little kitten. The mouth beneath the helmet bit its lip and didn't utter another sound.

Han Jun sighed, then said in a gentler tone, "Where is the USB?"

The drone swooped down to a desk across from Lu Qi. Han Jun glanced over and saw his USB. He picked it up and put it in his pocket.

"What's the matter with you?" he asked.

Lu Qi was silent for a moment. Then she reached up and took off her VR helmet, revealing a delicate, pretty face. She seemed about fourteen or fifteen. Because she'd been cooped up in her home for so long, her skin was pale white, and she must have been several years older than how she appeared. The VR helmet had left visible imprints around her eyes, like red circles left by a diving mask. Regrettably, her once large and shining eyes looked straight ahead, her gaze as slack and expressionless as a blind man's.

"Your eyes . . . " Han Jun waved his hands in front of Lu Qi's face.

"I can see. I'm a bit near-sighted, but I can see clearly at this distance."

"Then you . . . "

"You've flown a drone before, right?" she asked.

He nodded.

"When you're using VR to drive a drone, what do you pay attention to?"

He thought for a moment. "Potential collisions?"

"Yes. It doesn't matter what the drone collides with—it will always lose its balance, then lose control and crash." Lu Qi swiveled her head around, looking about her surroundings, then abruptly turned back to face Han Jun. "Sorry. Because of how the helmet sensors work, I'm used to turning my head when I look at things instead of moving my eyes."

"I understand."

"Also. How do you go down the stairs when you're flying a drone?"

"Of course you fly down."

"Now do you understand?"

"No, I don't," he said, puzzled.

Suddenly Lu Qi crouched down and lifted up her nightgown, revealing two pale legs.

"You . . . !" Han Jun hastily averted his gaze.

"It's fine," she said. "Take a look."

Cautiously he glanced back over at her legs, which were crisscrossed with scars, as well as the marks of past surgeries.

"I've flown down flights of stairs and platforms. Once, I even flew down a three-story balcony."

"I understand." Han Jun waved his hand, gesturing for her to rearrange her nightdress.

"VR is too realistic. It makes people . . . " She gazed at him. "I'm saying there are at least some people who get lost in virtual reality and have no way of distinguishing it from the real world. In the end, they can't find their way back."

Han Jun, thinking of the burning nightmare that had plagued him for so long, nodded. "No one in the planar network era has been able to solve the VR sickness problem in 3D gaming. Even though those cases are quite common, they're not that dangerous, so not many people have researched the question."

"But virtual reality is different," said Lu Qi. "To people like me, it's fatal."

"I really sympathize. I also agree with what you're saying," Han Jun said in earnest. "But I don't condone your actions. I've met a kid about your age before, who overstepped himself in the name of his so-called ideals and obligations. In the end . . . "

"You mean *him*?"

"Yes."

"Do you think I'm in danger?" Lu Qi smiled. "Everything's transparent on the Internet. Even NETLORD wouldn't dare do anything to me. Also, I used a fake identity, and I paid for an overseas proxy to post. They couldn't possibly find out who I am."

Han Jun gave her a grim smile. "How old are you? You're too young to understand how the world works."

As if to prove just how dangerous this world could be, the sound of screeching tires pierced through the window the moment the words left his mouth. Immediately after came the sound of striking metal and shattering glass.

Han Jun and Lu Qi peered out the window at the freeway overpass a hundred meters away. A black SUV driving the wrong way had crashed into a small, silver sedan.

"You see? They've already found you. Your security measures are of no use at all." Han Jun pointed to the NETLORD logo on the side of the SUV.

Lu Qi grimaced.

The door to the SUV opened. A tall human figure clad in dark green stepped out of the car.

"Fuck! Damn it! How is it him?" Han Jun took a step back, his face tight with anxiety. "Get away—quick!"

"What is it?" Lu Qi stumbled as Han Jun dragged her along. "Who is that?"

"NETLORD didn't come to find you. That person has a personal score to settle."

The green figure, ignoring the cursing driver of the sedan, jumped and landed lightly on the freeway barrier.

"He's called Zeng Ping. He's the burn victim. That thing is a holo-printed exoskeleton developed jointly by NETLORD and the military. It's a high-tech combat suit." Without thinking, Han Jun's voice grew louder and louder as he spoke. "Uploading that video caused a lot of bad repercussions for NETLORD. Now the company wants to get rid of their burden. Zeng Ping's free medical treatments and insurance, not to mention his unlimited time in virtual reality, are no longer available. You see why he hates you?"

Lu Qi bit her lip and nodded. "What now?"

"Now . . . "

The green figure bent its knees slightly, then leaped forward like a falcon lunging for its prey. But there were a hundred meters lying

93

between the freeway and the apartment building. Zeng Ping didn't make it even halfway before he fell over thirty meters and crashed into a street-side newsstand.

"We're lucky they haven't finished debugging that thing. We've got some time. Hurry!" Han Jun yanked Lu Qi out of the apartment. They hadn't made it two steps before he ran back to grab her VR helmet. "He must have tracked you using the serial number on your helmet."

"Then what are we taking it for?"

"Do you want him to destroy your house?"

"Bring it," she said curtly.

They ran out of the apartment, but the descending elevator was still stuck on the nineteenth floor, and it wasn't moving. Heavy, powerful footsteps came thudding from inside the staircase.

Han Jun nervously jammed the elevator buttons to no avail.

"Fuck that nondisclosure agreement," he said. "That battle suit is an experimental prototype. The military wants to develop battle armor that can be completely remote-controlled through VR, just like your remote-controlled drone. R-ARMOR can be worn, and it can also be operated remotely. Zeng Ping has been testing this battle suit for us." Han Jun thought for a moment. "He's a very good product tester."

The elevator doors opened. Han Jun hurried inside. He turned around and saw Lu Qi watching him. Her hands were pressed against the wall. She looked like she wanted to say something but couldn't.

"Come on, hurry."

"I . . . you . . . can you carry me?"

"What?"

"I . . . reality makes me dizzy."

The footsteps were sounding closer and closer. There was no time to hesitate. Han Jun yanked Lu Qi to him and slung her over his back. The girl was fortunately very light; carrying her took little effort.

"My dad takes me outside like this," she said.

The elevator doors closed. Slowly they began to descend.

"Right, I almost forgot—what about your dad?"

"He saw you, so he's probably hidden away. He's a little anxious."

"Why? What was there to hide from?" Han Jun gave a helpless laugh. "Get in touch with your dad. Tell him not to come home for the time being."

"Alright." Lu Qi put on the VR helmet.

The sound of the elevator doors ripping came from above, making Han Jun's teeth shake. He leaned against the elevator wall, glanced up, and waited.

The elevator shuddered violently as the R-ARMOR landed heavily on top of the carriage. A mechanical arm pierced through the carriage roof, groping around inside.

Han Jun crouched low, dodging the arm. Lu Qi lifted her head. The miniature drone was pinned to her ear like a hairpin, acting as her eyes.

"Does he want to kill us?"

"Probably. Why aren't you scared?"

"I encounter situations like this in VR games quite often," she said calmly.

"Well, don't think that we can just save and reload."

At last the elevator reached its destination. Han Jun charged out the doors as soon as they opened.

"We'd better get out of here as fast as we can."

"Let's take that car, then."

Lu Qi pointed to a light purple Toyota hatchback. The car flashed its headlights in response, its doors opening automatically.

Han Jun put Lu Qi in the backseat and slid into the driver's seat. The car engine started.

"Is this your family's car?" he asked.

"I like this color. I've hacked into all the smart devices in this building hundreds of times," she said.

"Alright, you can't do that anymore. That's illegal."

"No one says so in the games."

"VR games aren't everything!" he shouted.

He slammed down against the accelerator. The Toyota sped fast as lightning out of the underground parking garage. The R-ARMOR followed relentlessly behind them, but despite its massive strides, it fell farther and farther behind.

Han Jun let out a sigh. "We lost him."

"What now?"

"I have to go back to the NETLORD offices. That's where the R-ARMOR override device is—it can terminate Zeng Ping's remote access."

"You seem to know more than a regular programmer." The drone left the side of Lu Qi's head and hovered by the driver's seat next to Han Jun.

"I figured he'd come try to kill me sooner or later, so I did some investigating."

"You thought he'd try to kill you?"

"I don't know. I felt like he might." Han Jun ran his tongue over his lips. "After all, he has very strong antisocial tendencies. He's someone I selected very carefully. He does whatever he likes with no regard for the consequences."

The NETLORD office building appeared before them. Han Jun slowed down. Even from a distance, he could see that a huge gaping hole had been smashed through the windows of the building's southern wing, from which glass debris was still crumbling to the ground. There was a blurred flash of blue and red ahead, accompanied by the sound of police sirens.

Han Jun inched forward. The police had already crowded around the building, making the road ahead impenetrable.

"Fine, then," Han Jun muttered. He reversed direction, looped around, and parked the car at the back of the building.

Carrying Lu Qi, he snuck up to the building's northern wing. They didn't run into any other employees; they'd probably already been evacuated.

Han Jun opened the door to the high-tech equipment lab, revealing an utter mess within.

He put Lu Qi down and walked into the room. The main computer linked to the R-ARMOR had been thoroughly smashed to bits. All of his leads ended here. He'd only heard of the override device. But what did it look like? Was it a program? Or was it a button detonator like the kind suicide bombers used? He had no idea.

"Um . . ."

A groan sounded from within the room.

Han Jun walked around the table and saw his boss's boss—Director Daisy Fenton—sprawled on the ground, blood trickling from her forehead.

"Director Fenton—are you okay?" Han Jun lifted Daisy up. He thought for a moment, then did something he'd seen in the movies—he pressed his thumb against the acupuncture point at the middle of her upper lip.

Daisy sighed heavily, then opened her eyes. "Who are you?"

"I'm one of NETLORD's employees, Director Fenton. Is the R-ARMOR override device here? We have to stop Zeng Ping."

"Call me Daisy. And that's classified company information, you can't—"

"Director Fenton!" Han Jun gripped Daisy's shoulders. "There's no time. Zeng Ping wants to kill her, we have to . . . " He pointed to the door, where Lu Qi had been waiting, but the girl had disappeared.

"Lu Qi!" Han Jun ran out of the laboratory, but he saw no trace of her. All he saw was a green figure.

Han Jun retreated into the laboratory and yelled to Daisy, "Quick! The override device—shut him down!"

Shaking her head, Daisy pointed to the heap of computer wreckage.

The R-ARMOR strode into the laboratory.

"Where is the girl?" Its voice was low and muffled.

"You don't have to look for her," Han Jun said. As the R-ARMOR approached, he stepped back, deliberately drawing the battle suit deeper toward the side of the room to give Daisy space to escape. But Daisy only stared fixedly at the R-ARMOR, displaying no intent of leaving.

"No," said the R-ARMOR. "She's ruined everything. I want to tear her to shreds."

"It wasn't her. It was me," Han Jun said. "I'm the one who ruined everything for you."

"You?" The battle suit paused. "Who the hell are you?"

"You have one chance to do the right thing," said Han Jun. "Are you sure you can do it?"

"What?"

"You have one chance to do the right thing. Are you sure you can do it?"

"What the hell are you on about?"

"Dammit! Four years ago, I was the one who encouraged you to go protest at New Industries Corporation, don't you remember?" Han Jun straightened his back so that he wouldn't look so guilty. "We've only spoken online, but I know everything about you."

"It was you . . . " Zeng Ping was silent for a few seconds, thinking. "So you're the one who shot that video."

"Yes." Han Jun nodded. "But I never imagined it would end up like this."

Zeng Ping began to shake in mirth, which made the battle suit look very strange. When at last he stopped laughing, he bent down toward Han Jun. "You've given me a very good justification."

The R-ARMOR threw a punch at Han Jun's ribs. Han Jun had no time to respond. Only a single fact crossed his mind—the R-ARMOR could amplify its operator's strength by thirty-five times.

He flew backward. But he hadn't been struck by the R-Armor. There was a flash of silver between the fist and Han Jun, blocking the punch. The silver shape had thrown him back. It hurt, but much less than a hard punch from the R-ARMOR's fist would have.

He crawled upright. A silver-white robot stood facing the R-ARMOR, grabbing one of its arms with both hands.

"Who are you?" Zeng Ping demanded.

"I'm the one you want to kill." The silver-white robot responded in a clear, melodious woman's voice.

"Lu Qi?" Han Jun asked.

"It's me. By the way, your company's super-printer is great. I've wanted to print some big toys for forever."

"This isn't a game!" Han Jun exclaimed.

"I . . . " Lu Qi had just begun to speak when Zeng Ping struggled out of her grasp. The R-ARMOR twisted around, grabbed the silvery-white robot's arm, and ripped it out with ease. Then the R-ARMOR kicked Lu Qi's robot to the floor and pressed a foot against its torso.

"How could your hastily printed toy compare to mine? I put everything into creating the R-ARMOR!" Zeng Ping stomped on the robot's chest, forcing a deep hole in the 3D printed, multilayer cushion armor. "Everything! This is the reason for my existence! You've ruined it all. Do you understand? You've ruined it!"

Zeng Ping gave another stomp with every howl. He didn't stop until there was a massive crater in the robot's body.

"I want to see what you look like." Zeng Ping bent the R-ARMOR over and ripped the robot's breastplate open with both hands. But the control cabin was empty.

The robot had no control cabin at all.

"I'm over here!" Another robot appeared in the laboratory and charged the R-ARMOR. Once again, the silver and green robots were locked in a duel.

"You want to defeat me?" Zeng Ping's fists smashed against the robot's waist. The robot deftly twisted around and kicked the R-ARMOR in the chest. The R-ARMOR stumbled back a few steps, but Zeng Ping didn't stop talking. "I've trained in this suit for over a thousand hours!"

"And I've experienced the world like this for half my life." Lu Qi's robot continued its attack. Zeng Ping avoided a sharply thrown punch, then threw a side hook at the robot's head. The blow destroyed the robot's wireless system, and the robot toppled to the floor.

"You don't think this is funny?" Another voice sounded from the doorway. "You opposed 3D printing from the start, but now you grovel at 3D printing's feet."

The new silver robot launched another attack at the R-ARMOR. After a dozen exchanged blows, it fell defeated to the R-ARMOR's fists. But then a new robot appeared in its place.

Very soon, Zeng Ping became visibly tired. His reflexes slowed; his attacks lost their vigor. His raging battle cries became heavy gasps.

Lu Qi's robot seized the opportunity and sent the R-ARMOR crashing to the ground. The armor's left elbow joint twisted past its limit and broke, revealing the wires inside. A spark of flame emitted from the breakage. It was lucky that Zeng Ping had already lost his left arm long ago, otherwise he certainly would have suffered a ruptured tendon.

The R-ARMOR struggled to stand. It attempted a left hook, but Lu Qi knocked it down and forced it against the ground. Her robot's composite material mechanical hand pushed through the R-ARMOR's chinks and tore open the cockpit door, revealing the simultaneously malevolent and pathetically weak face of Zeng Ping.

Lu Qi extended her hand toward him.

"Lu Qi!" Han Jun yelled. "Don't hurt him!"

"No, no, I . . . I just want to look at him," Lu Qi explained.

"It's over," said Han Jun. "It's okay now, you can come back." He walked around both the R-ARMOR and Lu Qi's robot to Daisy's side. "Fenton . . . Director Fenton, that . . . "

Lu Qi walked into the laboratory, still wearing the VR helmet. The drone floated half a meter from her body, leading her forward like a guide dog.

"It was this girl that uploaded the video. Um, how do I explain this . . . " Han Jun twisted the bridge of his nose. "It was all a big mistake, this . . . "

"Enough, I don't care." Daisy gave a weary wave of her hand and turned to Lu Qi. "Can you see me?"

The drone moved up and down several times, indicating a nod.

"Did you design this robot?" Daisy asked.

"Yes. I designed it a long time ago, but the 3D printer in my house can only print items fifty centimeters or smaller, so I've never been able to test it out. Auntie, your company's 3D printers are great. I've wanted to try them out forever."

"Ah . . . right." Daisy took a look at Lu Qi's drone, then carefully examined the silver robot.

She had the sharp hunch that Lu Qi was a VR genius. Perhaps she could replace Zeng Ping?

"Ah . . . " Someone let out a long exhale. Zeng Ping had woken up. The R-ARMOR stumbled upright. This suit, NETLORD's finest technological achievement, was now broken beyond repair, teetering on the verge of collapse.

"Zeng Ping, enough." Han Jun stood, positioning his body between Zeng Ping and Daisy and Lu Qi. "I'm so sorry for all that you've suffered. If I can, I want to make it up to you."

"NETLORD couldn't even give me what I wanted. How could you?" Zeng Ping's lidless eyes roved back and forth at the three people before him. "I just want the ones who destroyed me . . . " The R-ARMOR raised a hand. It held a blue steel canister—one of the oxygen canisters from Zeng Ping's sickbed.

" . . . to get what they deserve!" Zeng Ping roared, and threw the oxygen tank at them.

"Careful!" Han Jun twisted around to shield Daisy and Lu Qi.

There was a great bang as the canister struck the wall and dropped to the floor. A crack split open in the canister on impact and oxygen began hissing out.

The tiny hexacopter drone fell to the ground.

In that instant Lu Qi switched her controls and manipulated the robot to block the canister. The canister rebounded and smashed against the R-ARMOR, which fell flat on its back.

Guided by reactive force, the canister rolled twice and stopped by the green robot's leg.

"Shit—it's going to explode." Han Jun quickly ran to the R-ARMOR's side and extricated Zeng Ping from the stabilization devices. Zeng Ping had taken a hard beating from the earlier attacks. Half of his already weak chest had collapsed inward, and blood trickled out the side of his mouth.

"Let me go!"

"Shut up! It's going to explode!"

Han Jun lifted him up. The limbless Zeng Ping wasn't heavy; it was like carrying a child. Indeed, Zeng Ping still was a child.

Zeng Ping struggled furiously, thrashing the stumps of his arms against Han Jun's face. "Let me go! I won't leave!"

"If you don't go you'll die!"

"I died a long time ago!" Suddenly Zeng Ping straightened up. His arm jabbed into Han Jun's eye. Han Jun's vision blacked out for a moment. He let go. Zeng Ping struggled free, rolled to the ground, and crawled on his ruined limbs back into the R-ARMOR's cockpit.

"Come on," called Daisy as Han Jun stood dazed before the R-ARMOR. "He's not going to leave."

"I won't leave. In here—this is my reality." Zeng Ping gave Han Jun one last look, then closed the cockpit door.

The canister whined as air continued to leak. Flames sparked out of the R-ARMOR's fractured left arm. Then the battle suit exploded.

Gusts of fire and air erupted outward, throwing Han Jun, Daisy, and Lu Qi to the ground.

Daisy climbed to her feet. Ignoring her scorched hair and the shrapnel wounds on her face, she stared in a daze at the blazing R-ARMOR. Zeng Ping gazed back at her through the cockpit window. He was embraced in flames, but he seemed calm; aloof.

Everything—the product of so many years of effort—was burning away.

Daisy turned. She walked out of the laboratory, down the long corridor, and back into her office. She poured herself a glass of whisky, then drank it down in one swallow. She took out a VR VISION set from the cabinet and put it on. Before her eyes appeared the moment she discovered Zeng Ping, that ugly, vulgar, wrathful child. She had stayed by his side while he recuperated. She'd helped him make peace with the rage within him. She'd watched as he entered the virtual world for the first time. She'd seen his face when he regained the limbs he had lost.

She left herself in that memory.

Han Jun lifted Lu Qi up. Her VR helmet had fallen off, revealing her face.

"Are these real flames?" she asked.

"They are."

Lu Qi reached a hand toward the flames, but quickly yanked it back. "Ouch!"

"Yes, they'll hurt you," said Han Jun. "That's the worst and best thing about reality."

Gradually the flames died out, transforming into black smoke, both at once illusory and real.

First Prize: 5th Lightyear Award for Best Short Story (2016).

Originally published in Chinese in *Whale's Route*, collection, 2018.

假手于人

By Those Hands

CONGYUN "MU MING" GU

慕明

TRANSLATED BY JUDITH HUANG

When Qingyun Tang walked into the house, Old Tang was bent over, cutting bamboo into strands. Heat was rising in indistinct waves from the stove where a clay pot stood, filled with simmering sausage, green beans, and white rice.

"Back home so late again? Come and eat," said Old Tang, lifting his eyes and peering at Qingyun's reflection in the mirror just above its frame. The girl had short floppy hair, thin suspenders holding up her jeans, and large headphones hanging around her neck, spewing what sounded to him like gibberish.

"I've already eaten outside." Qingyun walked over to the bamboo sofa to lie down and pulled out her phone. The chain around her wrist jingled loudly.

"Food from outside is not as good as food from home. Come on, at least eat a little if you don't eat it all. It's green beans and sausage clay pot rice." Old Tang stopped cutting with the knife in his hand and, by the light of the yellow lamp, examined the delicate strands of bamboo. The green part of the bamboo stems, which he had split so the yellow core was removed, was tough and strong, yet only half an inch thick. He had then further split it eight times into thin strips, carefully cut, which were all thin enough to be so translucent that you could read the small print of the evening newspaper through it if you held it up to the lamp.

Old Tang was trained in the art of bamboo craftsmanship and had finished his apprenticeship in the craft when he was just sixteen. Now, he had been weaving bamboo for forty-one years, and he was a master.

Qingyun dawdled, taking her time to get up and scoop a small bowl of green beans and a handful of rice dripping with pepper grains into her bowl.

"Why aren't you eating any sausage?" Old Tang lifted the intricate bamboo crock cover on the table to reveal a dish of preserved cabbage.

The cabbage had been soaked and preserved by Old Tang himself over a month ago, and the sausage had also been made by him last winter. Thirty-five pounds of lean meat, fifteen pounds of fat, everything diced and sliced with his skillful knife: lantern pepper, regular pepper, bright green sun-dried peppers, then passed through a grinder to form little tubes, then, with just the tips of the chopsticks, pushed carefully into little sausage cases, before being hung out on the balcony to dry. Because there were not many people in his family, the sausages lasted a long time. Since the sausage had been hanging to dry for quite some time, their surface was now covered with an ashy substance. When they were steamed, they were also brown, no longer the striking bright, oily red they had been while hanging from the window outside. Regardless, Old Tang felt that anything made by hand at home was bound to be better than anything bought from a store outside. As for what exactly made it better, he could not say.

"Next year, don't do it yourself anymore. You'll just tire yourself out. If you don't want to eat store-bought ones, then take the meat, bring it to the market, and use the machine there," said Qingyun, picking at the pepper grains while looking at her phone. "It's electric, and specially made for grinding meat and making sausages."

"What machine!" Old Tang's hands gathered the strands of bamboo, but because his hands were shaking, they clattered to the ground. He wanted to stand up in protest but found himself paralyzed, glued to the chair.

"Dad!" Qingyun threw down her chopsticks. "Another headache?"

Old Tang strained wordlessly for the teapot. Qingyun hurriedly handed it to him, and Old Tang gurgled and drank until beads of sweat rolled down the furrows all over his wrinkled face. He seemed to calm down a little.

"You'd better go check on it earlier. It's fine to leave these alone for now." Qingyun whispered.

"Don't bother, I have my own tally." Old Tang bent down and, not raising his head even once, began picking up the bamboo strands one by one. Qingyun picked up the rice grains silently. Between them, neither issued a sound.

The Tang family did not watch much television. For decades, after nightfall, the house was filled, in the early evening, with the sounds of Qingyun doing her homework—the rustle of pen and paper, while the later part of the evening would see the house filled with the sounds of Qingyun practicing guzheng, the plucked strings of the instrument resounding. These days, the sounds of keyboard and mouse were more likely, crackling on into the night as it got late. Interspersed with this was the rustling sounds of Old Tang cutting bamboo, making it into cylinders, weaving it into different patterns, and polishing. The sound of cars honking on the street and the music played by the little provisions shop in the alley made him feel frustrated and anxious, and it was only the subtle sounds made by his own hands and the objects he was working with that allowed him to concentrate and escape, to pretend that he had returned to his old home near the forest, where the wind rustled through the bamboo leaves.

"Leave it." The sound of water from the washbasin. Old Tang scolded, "Young lady, leave it. Hands made for playing the guzheng would get coarse by doing chores like washing up."

"Your hands are more valuable than mine," argued Qingyun, using the cylinders to brush the bowl. "You're able to weave bamboo using one hundred and eighty different methods, all by hand. Isn't that more impressive than playing the guzheng?"

Old Tang didn't say anything. He had started his apprenticeship at the age of fifteen and became a master at the age of twenty, and even his own master had said that he, Tang Hong, was the most accomplished bamboo craftsman he had ever seen. At that time in the old countryside, bamboo craftsmen had a good life. People who farmed the fields needed bamboo rakes, bamboo dustpans for drying grain, bamboo curtains for hanging in the summer, bamboo mats to sleep on, and bamboo cases for hand warmers. He still remembered the couplet that decorated the front door of his store: Branches and vines are shaped into tools, whether square or round; we, too, are shaped into worthy things of use. At that time, he took great pride in his role as a bamboo craftsman and had great regard for his craft. Craftsmen made an honest living, neither stealing nor robbing. He thought he was set for life and wouldn't have to worry about making a living. Little had he anticipated the world of today.

Old Tang reached his hand out to examine it. The many years of learning the art of a hundred and eighty methods of weaving bamboo had left his hands with cracks, scars, and bruises. The cold Chengdu winters also gave him frostbite, aggravating the cracks and making them itchy and painful, and no matter what medicinal balms he used, they never relieved his hands. But it was not frostbite that made his heart feel like it had been scratched by a cat's claw.

"Dad, next weekend, I want to bring Xu Xiao over for a meal," Qingyun said as she finished wiping the table and washing the rag. "We'll just eat at the restaurant downstairs and come back up here for tea afterward."

Old Tang frowned.

"Oh alright, alright, we'll eat at home, okay? Anyway, he keeps saying he wants to come and see you working at your craft. Maybe you could even take on a disciple!"

"Disciple?" Old Tang snorted. Since 1977, when he first started working at the bamboo factory, and in the two decades or more that he'd practiced his art, how many disciples had he taken on? But how many still practiced the craft today? Not to mention, the way young people were these days, they couldn't even sit still long enough to concentrate, not to mention learn the nuances of the art of bamboo weaving. Even his own daughter, who grew up watching him work, had never even tried her hand at it once, and was completely ignorant of the art. Take on a disciple?

It had gotten late, and Qingyun went back to her room. Old Tang was still under his lamp, his blade still open in his hand, but, instead of working, he simply sat and stared. Outside the window, the noise of commerce filled the street, and the glaring neon lights and shadows distracted passersby with their brilliance. Times had indeed changed, but at the bottom of the heart, there was always a shard of something hard, something solid and immovable.

Those with skills that the world requires prosper, while those without those skills are trapped with nowhere to go. Bamboo implements are cheap and lowly, unlike objects and precious things made of jade or silver. His master had said that if you wanted to be able to make a good living, to make a name for yourself, you need to rely on your own two hands. To this saying, Old Tang had tacked on, perhaps unconsciously, that no machine could equal the skill and finesse of a master craftsman of the art of bamboo. He just refused to believe it possible.

When I first came to New York City six years ago, I wandered around with no regard as to where I would end up. At the Rubin Museum of Art, my fingers stroked a tapestry from the Himalayas, and at a small Ethiopian restaurant, I rolled sour injera bread with tiny holes in it that evoked the texture of honeycomb. Truly, you can find something from every corner of the world in this city. In the subway, faces that emerged were varied and diverse, and in the plaza, every hand raised was a different color. After the initial shock subsided, I tried to find a common essence behind the differences, to find something abstract in common. This is the way I understand the world. It is the essence of my profession.

I studied applied mathematics at the Courant Institute. Applied mathematics is about abstraction and induction. If the beauty of pure mathematics lies in the creation of pure patterns in a concise system, unencumbered in any way by reality, as the mathematician G. H. Hardy said, or even the physical world itself, then applied mathematics is, I'm afraid, ugly, and concerned with trivialities. What I am after is not a perfect crystal in the void, nor a creativity comparable to that of a painter or a poet, but an explanation, a model, a new perspective that arises after careful observation and profound reflection. With this perspective, even ordinary things take on unimaginably rich layers and wonderful patterns may be observed.

In my second year, I started to decide on my research direction. Wall Street is the best testing ground for applied mathematics. The ever-changing market fluctuations and the richness and diversity of investment portfolios require precise descriptions in the language of mathematics. The pricing theory of securities was modeled by stochastic differential equations, and the value-at-risk of stocks was predicted by Monte Carlo methods. The models we play with in the lab, just a few miles away from the world's largest financial market in terms of volume, become real, huge risks, and commensurate huge returns. Hundreds of the brightest brains are fighting it out on this battlefield, and hundreds of megabytes of data are being captured, analyzed, and modeled as they speed through fiber optic cables. But for me, that's not interesting enough.

The research question I chose to answer was regarding the brain itself. In essence, it was not very different from the research my classmates were doing. If we look at the financial markets as a giant brain, then each trading decision that is made can be seen as a single disbursement of individual neurons, and each flow of information is analogous to the transmission of impulses between synapses. Deciphering the transmission process of a certain external stimulus along the "neural pathways" is also equivalent to deciphering the market shock that a certain piece of news may trigger. Understanding that the actual human brain is much more difficult and more interesting than understanding the financial markets. Not only because the average volume of transactions in the New York Stock Exchange is just forty thousand per second, whereas the human brain has millions of signals passing through it per second. But more importantly, the brain is not the only organ we use for this.

During my first year at the Courant Institute, I took an introductory neurology course in the medical school. In the class, I saw a diagram of a longitudinal section of the human brain, and above each brain region, other organs were drawn, in proportion to the size of the area of the brain responsible for the motor and sensory functions of each organ. This schematic diagram is called a cortical homunculus. On the diagram, I saw a hand that took up a larger proportion of the brain than the entire lower half of the body.

I have never forgotten that lesson. The old professor said in an incomprehensible Eastern European accent that the hand is the most delicate and complex organ that human beings have. There are a million nerve fibers in the human hand, a number unmatched in any limb of any other animal. The human being thus has the most complex and special functional relationship between organs, namely the connection between the hand and the brain. In addition, the human hand has an extremely special and delicate group of nineteen small muscles, each with a unique degree of freedom of movement. I reach out, flex my hands, and tighten them into fists again, imagining a torrent of data rushing into my brain at one hundred meters per second, lighting up one neuron after another, shining like a star.

The bamboo weaving factory was reorganized in 2003. The factory, which had employed five hundred people, was streamlined to less than one hundred workers. The old hands who had been doing it all their lives, and the young apprentices who only had a few years' experience, were all asked to leave. At the time, Old Tang was such a skilled hand at bamboo that he thought he would easily avoid this round of layoffs, but sadly, at the last minute, a relative of the director was given a spot in the quota instead of him, and Old Tang was forced out of his job.

His old colleagues lamented that if only he had presented two high quality Jiaozi brand cigarettes, or a bottle of Luzhou baijiu liquor to the right person, he would almost definitely have been able to stay on. But at the time, Old Tang was still young and stubborn, with an artistic temperament and a temper that refused to let him seek help from anyone. He thought he should be allowed to stay simply on account of his high degree of skill and craftsmanship. After all, which colleague at the factory could dispute that he was a highly skilled Master? With his skill, even if he lost his job at the factory, it was impossible to imagine that he would starve.

Reality hit him as he watched the decades-old company sign get replaced by a sign for a private limited company, thus changing its standing as a government brand. The cool wind that blew the street full of Chinese parasol leaves, flittering and clattering, blew just as cold a wind in his empty heart. That day he did not ride his bike, instead pushing it slowly along the south bank of the river, and, after he had passed the second ring road viaduct, he spotted the smoke spouting from the towering cranes, busy in the act of changing his city. When did his city change so much?

It was painfully obvious to Old Tang why he had been laid off. Although ostensibly the management had said the benefits of bamboo were not obvious enough, and that the staff were redundant, in the end, it was simply because bamboo weaving was far too labor intensive to be cost-effective. To make the same product, say, a rice sieve, required a skilled factory weaver a full day of work, whereas at the plastics factory, the same sieve would take just minutes to produce. Although the plastic was coarser, the holes rougher, and the feel less warm and inviting than bamboo, how many people would be willing to fork out a few times the price just to have the same item made out of bamboo?

Not to mention that, if you let the machines run for a few extra hours, you could double your output, whereas human workers needed to stay up until the light ran out, and when the sun set, blurry human eyes could not make out the fine, supple bamboo strands. Although he was reluctant to admit it, Old Tang had to say that even though machines could not attain the complexity and finesse of his bamboo weaving, in terms of speed, the machine was a million times better than any bamboo craftsman, no matter how skilled.

His old colleagues told him that these days, it was even possible to get out of Sichuan Province on a train or plane. A journey that used to take a whole month now took a mere few hours. How could a bamboo craftsman, used to laboring for a whole month to make a single item, keep up with the increasing speed and relentless change of times like these? He had to face it: their time had passed, and this age had replaced them so swiftly, they hadn't even had time to react.

A few of them left the factory with tens of thousands of yuan from the compensation they received. Some had enough savings and contacts to start motorcycle taxis or open grocery stores. The vast majority seemed to knock into insurmountable walls in every direction, losing all their money, and were reduced to doing odd jobs anywhere they could find them, working as security guards, masseuses, dishwashers, or vegetable sellers. The former bamboo artisans were now doing whatever they found their hand at, doing anything they could to survive. The only one who still refused to relinquish his bamboo carving knife was Old Tang.

Old Tang decided to invest tens of thousands of yuan, plus all the tens of thousands he had saved up over the course of twenty years, in opening his own store. He leased a small store on a tourist street where people came to buy gifts and antique wares and put up a sign saying "Chengdu Bamboo Weavers" above the door. From the moment he hung up that sign, it bought him another seventeen years in this line of business. Old Tang no longer worked for a factory, weaving coarse woven textiles, mats, and other household goods. Now, he specialized in intricate weaves and luxury products. Machines may be good at being quick and fast, and Old Tang recognized that. But it was different with fine work. This required finesse.

Bamboo weaving using the plants' fibers that were split as fine as silk is a craft unique to the city of Chengdu. All the skills that Old Tang had picked up over the years from the old masters in the village had really gone to waste in the factory since they were seldom required, but fortunately, with practice, these skills came back to him easily. The thicker weaves, using coarser bamboo, were the foundation of the art of bamboo, but these fine skills of manipulating thin threads of bamboo were like the pinnacle of a beautiful, jeweled pagoda. Bamboo is inherently tough and strong, but when the fibers are separated into fine threads, they are soft and pliable, and unable to hold their shape on their own. So porcelain or silver teapots and tea bowls are used as a base on which to do the delicate weaves. This is called bamboo weaving on a base. Each item contains intricate designs so that every inch of its surface is woven with a different pattern, all depending on the individual artisan's judgment and experience. This was not something that could be made by machine. Although he had left his master a few decades ago, in terms of fine bamboo weaving, few people could equal his skill since few people had received such training. In Old Tang's own eyes, there was none who met his standard. This was Old Tang's conviction.

Sadly, although his work was excellent, business was not so good.

The antiques and gift shopping street's location was less than ideal, and his small store was in an obscure corner. In the dim darkness of the evening, a single lamp illuminated Old Tang. He was in the middle of making an intricately woven bamboo tea set. The weave was so tight that he could accommodate twelve strands of bamboo within a centimeter. That was what was required to certify it a fine grade bamboo weave.

Old Tang had not yet found a buyer for the set. It had been an entire month since the last tea ware was sold. He was idle for two days but felt so terrible lying idle that he went to the wholesale market to put together a range of white porcelain that he could sell as a set to wrap in bamboo. For Old Tang, to weave bamboo was like playing basketball for a basketball player or practicing guzheng for a musician. A single day of missing his practice caused his hands to feel raw, and his heart to feel troubled.

The year he was laid off, it wasn't like it never crossed Old Tang's mind to do something else. But the more he thought about it, the more he was convinced that if he could do anything, he would still choose to weave bamboo. In the first few years of his business, he was losing money every year. Even Qingyun's school fees were paid with borrowed money. Even when his wife divorced him, he was still unable to let go of his craft. With one hand he grabbed his daughter, while the other hand still grasped his bamboo. When he got busy, he even brought his child to the store. By the time he had finally gotten a little famous for his work, Qingyun had grown up. They had a better life, but by then he had grown old. Under the clear light of his lamp, the bamboo his hands were weaving spread like a net. These days, when he looked back at the decades of life, he increasingly felt that while he wove, he was also part of a net.

A car honked.

Old Tang frowned and looked up. When he chose the store in the obscure corner of the tourist town, one consideration was the cheaper rent. But another was also that it gave him peace and quiet. Drunks were unlikely to be found this deep in the alley, and the quiet gave him the peace to concentrate on work.

"Shifu, it's me, Renjie Liu!" The car window rolled down, and the driver took off his sunglasses and waved, "Still recognize me?"

Old Tang opened his mouth, wanting to respond, but failed to make a sound. This disciple of his he remembered as being intelligent. However, when they worked together in the factory setting, his lively mind kept getting distracted with all kinds of schemes, so that he was completely unable to sit still and concentrate. One hot day, when Old Tang was sweating buckets in the factory while working on his weaving, Renjie was running to-and-fro, presenting Old Tang with a glass of chilled water. It turned out that this enterprising young man had secretly installed a refrigerator in the factory and was selling cans of soft drinks at one yuan a can to his colleagues, making more than any of them would on their salaries alone. Of course, the moment there was a series of layoffs, he was one of the first to be let go, and he went off to do some other kind of business. Old Tang had lost this particular apprentice a long time ago, and yet, the moment he heard him call him "Shifu," he found himself tongue-tied.

"This place can be really hard to find!" said Renjie as he entered the door, looked around, and pulled up a nearby bamboo chair to sit on. "How's business?"

"It's good enough." Old Tang continued to weave his bamboo. In the soft glow of the lamp, he saw that the skinny young boy he had known had since grown a beer belly, and that his business suit was straining to contain it. He himself was still wearing the old gray uniform from the bamboo factory that had laid him off.

"Don't you wish to do something else? Come over to my company and do something with me."

"I'm a craftsman. Not as good as you businessmen," Old Tang replied, not looking up at him.

"A craftsman lives by the work of his hands. Don't think too much! Isn't that what you used to tell me? I still remember, you know!" Renjie lit a cigarette, leaned nearer to Old Tang to watch his weaving, and said, admiringly, "Woah, it's like silk! That's unbelievably fine!"

"I didn't teach you these skills." Old Tang put down his work, coughed twice in response to the smoke, and asked, "Why are you here?"

"Can't I come just to see you?" Renjie put out the cigarette, "But if you must get straight to the point, then yes, there *is* a reason I'm here."

"I won't join your company," said Old Tang, bowing his head. Renjie had called him on the phone before, wanting to hire him as a consultant. But Old Tang simply could not imagine putting down his bamboo weaving and wanted nothing to do with machines. He had already hung up twice on him and had never expected him to track him down and turn up at his door. But even if he begged him a third time, he still wouldn't go. Old Tang had already made up his mind.

"I know." Renjie smiled. "Our company intends to sponsor the Cultural Heritage Invitationals Exhibition. It's a joint project with the Sichuan Department of Culture, and I immediately thought of you. Since you refuse to take my calls, I have no choice but to come here in person."

"Bamboo weaving counts?" asked Old Tang, his eyebrows raised in surprise.

"Of course! I've really not seen an equal to your exceptional fine silk weaves. The judging is primarily based on dexterity and complexity of skill, and your hundred and eighty methods of bamboo weaving definitely count as complex. The more methods you can show off, the better!"

Old Tang said nothing. In the past two years, his headaches were becoming more and more frequent, and the pain made his vision blurry and his hands shaky. Pain he could tolerate, and he was also used to hard work and setbacks. But the thought of the craft he took decades to master being lost, little by little, was truly the most bitter fate for him to face. Old Tang had long thought that, while he still was able, he really needed to make a masterpiece to leave as a legacy, so that it would still endure for those who came after him, even if he was no longer around. Renjie's offer spoke straight to his heart's desire.

"How about it, Shifu? Will you think about it? In three and a half months, give me a call if you agree." He put on his sunglasses, strode out of the little alley, and turned around for one last time. "I'll be waiting!"

Old Tang nodded his head, already planning what he would need to do. The sound of Renjie's car had long faded away when he remembered that tomorrow Qingyun would be bringing Xu Xiao home for dinner, and he had not even started to prepare the dishes he'd be serving. He rushed to his bicycle to ride to the market. Fortunately, he managed to pick up two celtuces and a handful of vegetables, including Chinese cabbage, and half a braised duck before closing time. He hung the duck from the handlebars of his bicycle and rode home slowly, humming songs from a Chinese opera as he went.

During my fifth year in New York, I felt overwhelmed for the first time.

For the past twenty years, whether it was studying for exams or fitting in during social activities, I was always able to quickly grasp the key to the puzzle and crack it with the absolute minimum of effort. Some say it's a gift, but to me, it's about thinking abstractly about a myriad of things, searching for the patterns that lie beneath, and applying your deductions. Just like mathematics. But that one time, I really felt as though I had hit a wall.

My thesis was about the neurology behind fine hand movements. Unlike in physiology and cognitive science, the language of computational neuroscience is mathematics and computer programming. The behavior of neurons, synapses, and neuronal networks become data that are analyzed to build mathematical models to imitate the workings of the cerebral cortex.

I don't have to feed mice or monkeys, or insert electrodes into their motor cortices, or send questionnaires to subjects. I deal with the data itself to build the models and write the code. It is just like what quantitative analysts in the financial markets do, except that we still know next to nothing about this "market." If you take the field of physics as an analogy, our field is still in its infancy, and has not yet seen our Galileo, much less our Newton or Einstein, when it comes to the quantifying of the human brain, much less the quantifying of the external world. It is both exciting and anxiety-provoking.

My data came from a collaboration with a group of researchers in the psychology department. Subjects followed instructions to perform certain hand movements, and MRI scans were taken, and data recorded. I mapped the hand movements to neural response signals, abstracted the key calculations, inferred the process of decision-making, built a model of the entire process, and coded algorithms to reproduce simple human fingertip movements into complex modeled signals. This was harder than I thought it would be. With millions of signals per second, identifying the signals that control hand movements is like finding a needle in a haystack. I tried various filtering algorithms and sequencing the subjects' pulses, but the results were not good. I approached my doctoral advisor for advice, and he listened to my presentation without saying much, just inviting me to coffee after.

"You are very intelligent and very hardworking," said my advisor. He was of Italian descent, a renowned scholar, with an outstanding mind, and discerning taste in both coffee and scientific research. I waited for him to continue with trepidation.

"However, being smart is only one aspect of doing research. Especially in this field." He put down his cup, "Intelligence, insight, analytical ability, these can all be called talents. Talent is valuable and essential, but experience, or rather, domain knowledge, is often needed if we are to solve practical problems. It gives us a deeper understanding of the underlying structure." He patted me on the shoulder, "Relax, I'll let you take a break. Also, regarding the problem of detecting signals, muscle nerve signals are probably simpler to detect than central nervous system signals."

I quickly figured out the mechanics of signal processing. But the domain knowledge my advisor spoke of still eluded me. Although I could extract stable muscle nerve impulses, the data were not significant enough to build a complete model.

I decided to take a break from work, hoping I could process things in the background like a program, as it were, while still doing my best to think. Then, one day, I casually flipped through the New York Times and came across a quote that jumped out at me.

The Devon-based [contemporary basket weaver] Hilary Burns recalls that observing Manthorpe [a master basket weaver] weave a herring cran was like "watching a dance; there was no wasted movement." Despite the loss of this know-how, what had already vanished long before was something more profound . . .

—*New York Times Style Magazine* Feature: "The Enduring Appeal of Baskets" by Deborah Needleman

I stood up and paced back and forth in my dorm until darkness fell. I went downstairs and asked for a bowl of Lanzhou ramen at my regular noodle bar. The short, lanky Mexican-born boy skillfully stretched, threw, and pulled the noodles, a craft that had survived for a century and across an ocean, and, more importantly, now reinvented in a way the original inventor could never have imagined.

I graduated a year later, after handing in a computational model and prototype to my advisor. He smiled and shook my hands goodbye.

I flew back to Chengdu.

Xu arrived at their place at noon. Carrying a basket of fruit, standing in the doorway, his face was still stained with sweat despite it being the end of October. Qingyun led him into the house and fussed over him, bringing him a pair of slippers to wear and pouring him tea. But all the young man did was sit there gulping water, not saying a word.

Old Tang also said nothing, only going to the kitchen to bring out plate after plate of food. The delicate green celtuce, the deep purple Chinese cabbage, plump pink meat slices, the glistening red duck, and of course, the thinly sliced homemade sausage. Because Xu hailed from the Southern provinces where food was less spicy, Old Tang did not put too much chili in any of his dishes.

"Xu came back from abroad, and now teaches at the University of Electronic Science and Technology of China. He is the youngest professor there." Qingyun clipped bits of food with her chopsticks while talking.

"It's nothing, it's nothing," Xu exclaimed while clipping rice toward his mouth. "I haven't been back in China long. I'm still working toward achieving something, unlike you, Uncle, Qingyun told me, your bamboo weaving craft, now that is . . . "

Old Tang looked at Xu's face, reddened with embarrassment, and it reminded him of himself when he was young. He gradually felt something indescribable grow inside him. "Ah, I know I'm old. Don't say that. Now you, on the other hand—you teach at UESTC. What do you teach there?"

"I'm in the field of neuroscience." Xu perked up. "Let's put it this way: If you think about it, even for an ordinary child to learn something, for example, how to type on a keyboard, takes them a certain amount of time. Not to mention specialized tasks. I study a new generation of human-computer interfaces, which aim to solve this problem. Even better, maybe machines could even . . . "

Old Tang's brow furrowed again. Qingyun winked urgently at Xu, and he hurriedly broke off mid-sentence. "Of course, sometimes manual skill is still irreplaceable. Mr. Lao She once said that we must use mechanical methods in large industries, and in small industries, we must preserve the skill of our hands. Things like the bamboo weaving you do, that's irreplaceable. Handicrafts are the embodiment of the human heart, and the heart is not something that can just be mechanized."

"That's well put." Old Tang chucked a chopstick's worth of Chinese cabbage into his mouth. "Qingyun said that you were interested in bamboo weaving?"

"Yes, I have an interest." He took his glasses off and wiped it of his sweat.

When they had finished eating, Old Tang took out his bamboo carving knife and demonstrated how he could separate a millimeter-thick strand of bamboo into four or five strands that were only the width of a human hair.

"This is called splitting to silk grade. The width of the knife varies from top to bottom, and since there's no scale, the evenness of the width of each strand is entirely controlled by hand. See, it's of even thickness. The cross-section of each strand is the same."

Then, he picked up the scaffold formed from bamboo strands, fitted it over the fine white porcelain tea ware, and picked up an even finer strand of bamboo to continue weaving along the porcelain. His hands moved up and down in waves, guiding the bamboo strands, lifting and pushing, applying pressure nimbly until the bamboo strands formed a fine mesh of a layer, securely clinging to the outside of the porcelain tea ware.

"Lift, press, twist: that's the basic technique. Whether it is plying or weaving bamboo, it is very difficult to vary the force your hands exert correctly. If you use too much strength, the weave around the porcelain would get distorted into the wrong shape or even break. With too little force, the bamboo will split apart and not hold its shape. When it comes to weaving on a base like this, there is no fixed formula. Every inch is different, and everything depends on an individual's discernment and experience. If you look at this weave carefully, you would be certain that no machine could make anything equal to it."

Xu didn't seem to have heard anything. He was staring at Old Tang's hands.

"I'll show you the ones that I've finished." Old Tang pointed to the porcelain cup and repeated himself, seeming a little out of sorts. He suspected this young man had only said he was interested in bamboo weaving to curry favor with him. And yet even Qingyun had believed him. He didn't really want to rattle on anymore, what he did for a living was his own business. As for what Renjie had asked him to do that afternoon, Old Tang was already hatching a plan in his heart.

When Qingyun pulled Xu into her own room and the sounds of the guzheng strings being plucked gently, Old Tang decided to put the whole thing behind him.

"Dad, come, dinner is ready." When he looked up, it was already dark. Qingyun had brought him some noodles. "He's already gone, you didn't even notice when he said goodbye."

"He just left?" Old Tang was a little embarrassed.

"He even gave you a gift." Qingyun handed over a string of beads. It was a bracelet of white chinaberries strung with a black tassel braided rope. Obviously of good quality, they were of equal size and when brought near, gave off the faint aroma of something bitter. "They were specially selected. It's said if you wear them in winter, they can prevent frostbite. I know you treasure your hands more than anything."

Old Tang took the bracelet and tried it on. The size was just right. He felt his heart soften a little. He also thought to himself, how likely was it that he'd accept a son-in-law as a disciple anyway? After all, he himself could barely earn a hundred yuan in a day. What he should really be worried about was disciples wanting to become sons-in-law. He would not want to let Qingyun suffer such poverty. Although the young man was a bit nerdy, at least he seemed decent, and he and Qingyun had also been together for quite a while. If they really could settle down, at least that would count as one less thing he had to worry about. As for the other matter, he would need to step up. Old Tang slowly turned his new bracelet, not noticing the faint green cast of the beads.

It has always been difficult to explain to people what I do. Ironically, this is because, unlike launching rockets or genetically engineering rice, what I do seems so simple.

"That's it?" Qingyun asked, pursing her lips, after she saw my first demonstration. The visual demonstration was of a 3D reconstruction of a human hand picking up a credit card out of a pile of other items.

"That project took me five years to do as a doctoral student! It was only after I put in a ton of work that it even managed to pick up that credit card. If you just replace the credit card with a rubber ball, it'll go back to not working," I said. "You may not know this, but it's much easier to predict the motion of a distant asteroid than it is to predict the motion of an object being pushed across a table by a model hand."

"But robot hands in factories have been able to follow instructions for movements in an assembly line for a very long time," Qingyun said, skeptical.

"It's true that robot hands perform well under strictly controlled factory conditions. But the world is not an assembly line. It's easy for people to interact with countless objects and an unpredictable environment. They can do so without thinking. But for machines, it's extremely difficult. Why do you think that's so?"

She tapped the desk, unconsciously playing invisible guzheng strings.

"That's because hands are soft." I tugged at hers.

"Hey." She shook my hand off.

"Flexibility. Tactility. The ability of the fingers to adjust in time to changes in the surface of an object is the most efficient way for a human to interact with the world. Man has invented countless tools, but the world, robotics experts say, is still designed for human hands. The reverse is also true."

She looked at me, then at her hands in wonder, tightening them into fists and then stretching them out again. Once, I had done the same. What appears inevitable and simple on the surface is both a trap and a shackle to our thinking. The more something appears simple and familiar, the later we as the human race come to truly understand it, because familiarity breeds contempt and stereotypes prevent us from examining simple things more closely. Such is the case when it comes to exploring our very bodies themselves. Our own bodies are like a far-off mountain, unknown and unexplored for thousands of years, despite being closer than our own skin.

"You've heard of the man from Qi who was afraid the sky would fall on him . . . " I teased.

"No, I'm not worried at all."

"The people who laughed at the man from Qi would never come to realize that classical mechanics, earth science, atmospheric science, many fields all have their origin in his very simple question. Now, like him, we have to do something similar."

She was still bewildered. I didn't say anything further. The first time I met her, I remembered her skillful guzheng-playing hands. But like the vast majority of people, she couldn't grasp this new paradigm, and her father, even less so. His gaze, though different from that of my advisor, made me incredibly nervous. Although he probably saw me as a traitor who wanted to take his job, that was not my ultimate goal. I was not out to simply complete a specific, tangible job. I wanted someone to understand my purpose, at least to the extent that that was possible.

In the blink of an eye, it was now winter solstice. If Old Tang had been walking down the streets, he would not find it cold, but because he sat for long hours at home, the cold soaked straight into his bones, leaving his joints with rheumatic aches and pains. Even so, Old Tang stubbornly refused to install central heating. In fact, he did not even turn on the electric stove he did have. He was concerned that the heating would dry out the house, leading his bamboo strands to grow too brittle to weave. He had already completed about half of his project. Judging from the rate he was progressing, he would just about make the deadline, but he could not procrastinate even a little.

Old Tang blew hard on his hands, and then rubbed them together to generate heat. This year, he genuinely seemed to suffer from less frostbite. The chinaberry wood beads had already developed a shiny patina from friction and being rubbed by his hands, and his hands had swollen with water retention so that he could no longer take the bracelet off. He thought of performing one of the time-honored rituals of a Chengdu winter—eating good quality home-cooked lamb soup— and put on his jacket before heading out the door. The university term wasn't over yet, so perhaps Xu could come.

At the market, he got a couple of pounds of lamb shank, slung it over his bicycle bars, and started thinking about the time Xu had come over for dinner. He had not even touched the Chinese cabbage, but at least Qingyun had eaten a bit of it. So he decided to select a few green celtuce. If he chopped them up and added them to the soup and boiled them until they grew tender and supple, they would make excellent comfort food. He thought about Qingyun, and how she had mentioned that Xu was a Southerner whose taste ran sweet, so he headed toward Wen Shu Fang on his bike.

The cakes and sweets at the Wen Shu Fang emporium had a decades-long reputation, especially their Peach Rose Cakes. When Qingyun was small, she used to cry because she missed her mother, and Old Tang had used those cakes to placate her. Now, Qingyun was fully grown, and her vanity meant she was watching her figure, so she didn't eat them anymore. But Old Tang still remembered the way to the little alley where the shop could be found.

He brought the paper box back to his bike and balanced it carefully on the back of his bike, then proceeded to ride slowly and carefully. He had not come to the Wen Shu Fang area for quite a long time. The formerly run-down alley outside the courtyard wall had now been renovated to resemble an ancient street for the sake of attracting tourists, with pink and white walls, ochre roofs, and red and yellow store signs installed all over the place. It looked surprisingly lively in the gloomy winter, with many tourists and locals milling about.

Old Tang got off his bike when he got to the entrance of the renovated street. When he was laid off, the renovation of Wen Shu Fang had just been completed, and the development was just starting to advertise for tenants. At the time, others had encouraged him to set up a storefront here instead of at his current store in Song Xiao Qiao. The asking price for rent then was about three thousand RMB a month, three times the asking price for the Song Xian Xiao store, and he considered and mulled over it quite a bit before ultimately rejecting the idea.

For one thing, if business was really bad, he would have to worry about not being able to make ends meet. For another, he really did not like the noisy sounds of a bustling street—it prevented him from concentrating on work. However, in hindsight, the poor foot traffic in Song Xian Qiao meant that the street became more and more deserted, and still, despite this, rent had risen to ten thousand RMB. The first few tenants had told him that traffic at Wen Shu Fang was now very busy. Just selling silk handkerchiefs with pandas embroidered on them or kitschy Sichuan opera masks would net enough to pay the rent, as well as a tidy profit. When Old Tang heard this, he had nothing to say. He thought back on the many decades of hard work he had put in to learning his fine bamboo craft, thought through every choice he had made from the beginning to this moment. At the time he made those choices, he always thought he factored in everything carefully before making a rational decision. But in hindsight, if he had the chance to choose again, he really had no idea what he would have chosen.

Old Tang stared for a while, and then continued to ride down the street. The street featured not just handicraft stores, but also a variety of high-end teahouses and restaurants, all sporting a "vintage," "rustic" bamboo hut look for people to eat cold noodles in. Young men and women dressed in fashionable clothing walked in and out of these establishments, and standing in the midst of them, Old Tang felt that he was the tourist.

Along the street, a black lacquered wooden door with gold trim opened, and a middle-aged man in a suit stepped out. Old Tang felt a flash of recognition. It was Renjie Liu. He did not see Old Tang but was chatting while walking toward his car. The door he had emerged out of was hiding what seemed to be a high-class club. Old Tang tried to glimpse inside, but only caught a flash of green, bamboo-like shadows.

"Manager Liu, thank you very much!" the person next to Renjie Liu said. Old Tang thought he sounded familiar.

"Professor Xu, please don't stand for ceremony! You're very welcome. With a young talent like you, the honor is all mine!" Renjie Liu was smiling ear to ear. Old Tang froze. He saw, through the crowd, clearly though he was at a distance, that the other person was Xu. He was wearing a dark gray tweed coat, half-frame glasses, and looked every inch the cultured gentleman. But laughing and talking with Renjie Liu, he seemed a completely different person from the red-faced young man who had sat down to dinner at his own table.

Seeing Xu get into Renjie Liu's car and drive over, Old Tang hurriedly turned away. How did they know each other? Why were they looking at bamboo weaves together? Did Qingyun know about this? Old Tang did not dare to think too much, got on to his bike, and peddled furiously until he got home. He hadn't ridden so fast for a long time, and when he got home and undressed, his undershirt was soaked in sweat. He sat down and looked at his half-finished bamboo weave. He didn't stop panting.

Qingyun opened the door, "Ah, so many dishes! Wow, you also got sweets and cakes from Wen Shu Yuan!" She circled Old Tang, "You sure are sincere in welcoming your future son-in-law."

"What son-in-law!"

"What?"

"You know what! No!" Old Tang was angry. "I don't know what kind of people he mixes with!"

"What's wrong with him all of a sudden? He's a university professor—how the hell is he not good enough for the bamboo weaver's daughter?" Qingyun exploded and took a step back, her face red with anger, "I always do what you want, but just what decade do you still think this is? Even the electric heater is not even on! It's like I'm walking on eggshells all the time!" Her eyes were bloodshot. "Even Mum couldn't stand you."

Old Tang stood up to his full height, beads of sweat beading on his face. "So you look down on bamboo weavers now—" He felt a stab of pain in his head, and in a flash, he was sprawled all over the chair.

This time, the pain was stronger than it had ever been, and it would not go away. It was as though there were countless tiny bamboo strands stuck into the furrows of his brain. Old Tang wished to grit his teeth and bear it like he had every other time, but this time he was past the point of endurance.

That wonderful solstice family dinner went uneaten. Old Tang was sent to the ICU at the hospital, and then transferred to the general ward, where he stayed for four days and where his whole body was examined. In the large general ward, there was a constant stream of people coming and going. Along with the sound of doctors talking, the beeping of various instruments, the moaning of patients, the anxious inquiries of family members, and the sounds of weeping disturbed Old Tang, so that he slept fitfully, if at all. Finally, at long last, it was time for light's out, and the hospital grew a little quieter, and still, he was disturbed by the sound of snoring coming from the next bed.

Every morning, Qingyun brought him a thermos filled with a generous amount of chicken soup, and at noon it was seafood noodles. But she refused to tell him the illness he had been diagnosed with. While peeling an apple, Old Tang got about half a question out of his mouth, but when he saw how red her eyes were, he did not continue. He knew very well that although he was still able to work, he was, after all, getting up there in years. When people grow old, like machines that have been working for a long time, they need to be oiled regularly, and human organs and body parts, used for decades, that look perfectly functional from the outside and seem to be working well, could still be atrophying or rotting away on the inside. It was only a matter of time. For the past two years, deep down he had known that he was unwell, but had been in denial, refusing to come to the hospital to confirm his suspicions.

Father and daughter faced each other, each unable to say a word, until the doctor arrived.

"So have you considered the options? We still recommend surgery first, then chemotherapy." The doctor was quite young, and the name tag on his chest indicated that he was a neurosurgeon.

"What disease do I have?"

"The patient still doesn't know?" The doctor wanted to tell him but held back. "You need to talk it over properly and consider all your options. Of course, if you want to keep to really conservative treatments,

you can also go that route . . . after all, you are on the older side and the condition is complex."

The doctor walked away. Old Tang looked at Qingyun and said nothing, just waiting for her to speak. The girl had been biting her lips the whole time. Finally, she could hold back no longer, and tears fell from her eyes. Through her sobs, Old Tang made out that his intermittent headaches and fainting spells had been due to a brain tumor. Although technology had advanced greatly, his disease was still incurable. At his present age, the prognosis for survival in the next five years was bad, at only ten percent; the average length he was expected to live was less than two years.

It was just a few numbers, but the effect they had on Old Tang was to make his heart feel as though a rope were tightening around it, squeezing tighter and tighter. Qingyun had dissolved into a crying mess, leaving tissues all over the floor. "I'll take you to Beijing, to Shanghai for the best treatment."

"Forget it." Old Tang surprised himself with how calm he was. "Old age, sickness, and death, these things can't be helped."

"No . . . " Qingyun's tears kept falling.

Old Tang said nothing, only reaching out to smooth her hair. Qingyun's hair was good, black, bright, and thick. When she was young, he braided her hair every day. With all the fancy hairstyles: princess hair, ponytail braid, fishbone braid, twisted braid, many people could not believe that the little girl was brought up by her father. Now that Qingyun was taller than him and had been for more than a decade, she no longer asked him to braid her hair.

"Let's go home first."

"Dad . . . "

"Let's go home first. It's just a small request . . . please, can't you do even this small thing for me?" Old Tang deliberately raised his voice to appear as though he were losing his temper, "What's the point of living at the hospital?" At this, his voice seemed to crack a little.

The moment Old Tang arrived home, he picked up more than half of the bamboo weaves he had completed. Although it had only been a few days in the hospital, his hands were already itching to work again. The second layer of weaving was almost done, and he had reached the part that would bind off the weave. In silken bamboo weaves, the binding off is also known as "locking off." In high quality weaves the final strand is hidden. The excess bamboo is clipped off, and then a thin layer of craft glue is applied onto the strand with a brush at the spot where it would be bound, or "locked off." The way the cut is made must also be done with care and precision. Cut too short, and the head would be exposed, but cutting more could endanger the structure of the weave and cause it to unravel. Old Tang took out a small file and meticulously filed off the exposed head little by little and felt a little of his former spirit return to his body.

As the moon waxed to fullness, the artwork gradually started to take shape. His anxious heart, which had felt as though it were hanging by a thread, also seemed to settle down, coming to rest a little more steadily in his breast. Invitations to exhibit at the show were supposed to pass public review as well as the province's panel of experts in the field, but Old Tang, not knowing what other contenders were doing, decided not to worry too much about the process. He also didn't return Renjie Liu that phone call. He simply thought that as long as he did his best with the work, and presented it at the time of the exhibition, things would naturally fall into place.

Qingyun stammered something about Xu wanting to come and see him, but Old Tang ignored it. What he had seen in Wen Shu Fang that day, he had never related to Qingyun. Even though he was not entirely certain what he had seen, his heart felt like it had been tied into a knot. In any case, he had better not think too much—it was all too overwhelming.

Three days before the launch of the exhibition, Old Tang finished the artwork. He checked it over carefully, and it was all to his satisfaction, so he put on his coat and went out the door. For the first time in months, he felt lighthearted enough to enjoy some time in a teahouse, so he took a different turn on his bike and headed to Huanhua Brook.

These days, the famous teahouses that had long lined the brook had been transformed into high-class establishments, with expensive menus. In the past, he always favored the quieter ones, but now even these were newly renovated and serving high-grade, expensive teas. At night, they were even transformed into bars playing loud music and serving alcohol. No one drank the traditional Lao San Hua tea anymore. In the several crowded parks he passed on his way, he could hear the sounds of noisy mahjong games, making him feel uneasy.

Old Tang sat down in a small courtyard, soaking up the rare sunshine. The sun shone through the gaps of the leaves of the Chinese parasol trees, green and gold, spilling into deep and shallow shadows. He gathered his cotton jacket around him, closed his eyes, and curled up in the bamboo chair. The guzheng on the stage began to play, and he was almost lulled to sleep.

"Old Tang! It's been a long time since you've last come here!"

He opened his eyes to see the teahouse owner pouring him a bowl of tea from a large, long-spouted copper teapot before bringing it to his table. "Still weaving bamboo?"

"Yes."

"It's been a long time since I've seen Qingyun too, and I was wondering what happened to the two of you." Qingyun sometimes played the guzheng here. When she performed on stage, she wouldn't be wearing her usual jeans, instead putting on her earrings and bracelets, putting on her elegant full-length spring green dress, and lowering her brow while she plucked the strings, her fingertips fluttering. According to Qingyun, she had met Xu Xiao for the first time in this teahouse. Old Tang could understand *that* for sure. When Qingyun played the guzheng, every teahouse guests' eyes were riveted on her. Even modest Old Tang himself could not hold back his praise when he saw her at that guzheng.

"Young people are busy with their own things." The thought of Xu had upset Old Tang a little. It was like poking a sore spot, and yet his suspicion was something he couldn't really explain.

"Has she found herself a boyfriend? I've told you before, a girl like Qingyun, with her looks and her talent at the guzheng, and not to mention, she's filial to boot . . . like I said, don't be too worried about her or try to control her too much." The teahouse owner peeled a tangerine while he talked. "Your little girl has grown up. Your thinking is too old-fashioned . . . "

Old Tang coughed a couple of times, so the teahouse owner did not continue. The guzheng on the stage was now playing "Lament of the Peach Garden," the song from the part of the story in the *Romance of the Three Kingdoms* where Zhang Fei had just received news of his dear sworn brother Guan Yu's death. Zhang Fei rushed for a day and a night to Chengdu, begging his other sworn brother Liu Bei to appoint the troops to attack the Eastern State of Wu. The two sworn brothers meet outside the city and weep for their fallen third brother. Zhang Fei sang this song of sorrow for his older sworn brother, lamenting the vicissitudes of age. Old Tang was moved, his heart troubled by the song, and found he could not sit there any longer. So he rode his bike home and opened the door to hear Qingyun clattering around inside her room.

Old Tang sat down and stood up, then sat down and stood up again, before finally making up his mind and knocking on Qingyun's door. Although he could hear the guzheng being played inside, the door did not open.

"Qingyun, I want to tell you something." Old Tang finally opened his mouth. But only the plucking strings of the guzheng replied.

Old Tang was both a little angry and a little anxious, so he twisted the handle.

The door was not locked.

"Why wouldn't you open the door?" Old Tang asked.

But there was no one was in the room. On the ebony instrument, the delicate strings pulsated, and music flowed from it. When Old Tang looked closer, he saw tortoiseshell nails were plucking the strings, as though an invisible person were playing the guzheng with invisible hands.

Old Tang felt that the sky was spinning. He felt his legs buckle under him, and he hit the speakers with a thud.

It had been quite some time since Qingyun came to see me. Her father had been hospitalized. Data package updates received were less frequent, but the line of communication was still stable. I offered to visit him, but she didn't give permission, and so I didn't try to force it.

When I was still working in the Courant Institute, the psychology department's experimental animal laboratory was just upstairs from where I worked. Of all the animals in there, three Tibetan macaques were the most precious. They had been raised since infancy as lab animals and each was worth tens of thousands of dollars. They were experimented on four times a week, for four hours each time. The experiments did not last for very long, but each time they had to be immobilized, their hands and feet tied down while electrodes were inserted below their cerebral cortices. Every few months, animal rights activists who opposed animal experimentation would hold signs outside the building in protest. They were not being unreasonable. These monkeys' only purpose in life was to be experimented on, and they also sacrificed their lives for the sake of these experiments, when their cerebral cortex was exposed to the electrodes for long periods of time. Most lab monkeys die from the complications of infection within a few years.

Although my prototype was lightweight and noninvasive, since it only took in signals through contact with human skin, collecting EMG signals without causing actual damage to the subject, I was no different from my colleagues in the psychology department when it came to ignoring the will of the subjects of my experiments.

Renjie Liu was the flip side of it all. I was not one to refuse novel sources of funding for my research, but his ways and methods of getting things done were particularly unorthodox. Perhaps these were simply the rules of the game. The many stories told by my classmates who worked on Wall Street seemed to suggest this. My aim had always been to understand, to integrate, in order to reach a new paradigm in my mind. Because what I envisioned was more than just a doctoral thesis, a product, or even just a theory. A vast new paradigm, a completely new world filled with infinite possibility, must necessarily accommodate all the dimmer corners of reality. I just hoped I hadn't sacrificed too much.

On the day Qingyun came to me, I was in the middle of correcting the fit of the prototype. She didn't sit down. Instead, tears fell continuously as she spoke. "Neuroscience is your field, and even you can't do anything about it?"

"I merely do the calculations," I laughed bitterly, "Extraction, abstraction, mathematical modeling: It is called applied technology, but it is still just a means of understanding the theory. It's like Newton coming up with the three laws of motion and giving us a way to understand physics and our external reality."

"But, other programmers' AIs can play Go and even win the world championship! You're working in this field, but you still can't do anything to help?"

Little had I known that even after doing applied math, the old problems would still be present. I was reminded once again of the G. H. Hardy quote that the most beautiful mathematics would have no application in the real world. When I had first heard that quote, I had laughed at his stubbornness, but now my heart was in knots because of it. The application of mathematics to build a new framework for understanding the human self, which he would probably have deemed already too "useful," was still miles away from solving Qingyun's very real problem.

I didn't care. When Descartes invented the Cartesian coordinate system and Einstein discovered the theory of relativity, I didn't care either, because the new perspectives and methodologies they brought to humanity itself was enough to put us all in awe. But at this very moment, I could find no way to face Qingyun.

"Human perception, including the connection between the hand and the brain, can be seen as an interface between human beings and the external world. It is a layer, the same way that text and images are a layer between people, or how the keyboard and mouse are a layer between people and machines. What I do is to mathematize and generalize this layer so that eventually one can get rid of the interface . . . " I struggled to find the words, "to move matter with the mind, like . . . *qigong*?"

But this was useless to her.

On the screen, the prototype flickered on and on. After she left, I thought long and hard and picked up my phone to dial a number.

Old Tang didn't have the energy to try to understand what had gone wrong. His head still hurt from time to time, but he insisted that he wouldn't go to hospital no matter what his condition; instead, he downed vat after vat of thickly brewed tea and soldiered on. When it came to bamboo weaving, the most important and difficult part was to lock the final strand securely; and so, in the same way, he would give it his all to the end, not stop at ninety percent. Tomorrow was the Exhibition for the Invitationals—no matter what, he had to finish the work he had started.

The crescent of a new moon hung in the sky, and the days were short while the nights were long. Even before dawn lightened the sky, Old Tang gathered up his artwork and left the house. He didn't ride his old faithful bike, instead getting Qingyun to hail him a taxi. The item that he hugged in his arms was not big, but it was wrapped in several protective layers. He carried it into the car.

"Why are you going to Chongzhou so early in the morning?" The driver looked at Old Tang, wrapped in his tattered cotton jacket, "What are you up to?"

"Exhibition." Old Tang stroked the precious artwork in his arms. "Handicraft exhibition."

"Handicrafts." The driver nodded, "What a time-consuming thing to do . . . and a waste of expensive taxi fare . . . "

"Whether it's a big or small thing, someone has to do it." Old Tang didn't feel like making small talk.

"I suppose so." The driver nodded, "Our fates are determined by our talents—each according to our ability, right? Sought-after, highly skilled talents get sought-after rewards and earn big bucks. Look at me, for example. I can't do anything else, but I know the roads well, and I know how to drive . . . I know the maps like the back of my hand, and so I drive a taxi. You, you have your handicraft skills. Maybe it's a little difficult to make a living . . . "

Old Tang did not answer again. After a while, the taxi had quietly left the old town behind. It had been several decades. He had gone from being the famous young bamboo artisan whose name was known in every village for miles around, to the respected old master craftsman at the bamboo factory where everyone called him "shifu," and now, here he was. He thought his work was refined, and that he had reached the pinnacle of his craft, but the people and things that surrounded him now confused him more than ever.

The car drove for an hour, to a town just beyond Chongzhou. This place resembled his old home a lot. Just on the edges of the town was a lush bamboo grove. It had been an age since he walked in such a bamboo grove. Walking through the fine mist, watching the sky gradually turn white, Old Tang touched the cold, green bamboo on its nodes, listening to the wind playing in the leaves of the bamboo, the sound of the gurgling stream as it ran over a gap, and was struck with a feeling of timelessness.

The exhibition hall was located deep in the bamboo forest and took the form of a circular house with many long corridors. It was said that it had been built by a professor from Shanghai, and although the material was prefabricated in a factory with machines, and the structure had been assembled in just a few weeks, it had won an international award. Old Tang walked one round around the exhibition hall and noted the delicate traditional cascading green tiles, which reminded him of old Chinese mansions, but the ultramodern steel and wood structure and the shiny floor-to-ceiling windows made him feel a little uncomfortable. Through the window, the green trees in the central courtyard and the green fields and hills on the outside of the building unfolded in layers to his eyes, like a painting. It felt far more exposed and transparent than traditional old, dark mansions, and this made him feel a little ill at ease.

The exhibition officially began at ten o'clock. The Shu (traditional Sichuanese) brocade and embroidery was spread out for all to see, so bright and intricate they dazzled the eye. The lacquer art was carved and inlaid with a multitude of beautiful and intense colors. There were also exhibits for silver thread embroidery, sugar painting, traditional New Year paintings, paper cutting, and various forms of printing and dyeing. The bamboo weaving exhibits, moldering in a dim corner, looked rather dull. The expert judges arrived, and Old Tang clutched his thermos and stood waiting in front of his artwork.

There were quite a lot of bamboo weaving entries, and there would only be one award in that category. Old Tang's eyes followed the judges. The first piece they looked at was a bamboo pagoda that stood a whole foot high. It was a four-story pagoda, with two layers of four-sided flying eaves. The upper roof was octagonal and reached a graceful tip. On every layer of the ridge, tiny birds and animals were woven according to what you would find on a real pagoda. In terms of coarse silk bamboo weaves, this would be considered a top-grade quality weave.

The second item they examined was a one-foot high, three-foot wide bamboo calligraphy scroll. It featured a fine silk bamboo weave, so it was light as silk and yet as flat as paper. Instead of ink forming the words, different colored bamboo strands wove out the script of the incident from the *Romance of the Three Kingdoms* known as "Before the Table of Division." The calligraphy was done in the style of Yue Fei. Old Tang did not know much about calligraphy, but even he could see that the variation in the strokes and their stately look had been successfully achieved using just bamboo.

The judges moved on to the third, fourth, and then the fifth exhibits. Finally they turned to where Old Tang stood. He moved to take out his work—a paltry less than half a foot of bamboo weave that he had tucked over a porcelain tea ware, short in the middle and fine at the ends. It was so intricate that only if you picked up the tea ware would you realize that what appeared at first glance to be just a varied selection of patterns woven into the weave were actually an accurate miniature replica of Su Dongpo's famous painting "Folded Bamboo." Seen from a distance, it was an unremarkable piece of work, but up close, with the shifting light casting delicate shadows, the outline of Su Dongpo's masterful strokes that had created the bamboo leaves appeared, even more vivid than the original painting.

"Not bad at all." The expert judge put down the basket, "We get to see some top-grade examples of fine bamboo weaving on a base."

"Wait a minute." Old Tang reached into the belly of the porcelain tea ware and pressed gently, removing the bamboo weave so that the porcelain and the bamboo basket were separated.

"It's woven on a base, and yet if the base is removed the weave still holds its shape! That's really skilled work!" The judges looked even more interested.

"One more thing." Old Tang held the bamboo basket in one hand, and with his other hand, he unscrewed the thermos and let a few little red goldfish pour into the bamboo basket along with some water. The basket held the water and fish, which were waving their tails happily, without leaking even a drop, and you could see the intricate pattern of the weave clearly through the water.

"A good bamboo basket for fetching water!" the crowd that had formed around him applauded, and Old Tang smiled. He was filled with pride. The basket itself might be small, but its construction was ingenious, composing of three very thin layers of silken bamboo weaves nesting inside each other, every layer using a different pattern so that the weave would be so tight water would not leak out of it. With this particular artwork, even if he never managed to train another disciple, he could feel like his lifetime spent mastering his art had not been lived in vain.

"Shifu, how about *this* piece, was it made by you, or made by your disciple?" Just at the moment he had reached the pinnacle of fulfillment, Old Tang heard this question pelted at him, and his hand shook when he saw which piece they meant, causing him to spill the water all over the ground.

In an identical bamboo basket, there also swam a few tiny fish waving their little tails. Old Tang picked it up and examined it carefully. Every feature: the coiled silk strands, the triple layer structure, the stacked patterns, and the hidden bamboo head in the "lock," was exactly the same, just like there had been an assembly line creating baskets using his methods. But when did machines learn how to braid so finely in his style and using his painstaking method? What were they trying to do? Old Tang put down the basket, his eyes searching through the crowd. He spotted them—and they dare not look his way.

"Abomination!" Old Tang was furious and wanted to chase them down but lost his footing on the puddle and slipped.

"Shifu, Shifu!" The buzzing sound of the crowd made his head ache as though there were an earthquake in his brain. Slowly, his eyes shut.

I had never been so nervous in my life. Not during my doctoral defense, not during my oral presentation for my selected thesis topic, never. Nothing compared to how nervous I was in this moment.

Renjie Liu was talking to the doctor. Qingyun was asleep in the corner, the tip of her nose still red from crying. I sat down, put my coat over her, and took the string of beads out of her hand. The bracelet had been disassembled and the beads split in half, revealing a set of fluorescent green chips hidden within.

The prototype worked by intercepting the motor signals sent from the central nervous system to the nerve ending inside each finger before transmitting them wirelessly to the computer terminal. It was like bugging the central nervous system with a wire that tapped into, tracked, and recorded the movement of the hand that had worn the bracelet without the need for a camera. For the past three months, every push, lift, press, and twist the hand had made upon the bamboo strands had been recorded, and every nerve impulse captured, abstracted, and modeled.

A working, movable model that could articulate up to twenty degrees of signal flexibility, which was more flexible and powerful than any existing technology, was then built out of this data, which all had its origin in a place time had nearly forgotten.

The human brain is extremely plastic. Types of sensory input that are repeatedly reinforced over long periods of time occupy a much larger area of the cerebral cortex, and there, neural signals are able to express far more nuanced and sophisticated degrees of control. Moreover, only with signals that had been captured from twenty different planes combined together rather than a single-dimensional model—as well as the daily practice of the hand that had repeated the motions every single day—could such a model truly become an interface that could interact with the outside world with the kind of precision it required. This was unprecedented.

Old Tang, the old shifu, now lay unconscious. He did not know that when it came to interacting with the external world, his hands had reached a level so sophisticated that they could move in more dimensions than any of ours.

What he had wished to preserve may have been a tradition, his own self-respect, and a way of life. But for me, what was precious was the vast ocean of knowledge and skill that had been accumulated over thousands of years in the traditional craft he had mastered, and the related patterns of brain function that had arisen. This is our human potential, which was passed down by both the culture collectively and through individuals, developed through the millennia-long process of natural evolution and cultural transmission. Now, this knowledge would be converted into the pulsing signals that jump through the crystalline grooves of computer chips, a very precious legacy that Man can be proud of. And what I have done is to liberate this knowledge from the limiting, ancient shackles of oral transmission. Extraction, modeling, digitization, generalization. To transmit a signal from the central nervous system to the nerve ending in a finger takes time, yet my prototype was able to capture the signal before the hand even made the actual movement.

The key is not in the hand, but in the brain. I had confidence in my ability to reconstruct the brain but taking the reconstructed brain and attaching it to another hand was where the applicability of my model would be put to the true test. Just as it was not hugely difficult to build an identical bamboo basket with identical bamboo strands, it was using my new creation in an operation on an actual, living brain that was the ultimate challenge I faced now. I had done everything I could.

"Professor Xu? Let's get ready and get started."

"Renjie Liu, tell me the truth, how confident are you that this is going to work?"

"Professor Xu, I was his apprentice for five years and knew him personally for twenty-one years. To be honest, I don't believe in you. I believe in him."

There was not a single soul in the operating theater and the lights, which were out, cast no shadows. In the darkness, a hologram came to life and grew to fill the room with light, as Old Tang's brain and body appeared before our eyes. A cluster of malignant red gliomas was entangled between a jungle of blue nerves. The hideous tumor wrapped its many strands around the slender blue branches like a mesh, defying radiation therapy and chemotherapy, and making it extremely difficult to completely remove via surgery, as it was all too easy to injure the healthy brain tissue.

Even if healthy tissue was not injured, if the removal was not complete, the possibility of recurrence would be extremely high. I stared at the giant brain, and it was as though the blue parts were fading before my eyes. I blinked. The lead surgeon pulled up an interface in the control room and two tiny silver fibers appeared in the middle of the brain area. He waved his hand to zoom in on that part, and at the tip of the fibers appeared a mechanical hand with five long, thin, rounded fingers. The doctor adjusted the angle and began to send instructions.

I saw the hand, covered with its distinctive wrinkles and scars, come to life again in the hologram of the brain. Dissecting the adhesions, twisting the nodes, weaving in and out of the weak nerve fibers, moving with great flexibility between the dense weave of the cerebral cortex. Every incision was tailored to that particular case, and every measure of force was applied to just the right degree. The tumor was like a bamboo strand in a hidden head "lock," finely excised without missing a single hair, without hurting the integrity of the structure it had wrapped itself around. In these hands, the sinister, malignant red was reduced little by little, disappearing strand by strand.

Qingyun woke up at some point. She watched the rapidly weaving hands, staring at that fluorescent, flickering brain, and heaved a sigh of relief.

"It's okay. You must believe in your dad." I held her close.

When he next opened his eyes, all Old Tang saw before him was a white blur. It was only when he tried to concentrate a little more that he realized what he was staring at was a snow-white ceiling. Pale green walls, deep green curtains on the windows. He realized that the air-conditioning unit was turned on and he was covered by a blanket to keep him nice and warm. He also heard instruments and machines whirring and beeping. So he was at a hospital.

How much time had passed? Old Tang tried to think back to the last thing he could remember, which was falling on the floor. At the time, he had felt a hundred times more pain in his brain than in his bones, but now, he found that his ankle was bandaged so much that it was immobilized, whereas the pain in his head, while still there, seemed to have subsided somewhat. Old Tang tried to move his fingers, and they seemed to be working fine, but it felt like something was missing. When he raised his head to check, he saw that the chinaberry wood bracelet he had gotten so used to wearing was resting on the bedside table. The ivory-white beads were emitting a strange green light.

Old Tang felt a little dizzy. He touched his scalp and found it completely bald, which gave him a shock. After years of having a Mediterranean Sea bald patch, now his scalp was completely naked from the top of the head to the bottom of his ears, and he could also feel a thin thread that sewed up a wound. He asked Qingyun, "Didn't they say that neither man nor machine could get rid of my tumor?" Qingyun turned her head to look outside the door.

It was Xu who walked in. He explained what had happened. Old Tang didn't quite understand. It was like watching a magic trick in a magic show, where the puppeteer wears a bracelet in order to manipulate the little puppets tumbling about and jumping, while the hand that controls them only twitches slightly. Xu said, what was more important than the human brain, was the human heart. Old Tang completely failed to understand any of his explanations, but at least he sensed that what he said seemed good.

In the end, it was still with the help of a machine that they had snatched his life back from the brink. That stony thing that had laid in his breast for so long melted, just like ice in a heated room, and Old Tang heaved a sigh. He had indeed gotten old.

"You were the one who saved yourself," said Xu.

"Just think of it as having taken on a disciple, except that your disciple can not only weave bamboo, but also a lot of other things . . . " Qingyun said while carrying a bowl of porridge over to Old Tang and placing it into his hands.

Old Tang looked at his daughter, then looked at Xu, and said nothing. He scooped up the porridge. The porridge was still hot, and the fragrance of peanuts, sweet red dates, glutinous taro, and soft kidney beans comforted him as he took it in. It was when he tasted those autumnal flavors that he realized that the Laba Festival had already passed.

Chengdu winters bring with them a special warmth in the air. It's like Sichuanese pancakes, stewed dishes, and sausages all mixed together, but without the smell of oil and smoke, as though the fragrance has been cleansed by the Sichuan rain. Against the dark sky, raindrops slip from the tips of verdant banana leaves, and red and brown sausages hang from balconies.

I put down my chopsticks and refilled the two shot glasses.

"A toast! To you, and to your art!"

"Handcraft. These past few days, I've been pondering what 'craft' actually means." Old Tang, the master, did not raise his glass.

I raised my eyes. "And what do you think?"

"When I first learned my art, my shifu said a bamboo craftsman must have a deep soul. It takes many years of practice before your two hands can truly work together, and even more before the soul and the hands work as one." He sipped his wine. "Although I do not understand all your explanations, this is something I do understand. The reason why people these days cannot do what we could before is because they all lack a stillness of the soul. When it comes to my art, there is nothing that complex about it. But to do it, you do need to be still in your soul. Your heart must be quieted before inspiration can strike, before your hands can move with skill."

"Well said. The most valuable thing is that heart of yours." I tilted my head back and drained my glass of wine.

"You're leaving on the sixth day of the new year?"

"Yes." I nod my head. "I'll be traveling the country, traveling all over the world, in search of hands, in search of hearts."

A year ago, I set out from New York. A year later, we will set off once again, this time from Chengdu. From the ancient masters who repair the exquisite clocks and watches housed in Beijing's Forbidden City, to the oil-paper umbrella makers who work in Yunnan's rainforests, from the guqin players keeping a thousand-year heritage alive in Yangzhou, to the nearly extinct sculptors of sea willow in Fujian, we will visit them all and record the skills that reside in their talented fingers.

Then we will go even further, and model, analyze, and record traditional crafts from all over the world, such as the spiral weaving of southern France and the winding techniques of South Carolina in the United States. It is our aspiration to build an enormous, comprehensive database that connects human hands, brains, and countless man-made artifacts in a vast treasury, which will be permanently preserved on the Internet. Even in a thousand years, when the artifacts themselves have turned to dust, these models of human movements will live on, carrying with them the rich history of thousands of years of civilization and evolution, expressed either in flesh and blood, or perhaps in a body composed of metal and electric circuitry.

And then, when even that has been completed, we will search for the most excellent eyes, ears, noses, and tongues. We will redefine all the senses, the senses that compose the interface between Man and the world he inhabits. We will build a new layer of interfaces that are parallel and complementary to the physical world. We will create the only world that Man can know, a world that will allow Man to escape the boundaries of the physical body nature had bestowed on him, so he can become the True Man. After millions of years, Man will finally see the day he receives true freedom.

That day is not far away.

Old Tang, sounding conflicted, spoke again. "You said . . . you said that the hand doesn't need me anymore. Then, in the future, why would people still want hands?"

I laughed but said nothing. Instead, I poured more liquor, and waited silently for him to finish. He had woven bamboo for over forty years now and understood the nature of the craft—its meditative quality and the need to go slow to master it. But at the same time, it also required speed and skill. He sat in silence for a while, then picked up his glass. We clinked glasses again and drained the shot glasses bottoms' up.

On the afternoon of the Lantern Festival[1], Old Tang went to the teahouse again. He didn't ride his bike because his feet were not yet back to their old selves. There was no one else in the small courtyard. He spotted a few gnarled old plum trees and the hanging vines were budding with

1 The Lantern Festival takes place on the fifteenth day of the Lunar New Year and is part of the Lunar New Year festivities.

half-opened buds, while the black and brown branches sported the bright yellow furry buds of spring. Old Tang found himself a chair, and, as usual, ordered a pot of traditional Lao San Hua tea.

The results of the Invitationals Exhibition had been announced. Old Tang had won second prize. Before, he would have sulked about it, but not now.

Renjie Liu had paid him a visit on the fifth day of Lunar New Year, bearing all kinds of gifts as both apologies and tokens of gratitude. He said that now that the surgery machine had been upgraded with Old Tang's skill, and had also demonstrated its first successful operation on him, orders had gone through the roof and would keep him busy all the way until the next Spring Festival. Old Tang waved away the consultant's fee Renjie Liu had stuffed into a red packet, only accepting the magnified model of the machine hand. Ten metallic fingers and claws were encased in a three-inch high cube of transparent, extra-strong glass. No matter how long he looked at it, Old Tang could simply not see the resemblance to his own hands.

Qingyun and Xu spent the first few days of the new year at home and went out on the sixth day. That night they talked a lot, and drank a lot, and he could no longer remember exactly what had been said. When he woke up the next day, he felt as if there was something different about himself, although he could not quite put his finger on it.

As the teahouse owner poured Old Tang tea, he remarked, "How strange . . . Why did you come over today? Surely, as head of the household you should be rolling tangyuan2 tonight, right? Filling them with sesame and rose fillings . . . wetting flour with water . . . "

"I won't be doing it by hand this year. Tonight, I'll just go out and buy some," said Old Tang. "Not many people in our household anyway, so it'll save some time."

"You're not doing it by hand?"

"Machine-made is still more convenient!"

"Wow, I'd never thought I'd see the day. Here's your tea, take your time and enjoy!"

On the stage, the old huqin was playing "Eight Trigrams Forma-

---

2 Tangyuan are traditional sweet flour balls eaten on the fifteenth day of the Lunar New Year. Sometimes they have fillings like peanut, sesame, etc., and it is a traditional family activity to make them together.

tions" from *Romance of the Three Kingdoms*. In this part of the story, the military leader and enemy of the three sworn brothers, Lu Xun, had just burned the joint forces' camp, which had reached around for seven hundred miles, and he chased the escaping hero Liu Bei through the smoke and fire to the Yufu Waterfront. But there, Lu Xun fell into the ambush of master strategist Zhuge Liang's Eight Trigrams Formation. A gentle breeze blew, dispersing the delicate fragrance of the wax plum blossoms, and a little petal fell in the half-open tea bowl. Old Tang drifted to sleep.

In his dream, he seemed to enter a dense, primeval bamboo forest, where he moved through the deep twilight, and where there was hidden a secret structure of white walls and black tiles. Lights flickered here and there, but no matter which direction he walked in, bamboo branches grew, blocking his way out. But regardless of what he did, he found his hands fixed firmly to his sides, unable to move. Then, it dawned on Old Tang like a flash of lightning that he was a master of the art of bamboo, and out slid his bamboo carving knife from its sheath. His conviction slid like a knife through mud, and within seconds a new path had been cleared out of the darkness. All throughout, his hands had not moved an inch, still fixed by the sides of his body. And yet bamboo leaves tumbled to the ground and great stems were felled before him. He raised his head to the skies and yelled out loud, before striding forward, his face to the wind.

Author's Note: The noninvasive neural interface technology in the story that enables control through intention alone is inspired by the real-life work of CTRL-labs. The techniques of bamboo weaving in the story are based on the art of Chengdu porcelain bamboo weaving, Yunnan Yiliang bamboo weaving, and Hunan Huitong bamboo weaving, among others.

First Prize: 7th Future Science Fiction Master Award (2018).

Originally published in Chinese in
2018 China's Best Science Fiction Works, anthology, 2019.

济南的风筝
The Kite of Jinan
LIANG QINGSAN
梁清散

TRANSLATED BY EMILY JIN

I have to admit, it's hard to set aside emotions—such as spontaneous curiosity and impulsive doubt—when I examine historical archives. I know some people would call this unprofessional. Thank god I was never a "professional" to begin with, and I don't have to play by the rules of academia.

Anyway. My so-called unprofessionalism came back to haunt me once again when I set my eyes upon the news report for a case in Jinan that took place more than a century ago.

In 1910, there was an explosion in Luokou, north of the city of Jinan, Shandong province. It happened at a small factory named Luonan Firearms Factory and the collateral damage caused at least fifty deaths, including the people of nearby villages and factory workers. Normally, this kind of incident would've wreaked havoc in the capital, however, the Qing Empire was dealing with the fallout following the unexpected death of Emperor Guangxu and the hasty ascension to the throne of the young Prince Xuantong. Thus, the incident barely impacted the court and was quickly forgotten, its traces dissipating like gunpowder and smoke.

Shortly after the explosion took place, the Qing police force—which, at the time, was going through a systematic reformation by imitating the model of European police forces—caught the culprit. The unwitting perpetrator's name was Chen Haining, a technician at the factory. He died in the explosion. The police determined that he was the cause of the explosion because they had discovered clothes at the crime scene that belonged to Chen Haining, embellished with customized metal accessories. The explosion was caused because a few of those metal accessories had fallen off and became caught in between mechanical gears. The sparks generated eventually detonated the ammunition stored in the factory.

Two photos were attached to the news report, respectively portraying Luokou, in ruins and scorched black, as well as Chen Haining's clothing, blown to scraps save for some metal pieces stringed together that were fastened to the chest area.

Instinctively, I find those "accessories" extremely odd. Why were they attached to Chen Haining's clothing in the first place? It should have been obvious to a professional technician that those metal pieces could very well be a safety hazard. The news report also seems like it is hiding something.

Time for an amateur historian to demonstrate his close-read skills! The phrase, "serial explosion" attracts my attention. How did those serial explosions take place, in the first place? In 1910, a time when modern technology in China was still in its toddler phase, how could there have been so many factories carrying highly explosive material in such close proximity to one another?

After I examine the documents on industrialization in Luokou, Jinan, I realize that it was indeed possible. In fact, Luokou was a major industrial town of the Late Qing. In 1879, Ding Baozhen, immediately following his appointment as the governor of Shandong province, invited China's science and technology gurus at the time, Xu Shou and Xu Jianyin—a father-and-son pair—to establish the Shandong Bureau of Mechanics. Later, Xu Shou was transferred over to the famous Jiangnan Arsenal in Shanghai and put in charge of shipbuilding. Xu Jianyin, more experienced with chemistry, took over his father's role. From that point on, the Shandong Bureau of Mechanics specialized in the research and production of weapons and ammunition.

The establishment of the Shandong Bureau of Mechanics took place when Emperor Guangxu first ascended to the throne. By the end of Guangxu's reign, the military industry had already become a part of Jinan's tradition. Beyond the walls of the Shandong Bureau of Mechanics, local factories big and small, harboring the dream that the Great Qing Empire could one day recover its past glory, invested their energy and resources in producing black powder. Though most of those factories were undocumented, I can easily piece together the scale of ammunition production in the Luokou area from the information I have on hand. From my perspective, it's very likely that those black powder factories, in their rudimentary stage, took little to no safety precautions. Even Xu Jianyin himself died from an explosion accident in 1901, during an experiment on smokeless powder.

The demand for high-efficiency ammunition rocketed alongside the demand for more guns and cannons. In the years leading up to the fall of the Qing Empire, the entire city of Jinan was permeated with the acrid stench of gunpowder. North of Jinan was a large piece of land encircled by short stone walls, and within those walls lay the Shandong Bureau of Mechanics, long abandoned after Xu Jianyin's death. Adjacent to the Bureau was a swarm of small, tightly clustered black powder factories—no, perhaps *workshops* is the right word to put it.

What a shame that photography was so expensive and hence used so sparingly back then! Yearning for more pictures, I take a dive into my go-to data bank. The only results that my blanket search yields are some photos of the Shandong Bureau of Mechanics itself, most of which depict the Bureau's front door, an arching gate with a plaque inscribed with the phrase "The Beginning of Creation," as well as a handful of workers there with awkward expressions on their faces, clearly uncomfortable in front of the camera. I cannot find any records of the smaller workshops on the peripheries.

Numbers can be telling. A simple calculation of the total documented workshops and Luokou's land capacity reveals how those workshops overcrowded the small town, leaving no margin for safety whatsoever. Technically, the possibilities of serial explosions taking place in a setting like that would be well above fifty percent.

My lead on the factories is soon exhausted and my only other clue is the name, "Chen Haining." Returning to my data bank, I plug the name in as the new search keyword.

To my surprise, the data bank immediately picks up a useful piece of information: three decades before the fall of the Qing, in the year of 1880, "Chen Haining" appears in a long list consisting of the names and job positions of the Shandong Bureau of Mechanics' new recruits.

A year after the construction of the Shandong Bureau of Mechanics was completed—which was in 1879—it welcomed a group of low-ranked technicians to their new posts. Chen Haining was one of them, put in charge of mechanical engineering. Someone in this position would have been an expert, unlikely to have been reckless enough to have worn such clothing while operating one of the machines.

Now this is getting interesting.

I recognize, however, that I must proceed carefully. Even though the location and the profession both overlap, it is possible that the Chen Haining mentioned here isn't the one who died in the accident. I need more data.

The next batch of survey data, however, yields little of value. The only other record I can find on the name "Chen Haining" is from a list of students who studied with Xu Shou and graduated from the Jiangnan Arsenal in Shanghai in 1879.

Out of the three search results for "Chen Haining," two of them are appearances in lists of names and contain no further demographic information. I'm fairly certain, however, that both the 1879 document and the 1880 document are referring to the same Chen Haining. Xu Shou, the father of Xu Jianyin, was at the forefront of China's shipbuilding sector. As one of the main officials of the Jiangnan Arsenal—a major local manufacturer of military equipment as well as an academy of Western languages, science, and technology—Xu Shou was a top-tier researcher of mechanical engineering. It makes sense that Chen Haining, one of Xu Shou's students who was presumably trained in the same field, would eventually end up working for the Shandong Bureau of Mechanics, which was spearheaded by Xu Shou's own son. However, the real question lies in whether Chen Haining, Xu Shou's student, is really the same man who caused the Luokou serial explosion incident three decades later.

With a sigh, I exit the data bank and open my inbox. I attach my three findings to a new message and type Shao Jing's email address into the recipient field.

Shao Jing is a friend from college, my partner-in-crime in the field of historical research. He eventually went off to graduate school and landed a position at the office of historical archives. I, on the other hand, wandered around listlessly and made a meager living out of writing stories. Thank goodness Shao Jing never viewed me as a less competent researcher because I came from a nonacademic background. Years of working together has guaranteed a mutual understanding so deep that he was able to get my point the moment I open my mouth.

I was going to leave the body of the email blank, but I find myself hesitating before pressing "send." Though we both indulged in the game of sending historical riddles back and forth, I know that he is in the middle of organizing a national academic conference, and very much likely preoccupied with logistical "riddles" to make sense of. I end up writing down my entire deduction process, closing the email with a lie that the only reason I became invested in the story of Chen Haining is because I want to write a story about the incident. Hopefully this excuse is enough to justify my intrusion upon his packed work schedule.

Ten minutes later, a new email notification pops up.

His response, drafted as timely as usual, contains two attachments. The body paragraph, written with his classic sarcasm, mocks me for my "unprofessionalism" in ineffective data searching.

The attachment files, however, make my heart leap. In merely ten minutes, Shao Jing was able to find more information using a method completely different from that of my own—he turned to non-Chinese primary sources.

The first document is a news report containing two blurry pictures. The report itself is written in German, which I cannot read; however, the headline indicates that the report is from *Rheinische Industrie-Zeitung*, a medium-sized industrial newspaper in nineteenth century Germany.

Unlike its contemporary *North-China Herald*, an English newspaper based in Shanghai's British concession that primarily targeted British readers living in China, *Rheinische Industrie-Zeitung* was a German newspaper that has never left Germany. Why would it be interested in reporting news from China? I cast my eyes on the citation column.

From my modest knowledge of print history, I recognize that the news was written by a journalist of Wolffs Telegraphisches Bureau, the leading press agency in Germany at the time. No wonder *Rheinische Industrie-Zeitung* would publish the article.

The news report was written in May 1881, during Chen Haining's second year at the Shandong Bureau of Mechanics. Even though Shandong province was already more or less under German control in 1881, German press rarely paid it any attention, which made this article somewhat unusual.

The pictures are even more bizarre. Both photos are horizontally composed. In the first, over half of the frame is overexposed, displaying nothing but pale blankness and a few indistinct lines. I can discern a large empty field and a handful of short buildings stacked on one side of the field. In the bottom left corner is a machine that resembled a suspended windlass. A man with braided hair and a Qing-style long gown is operating the machine, his mouth hanging open in shock. I can catch a faint glimpse of a rope attached to the windlass, crossing the entire picture diagonally and extending all the way to the top right corner, arcing from the pull of gravity. At its other end is an enormous kite—or rather a set of huge kites. Though the kites are out of focus, their colossal presence is unmistakable.

I reckon that kite-flying can be quite popular in Jinan, in the springtime. The arrival of spring in Beijing usually brings crowds of people to parks and plazas to fly their kites. Perhaps Jinan, a northern city just like Beijing, has a similar culture.

I zoom in on the photo, trying to examine it more closely. Beneath the set of kites is a chair. The chair is blurred out, but I can distinguish a pair of dangling legs, which means that someone must be sitting on the chair. At the bottom of the chair hangs something dark and clunky, reminding me of a weight.

The second photo, on the other hand, depicts an odd-shaped chair in the middle of two men. The chair has no legs, but bits and pieces of what seems to be mechanical components are protruding from beneath the seat. It must be the same chair as the one in the first photo, except that the weight had been taken off. The man on the left, in a long gown, is the man who was operating the windlass in the bottom left corner. Then, the man on the right must be the one sitting on the levitating chair. Behind them is the Shandong Bureau of Machinery's front gate, as I can easily distinguish the plaque that said, "The Beginning of Creation."

I can't read the German captions, but I can identify a name written in pinyin: HAINING CH'EN. I type the German sentences into an online translation software and discover that the man on the right is Chen Haining, presumably Xu Shou's student who worked at the Shandong Bureau of Machinery. At the time the photo was taken, Chen Haining was dressed in a Western-style suit and a top hat. His youthful face was beaming with confidence, a stark difference from the awkwardness of his contemporaries in front of the camera. I finally know what my protagonist looks like.

The translation software tells me that the strange chair was named "the kite of Jinan."

Shao Jing's second attachment is a PDF file consisted of an English article in *The Illustrated London News* and a French article in *Le Petit Journal*, both published in 1881. Evidently, those articles were derived from the original German news report, and of course the reporters cared more about the photos' shock value than the machine itself. I don't read French either, so my only option is English.

The caption of the photos reads as: "The Kite of Jinan—the miracle of the Qing Empire—man-lifting kite launches!"

I let out a sigh. Sure, it is unusual for a Chinese technology to be noticed by Western press more than a century ago, but man-lifting kites are nowhere near a groundbreaking invention, even in the year of 1881. In fact, they have existed throughout Chinese history. In ancient times, manned kites have been widely applied for military use, especially in espionage. The only difference between the kites in the photo and the kites I know from books is the strange look of the attached chair. *What on earth are those mechanical appliances for?*

Though Shao Jing's contribution now provides me with more information on Chen Haining, I am still missing the last puzzle piece. Even if we now know that Chen Haining, the student of Xu Shou, had once been the center of Western media's attention for his achievements, how can we prove that he is the same person as the culprit of the Luokou explosion incident?

It seems that I have driven myself into a dead-end.

"I know that you must be busy, but I need to follow up with you on some additional questions . . . " I type.

Then comes a long period of silence. After waiting for more than an hour, I finally decide that Shao Jing is occupied with work and won't be able to get back to me any time soon.

I can't imagine being in his shoes . . . as I contemplate, I realize that a new text message has been sent to my phone. It's from Shao Jing, "Why don't you go to the Luokou archives and see for yourself?"

He's right. It's worth a shot. I respond with a quick thanks and start planning my trip to Jinan.

Many years have passed since I last visited Jinan. I vaguely remember a street of old bookstores outside of Zhongshan Park, but the street of my memories is no more, leaving only boring-looking residential buildings and bleak, withered locust trees.

My research tells me that none of the factories and workshops in Luokou are still operating. However, harboring a faint hope that I might come across remains of century-old buildings and traces of the Shandong Bureau of Machinery, I embark on a journey to Luokou. Though, I clearly haven't done my homework on geography: Luokou appears to be a district of Jinan, but it's hours away from downtown. By the time I arrive in Luokou by bus, it is already three in the afternoon.

Jinan, like any other northern city, has its sun setting at a little past four. The twilight casts a glorious golden glow on the buildings, as if to inject new vitality into their veins.

Realizing I don't have much time left, I hurry over to the local archives. Shao Jing had contacted his work connections in advance for my sake. When I arrive at the office, I see a middle-aged man waiting.

"I really appreciate your help," I stutter. "And so sorry to keep you waiting."

"No worries at all," said the man, smiling warmly. "Shao Jing told me that you are working on a presentation for the conference that he is organizing, and you are in need of our archives. I'm touched, really—people nowadays never have the patience to polish their research!"

Scratching my head, I follow the man into the archives room. After giving a basic introduction, he nods at me and says that he will leave me to my work.

I am left in silence, alone with a room full of index card cabinets that remind me of herb trunks in Chinese medicine clinics.

Starting with biographies, I begin to search for the name "Chen Haining" by year and by the first letter of the pinyin of his surname. With every page I turn, I feel myself tensing up. What if I can't find anything? I will be utterly out of leads, then.

Fortunately, I spot the name in a file written more than a century ago. I give the index card to the middle-aged man in charge, who then brings out a thick, bound volume of biographies for me to examine.

Leaning over the closest table, I begin to flip through the pages, finally landing on the entry that contains "Chen Haining." His biography, like the people preceding and following him, is quite short and concise; there are no descriptive language save for a few key dates and events about his life.

Perfect—this is exactly what I need. Immediately, I turn my eyes to 1880 and 1910.

I am relieved to find that the various mentions of Chen Haining that I have been encountering are, in fact, about the same person. The biography indicates that Chen Haining was a new recruit at the Shandong Bureau of Mechanics in 1880, died in the Luokou explosion of 1910, and was suspected by the Qing police force as the culprit.

I begin to take notes on Chen Haining. According to the biography, his life between 1880 and 1910 was full of ebbs and flows. In 1881, he went abroad to study at the University of Bonn in Germany, majoring in mechanical engineering. I am surprised to discover that the year of his arrival in Germany coincides with the year in which the news report on *Rheinische Industrie-Zeitung* was published. This means, to Chen Haining, that news report wasn't merely a one hit wonder; rather, it marked the beginning of his journey beyond the horizons of the Qing Empire.

The only other person I can think of who was also in the West at the time when Chen Haining was studying abroad is Yung Wing, who led a group of talented teenagers from the southern province of Fujian to Yale University, where Yung Wing himself was a student. Amongst those teenagers was Jeme Tien-Yow, who eventually became one of the founding fathers of Chinese railroad engineering technology. Cross-compared to his Chinese contemporaries, Chen Haining was definitely a pioneer in studying abroad.

I can't help but feel sorry for him though: not only that history had wiped him out, but that he also died such a painful death.

The biography doesn't mention whether Chen Haining completed his studies at the University of Bonn. The only thing I know is that he returned to Shandong from Germany in 1884 and reentered the Bureau of Mechanics.

Not wanting to miss a single detail, I continue to take notes. In the years after Chen Haining's return, he was sent away from the Shandong Bureau of Mechanics on multiple occasions—Xinjiang in 1895, Jiangxi in 1898, Hanyang in 1900—but somehow, every time he was "exiled," he ultimately managed to make it back to Shandong. After spending a year in Hanyang, he returned for the last time in 1901. This time, he was placed in the Luonan Firearms Factory instead of the Shandong Bureau of Mechanics, where he remained employed until the day of his death.

This is all there is left to remember him by.

I return the book of compiled biographies to the man who accompanied me, thank him, and leave the dusking sky of Luokou behind.

The tedious bus ride back to downtown is enough for me to reconsider the new leads on Chen Haining again. Gazing out the window at Jinan's splendid, luminous skyline, I have a vague feeling that I am onto something.

The first thing I do upon stepping into my hotel room is to turn on my laptop and pull up the *Rheinische Industrie-Zeitung* news report. After another peek at the two photos, I begin to type the German article word by word into my translation software. The most that the software can manage is a couple of incoherent sentences, littered with words left untranslated. Fortunately, from the broken Chinese version of the text, I find what I need.

Just like how Chen Haining's presence on a foreign newspaper was merely a beginning to his adventures in a greater world, "The Kite of Jinan" was nowhere near the epitome of his engineering talent. The German article indicates that the peculiar machine was only one of Chen Haining's many innovations. Those kites were not solely there to lift the chair into air, but rather to measure a set of more complex parameters related to flying. By the time that the news report was written, his experiments had yielded an equation that could account for the mass of the chair, the weight of the pilot, and the flying parameters. In an era without digital simulation and modeling, in order to obtain enough data, physical experiments were the only way out.

In short, Chen Haining's goal was to build a real aircraft.

With hovering fingertips, I trace the arc of the kite string that stretched across the photo. *Who cut the strings?* I wonder to myself.

After I return home, I send my new findings in an email to Shao Jing and express my gratitude once again for his help. Much to my surprise, Shao Jing texts me back in no time. Congratulating me for my new breakthroughs, he asks me whether I would be interested in meeting an associate professor at the Shanghai Jiao Tong University, specializing in the history of science and technology, who would soon arrive in Beijing for a preconference meeting. "Professor Ding might have interesting things to say about your research," suggests Shao Jing.

I can't say no to the opportunity. A few days later, I arrive at a café next to the office of historical archives. The café, on a workday afternoon, is packed with people. Fortunately, I am early enough, and I manage to find an empty table in a quiet corner.

At the minute of our arranged meeting time, the café door swings open, and a man walks in. His eyes dart back and forth, clearly looking for someone. Upon meeting his gaze, I raise an arm to wave.

After Professor Ding and I introduce ourselves to each another, he gives me a look, as if I am one of his students waiting in line to do a class presentation. Battling my nerves, I pull up the documents on my laptop and begin to ramble on about my deductions, pointing to the name lists and the photos.

"Can you show me the article on *Rheinische Industrie-Zeitung* again?" asks Professor Ding, right when I finish my talk.

He reads the German article thoroughly, then takes off his glasses and leans forward. Almost pressing his forehead into my laptop screen, he scrutinizes the two photos, paying special attention to the one taken by the front gate of the Shandong Bureau of Machinery. He enlarges the low-resolution photo until every pixel is visible, focusing intently on the chair and the various protruding mechanical components on the two sides of the chair. He zooms out, zooms in again, smacks his lips, and shakes his head. Finally, he puts his glasses on and looks up at me.

"The translation software did a fine job," he says. I realize that he is a fast speaker, as I can barely keep up with what he is saying. "Funny thing, though, the British and the French newspapers completely misinterpreted what the German original was trying to do."

I nod.

"I'm interested in learning more about this man. I think you're on to something here," he explains. "I have no spare time on my hands to take on new projects, though, and I would hate to force myself onto a project that you are so invested in. By all means, you have my full support, and I am looking forward to seeing what else might come out of your research."

Judging from the look on Professor Ding's face, however, I can tell that he has another point to make. Reading the anticipation in my eyes, Professor Ding chuckles. "I was going to ask whether you would be interested in applying to Shanghai Jiao Tong University. You know, I would love to take on a student like you who demonstrates resilience, curiosity, and academic sensitivity."

"I . . . I'll have to see," embarrassed to tell him that I am actually more intrigued by the unsettled case of the serial explosions than Chen Haining's contribution to the history of science and technology, I nod again, awkwardly. I am almost certain that my niche is unworthy of scholarly attention. "If given the chance, then, well, maybe . . . "

Professor Ding smiles, a knowing look emerges on his face. No longer pushing on the issue of graduate school, he turns back to the news article again. "'The Kite of Jinan' is what the Germans called it, isn't it? I have certainly come across this name before, when I was browsing through archives," says Professor Ding, clearly confident about his own memory. "It's out of the parameters of my own research, though, so I didn't really pay much attention to it. Why don't you go look it up yourself? The library of the Chinese Academy of Sciences has the official journal published by the German Society of Industrial Science, *Industrie und Wissenschaft*. You'll find what you need in there. Given your talent in conducting historical research, I'm sure the task won't be difficult."

I thank Professor Ding again before we part ways. "I'm so glad that Shao Jing put us in touch. You're a brilliant young man," exclaims Professor Ding. "Please send him my regards."

• • •

The library of the Chinese Academy of Sciences has moved to a new building outside of the North Fourth Ring Road. The new building is much taller and more magnificent than the previous one, exuding an air of superiority tinged with mysteriousness.

Periodicals from over a century ago are only available by request. After entering the reading room, I hand the index number for their complete volume of *Industrie und Wissenschaft* to the librarian, a middle-aged woman wearing the library's uniform, which includes a pair of blue protective sleeves. Her hair is pulled into a tight bun, revealing a stern face. She acknowledges me with a slight nod, then turns on her heels and disappears into the storeroom behind her desk.

Left alone, I look around and find that I am the only person here. The wait, however, is exceptionally long. After a good forty minutes, the librarian reappears with a look of fatigue and frustration on her face.

My heart sinks as she opens her mouth, "What you're looking for isn't here."

"How come?" I'm taken by surprise. Speeding over to the reading room's computer, I search for the index number and point to the "in store" mark behind the title *Industrie und Wissenschaft*, gesturing for her to take a look.

She shakes her head. "I didn't find any of it in the storeroom, though. Maybe the periodicals were sold at the big garage sale when we moved into the new building, and we haven't had the time to update the system."

"You sell century-old historical archives at *garage sales*?"

"Fine, that's impossible. Then maybe it got lost during packing."

I blurt out, "do you mind if I . . . " then I cut myself short.

"Do you have a letter of introduction from an institution?"

I shake my head and look at her pleadingly. .

"Are you a tenured professor, then?"

I shake my head again. Not wanting to give up just yet, I maintain eye contact, praying silently that my expression is genuine enough to move her.

However, she seems to have already expected my response. "Sorry, I can't let you into the storeroom. Do you have any other information on the title you're looking for besides the index number? There's also a chance that the periodicals haven't been added to the stacks yet, and they are lying around somewhere in a box. We did just move into our new building, after all."

A sliver of hope rises in my heart. Grabbing a pen, I pull out the small notebook that I have been carrying around and copy the German title down for her on a sticky note. "This is the name of the journal I'm looking for. It's in German," I stammer. "Would this be helpful?"

The librarian frowns at the name. She turns around and reenters the storeroom.

Another forty minutes or so pass, and the tiny storeroom door creaks open again. Immediately, in the librarian's hands, I spot a thick, hardbound volume with a dark-brown cover.

"Finally! There are only three of them in total, and they come in bound books. Why, I bet that if you stick them in a corner, it would take another century for someone to notice them. They must be glad to catch a breath of fresh air, too, thanks to you!" She walks out from behind the librarian's desk in front of the storeroom and solemnly places the volume in my hands. "It's our rule, you can't possess more than one book at a time. I'll grab the second volume for you when you're done with the first one."

The weight of the volume on my palm gives me the feeling that I am holding on to a precious treasure. Not wanting to waste any more time, I sit down at the closest table and begin to read.

The paper in the volume has been yellowed by time, but the pages feel firm and smooth beneath my fingertips. "The library should laminate or digitalize these books," I mutter as I flip to a new page, extra cautious of my movements.

"Easier said than done. Lamination can also damage the original copy. These books will fade away with time anyway, and there is no perfect way to preserve them," responds the librarian.

The title *Industrie und Wissenschaft* is printed in cursive letters on both the dark-brown front and the spine. No wonder the librarian went through so much trouble—identifying an unfamiliar language is already a difficult feat, let alone half-faded prints. Beneath the title is the periodization of the bound volumes, respectively 1877–1897, 1898–1918, and 1919–1936. Spanning six whole decades, this journal

THE KITE OF JINAN

is unarguably a key witness of Germany's rise to industrial power. It survived World War I, but ultimately met its demise in the impending doom of World War II.

The journal is entirely in German. I start from the table of contents. As I have expected, I notice the name "HAINING CH'EN" in the table of contents of the 1884 volume, the year in which Chen Haining left University of Bonn and returned to Shandong. The paper he published in here should be the first fruit of his three-year-long academic training in Germany. Of course, I can't quite tell what the paper is about from its German title. I flip to the corresponding page, in hope that there would be more comprehendible information.

The paper is only seven pages long, too short to be Chen Haining's dissertation. The paper consists primarily of formulas and diagrams, save for a few explanatory paragraphs. Though I can't understand anything else, it is clear that the diagrams, despite being covered in auxiliary lines, resemble "The Kite of Jinan."

Encountering something familiar in this obsolete journal gives me the same feeling as running into a friend in a foreign town. With the help of diagrams, online translation software, and my close-to-nonexistent knowledge of mechanics, I am finally able to piece together the main idea of Chen Haining's paper: a hypothesis of using kites to measure aircraft-building parameters, as well as a documentation of his past experiments.

I recall what Professor Ding has told me about the news report on the *Rheinische Industrie-Zeitung*, and I'm baffled by his extraordinary memory. It looks like Chen Haining spent his years in Germany working on his aircraft project.

I expect the discovery of Chen Haining's paper to be a beginning, yet when I continue flipping through the pages, a sense of dread emerges. After Chen Haining left Germany, he disappeared completely from the journal. Was he so sick of doing research that he quit his projects the moment he left school? Did academia dishearten him so much that he degenerated into a fool who arbitrarily set off an entire factory?

No, no, it can't be. For some reason, I can't help but feel a fundamental trust for this man who lived more than a century ago. Inhaling deeply, I turn to the next page.

Out of the blue, I see Chen Haining's name again.

My heart misses a beat. Overcome with joy and excitement, I turn to the cover of the issue to check the date: 1895.

Staring at the numbers, I'm overwhelmed by the sense that I have found what I was looking for.

The librarian, seeing the look on my face, walks over to me. "What is it?" she asks eagerly.

Just when I am about to utter, "I'm not sure," a spark of inspiration hits me.

"It's an ornithopter," I say, a little breathless, my heart pounding in my chest. "A manned ornithopter."

I photocopied all of Chen Haining's papers before I left the library. Sitting down at my own desk, I begin to arrange the papers in chronological order. The ornithopter design itself isn't exactly the focus of my investigation; however, from the publication date of these papers on the ornithopter, I can finally see the hidden picture behind the serial explosions that took Chen Haining's life.

1884, 1895, 1898, 1900, 1902, 1910. Six different years, and six papers. Including the first paper on "The Kite of Jinan," Chen Haining published a total of six high-quality papers in *Industrie und Wissenschaft*, a highly professional European annual journal, in fluent German. I find myself marveling at this man. Even with my limited historical knowledge, I can tell that these results—produced in a time like the late nineteenth century—are enough to place Chen Haining amongst the top-tier scientists and engineers of pre-Republican China.

The key to assembling the miscellaneous puzzle pieces that I have discovered one after another is *time*. The years in which Chen Haining published his papers correspond perfectly to the years in which he was sent away from the Shandong Bureau of Mechanics. I can't help but chuckle in awe of how obvious the secret is.

Chen Haining spent three years in Germany and published his first paper in 1884, the year he left Germany for China. After he was recruited again by the Shandong Bureau of Mechanics, his research of the ornithopter plateaued out: twelve years of silence. Without further information, it's hard for me to imagine what had happened to him and his enthusiasm for engineering. In 1895, he began to publish again. However, immediately following his second paper, he was displaced from the Shandong Bureau of Mechanics and sent off to Xinjiang all the way in the west, far away from the major cities that were home to academic resources.

I am sure that his dispatch is a penalty. But for what?

The answer is evident: his research.

Chen Haining was sent away a few more times in the next couple of years, but just like the first one, none of those "exiles of shame" lasted longer than a year. Perhaps this was a struggle between his mentor's urgent need to "teach him a lesson" and utter admiration for his talent.

Besides, the year 1895 already says enough about the context in which Chen Haining's work took place.

1895 marks a watershed in the history of the Qing Empire. In this year, the Qing Empire suffered its most demeaning defeat ever since the Opium War: the First Sino-Japanese War. The Qing Empire, under the proud impression that its modernized naval fleet was ranked amongst the top five in the world, ended up almost crushed by the Japanese, which possessed far fewer resources at the time. After the war, the Qing Empire was forced to sign the Treaty of Maguan, which requested the Qing Empire to cede the full sovereignty of various lands to Japan. It was a thorough, national-level humiliation. Following the establishment of the treaty, the voice of the foreign affairs movement in China, a set of institutional reforms that advocated for Westernization and military modernization, soon died down.

What is more noteworthy is that the two capital ships of the Qing naval fleet, respectively named Zhenyuan and Dingyuan, were constructed as a result of Xu Jianyin's personal visit to Europe as one of the military modernization project's supervisors. In the same year, Chen Haining made his grand reappearance in academia and published a paper that he had likely been withholding for more than a decade.

I don't believe that this is a mere coincidence.

1898, on the other hand, is an unforgettable year in Xu Jianyin's personal life. The First Sino-Japanese War was already a major blow to his career and aspirations, yet 1989 posed a direct threat to his life. At the end of the hundred days' reform, a nationwide institutional reform that aimed to modernize China socially and politically, the Qing Empress Dowager Cixi launched The Coup of 1898 under the support of conservative court officials. She forced the reform-minded emperor Guangxu out of power and executed the most influential leaders of the movement.

Xu Jianyin, a tech-advocate, also deemed himself a reformist. Having joined the main movement at a much later stage, however, inadvertently protected him from the sweeping arrest. He escaped the capital in time with the excuse of needing to return home for a family tomb-sweeping memorial. Of course, he had to leave his work in Shandong behind. In accordance, the issue of *Industrie und Wissenschaft* that included Chen Haining's article was published around the end of the year, which means that as soon as Xu Jianyin left for his hometown in July, Chen Haining sent out the most recent version of his paper to Germany. It would take about a month for his manuscript to arrive at the publisher via ocean shipping; given that Chen Haining has already had experience working with the journal before and made a name, it wouldn't be too surprising if the editors expedited their review process and managed to print Chen Haining's article before the new year arrived.

Then came 1900, when an alliance comprised of eight foreign nations invaded northern China, including Beijing, the capital. The life of the Qing Empire hung on a thread. Zhang Zhidong, a major official who spearheaded the military modernization movement, was sent to Hubei Province down central-south. Xu Jianyin followed along. He established the Hanyang Firearms Factory in Hubei and began his series of experiments on smokeless powder. Evidently, he had no time to spare for Shandong, let alone Chen Haining . . .

The pattern here is clear, then: whenever Xu Jianyin was too occupied to pay attention, Chen Haining would immediately begin to work on his own research, submitting papers one after another to *Industrie und Wissenschaft*, in a way that seems almost childishly rebellious. I can't help but picture a boy left home alone when his parents are out working. For sure, this is not the best impression to give your boss and mentor, but perhaps for someone like Chen Haining, who was obsessed with ornithopter research, he couldn't have cared less for what other people thought of him.

I turn back to the materials for 1879, the beginning of the story: the year in which the Shandong Bureau of Mechanics was established, which consequently led to the recruitment of Chen Haining, as well as the year in which Xu Jianyin was dispatched by the court to Europe for a four-year-long mission to thoroughly investigate European technology.

During his time in Europe, Xu Jianyin ordered the construction of Zhenyuan and Dingyuan—the two flagships of the Qing Empire's modernized naval fleet—and wrote "A Collection of Europe Travel Notes."

Browsing through Xu Jianyin's writing, I notice that he had copied down an excerpt of a letter from Li Hongzhang, a high official supervising the modernization movement. It mentioned that the court insisted on adding two more students in the study abroad program to learn about shipbuilding and firearms and sending more young representatives to intern at German and French factories. The rest of the notes are solely about Xu Jianyin's observations of German and French arsenals and firearm factories. Undeniably, he put the goal of enhancing the Qing Empire's military strength above anything else.

There is no way that Xu Jianyin never crossed paths with Chen Haining. First, Chen Haining was a student of Xu Jianyin's own father, Xu Shou, as well as one of the handful of Chinese students studying abroad in Germany at the time when Xu Jianyin was dispatched to Germany. Judging from Li Hongzhang's letter excerpt, sending students abroad was a major goal of the Qing court at the time, hence it would be natural for Xu Jianyin to pay them special attention—especially Chen Haining, who clearly demonstrated an extraordinary talent for mechanics. However, Xu Jianyin made little to no indication of Chinese students in his notes, let alone Chen Haining.

What does this say about their relationship? I wonder to myself. With the question in mind, I bring out Chen Haining's personal chronical again to examine.

The third time that Chen Haining was removed from the Shandong Bureau of Mechanics, shortly after 1900, he was sent to Hanyang, where Xu Jianyin was working. Perhaps it was a result of Xu Jianyin's own concern for Chen Haining—that he felt like the only way to put this talented young man back on the "right" track was to constantly keep an eye on him.

It seems like Xu Jianyin's efforts was not so effective, after all. In 1902, Chen Haining published another paper. By then, Xu Jianyin had died in Hanyang while experimenting with smokeless powder.

A similar explosion, a similar accident, and a similar smokeless powder experiment, I think to myself. *Chen Haining was a witness of Xu Jianyin's death.*

Of course, I don't have any evidence on whether Chen Haining was actually present at the Hanyang Firearms Factory when the accident took place, but I can sense the vague possibility of vengeance, which puts a frown on my face.

Would it be possible that Chen Haining ended up resenting Xu Jianyin so much that he murdered him, and then framed it as an accident? After all, we never found out who triggered the explosion that resulted in Xu Jianyin's death. I can't bear the thought of resorting to violence when there is a conflict in ideology.

If that's the case, then, perhaps Chen Haining eventually committed suicide to atone for his crime and ended up inadvertently setting off the entire Luokou. But he had already witnessed the terror of an explosion once in Hanyang; why would he want to put thousands of people's lives at risk again?

I recall the clothes of Chen Haining on that photo reporting his death, and the metal accessories decorating the chest area. No, no, it can't be . . . if he simply wanted to take his own life, why would he be wearing such a peculiar jacket? It's obvious that his jacket was designed for a purpose.

I find myself stuck again. My heart is heavy with confusion. The pain of the possibility that Chen Haining might have been Xu Jianyin's murderer seems to have crystallized into an uncomfortable lump in my throat.

Well, at least I have been making progress. After reviewing my notes once again, I outline my process of deduction and my conclusion in an email, and then send it to Shao Jing alongside the photocopies of Chen Haining's research papers.

The moment that Shao Jing sees my email, he asks me to meet him in person to talk about my findings.

The next day, I arrive at his office. He is already waiting in the common room with his laptop and two cups of water.

"Have you read all of Chen Haining's papers?" asks Shao Jing the second I sit down.

"Well, I skimmed through them, but honestly I didn't quite understand what he was writing about," I answer.

Shao Jing pulls up the photocopies I sent him yesterday on his laptop and turns the screen in my direction, displaying all of Chen Haining's papers at once. "I don't really know German, either, but after reading these papers more closely, I think I found what you're looking for."

"You mean that he's been obsessed with the ornithopter? I thought I had already written that down in my email to you."

Shao Jing shakes his head, "No, not quite." He points to a formula, "The P symbol here represents power output, right?"

I nod.

"When Chen Haining published for the first time in 1884, he neglected the power output of the ornithopter's wings. Instead, he chose to focus on calculating balance of the chair in air, as well as the optimal mass of the weight hung beneath the chair."

"This paper was born out of the experimental data that Chen Haining had gathered before he went off to Germany. I'm guessing that he produced his final draft while studying at University of Bonn."

"Which explains the photo in *Rheinische Industrie-Zeitung*. Remember the kites? Chen Haining managed to fly the chair to the sky and then brought it to a landing."

"What about it, then?"

"Look at his second paper, in 1895. Twelve years later, he ended up with a working design of an ornithopter. Even if you know nothing about mechanics, you can tell that he succeeded . . . "

I nod again.

" . . . which marked the shift in Chen Haining's research focus. See? In this paper, he barely touched upon issues such as component design, size of the wings, and the frequency in which they flap in."

"Well, the kinetic data should be from the kites, and he must have perfected the ornithopter's design over the years."

"Don't you find him extremely confident about his own design?" Shao Jing winks. "Starting from this paper, he threw himself entirely into finding an appropriate power source for his ornithopter—he made no mention of the design at all. Obviously, he considered his design near-perfect."

"True," I lean in to scrutinize the diagrams. "I see he mentions the steam engine here."

"Yes, the steam engine. In his paper, the mass of the steam engine is a constant value," says Shao Jing, pointing to various formulas. "From here, we can infer that the weight beneath the chair in 'The Kite of

Jinan' represented the ornithopter's steam engine, at its optimal mass. However, the 1895-version-ornithopter was doomed to fail, because a steam engine with Chen Haining's preferred mass would never be able to output the amount of power required to fly an ornithopter. I looked up models of other ornithopters in history, too. Apparently, the major reason that they failed was also because steam engines—the power source with the most power output at that time—were way too chunky," Shao Jing explains. "This resulted in another shift in Chen Haining's research."

"Another shift?"

"In his 1898 paper, he discussed the impossibilities of applying a coal-fueled steam engine to an ornithopter. The burn rate of coal is way too low to supply enough power. At the Shandong Bureau of Mechanics, with resources at hand, he was able to conduct a myriad of experiments on fuel. Gunpowder was one of the options. However, no matter what kind of gunpowder he worked with, it burned too fast for the ornithopter. Honestly, his paper was more about chemistry than engineering. Then, in his 1900 paper, he suggested the use of alcohol-based fuels. How clever! He must've come to the conclusion after countless failed experiments. Alcohol-based fuels can sufficiently solve the problem of low burn rate. Furthermore, if he modified the traditional steam engine so that it could run on alcohol-based fuels, I'm sure that the overall mass of steam engines would be significantly reduced. See what he wrote in the conclusion? My God, he was even speculating the likelihood of applying internal combustion engines!"

Shao Jing's fingertip slides over to the 1902 paper. I inhale deeply, curiously anticipating what he is going to say.

"Now, finally . . . " Shao Jing shuts off all the other articles and enlarges the 1902 paper on screen, as if to make a dramatic introduction. "*This dude!* Just look at him. Why on earth did he stop discussing chemicals altogether in this paper? For some reason, in the 1902 paper, he began to hypothesize the possibilities of using human power instead. Though he argued that the reason he gave up on steam engines altogether was to reduce the total mass of the ornithopter, this is clearly a step backward!"

I frown. "He doesn't seem like someone who would make such an irrational decision. Why?"

"*Why?*" Shao Jing smiles. "For Xu Jianyin."

I'm utterly dumbfounded. "What?"

"Remember that Xu Jianyin died merely a year before this paper was published? How did he die?"

"From an explosion—"

"—Exactly. From that point onward, Chen Haining started to reject fire-related power sources radically, in a way so nonsensical that it almost made him look stubbornly foolish."

I feel the uncomfortable lump in my throat dissolve at once. More emotions are surging up, swallowing me whole.

"Even without understanding German, I can see with my eyes how many times Chen Haining writes down the phrase, 'fire isn't necessary for the construction of machines,' in this paper. Honestly, before reading this paper, I could never have imagined that a paper on engineering would sound so . . . heartbreaking."

"But didn't Xu Jianyin send him away from the Shandong Bureau of Mechanics to penalize him?"

"Have you ever mentored a student who was talented, but rebellious? I suppose that was the relationship between Xu Jianyin and Chen Haining. To Xu Jianyin, Chen Haining was his father's student, as well as a major asset to the field of Chinese engineering. How could he not have taken the young man under his wing?" Shao Jing lets out a sigh. "But their ideologies—their entire worldviews—were utterly different. One valued military strength above all and considered science and technology mere vehicles of modernization and social reform; the other, I reckon, paid little attention to the rest of the world and cared for the purity of academic research. Perhaps, in Xu Jianyin's eyes, Chen Haining has always been a piece of peculiar raw jade that needed to be carved into proper shape."

I am left speechless. Of course, I can refute Shao Jing and call his theory an unfounded speculation, but I can't turn a blind eye toward the overwhelming sadness seeping through every word and number of the incomprehensible article in front of me.

"There's more," says Shao Jing, opening Chen Haining's last paper written in 1910, shortly before his own death. "You and I both missed an important detail when we were reading this paper the first time. The year in which it was published was too much of a distraction. What do you think of this?"

He points to a word comprised of two letters: *Po.*

To be frank, I wouldn't have noticed it amongst all the German words anyway, let alone recognizing its meaning. *Is Shao Jing trying to show off that he knows German or something?*

Po. Surely it doesn't look Chinese or English, but it doesn't look German either . . .

Wait.

"This isn't German," I blurt out. "*Po* stands for polonium!"

Shao Jing grins. "Precisely!"

He pulls up another image on his laptop, which is a scanned version of a Late Qing newspaper. "*The Globe Magazine*, founded by the missionary Young John Allen to report on news in Western countries, wrote in 1905 that the Curies had discovered polonium. Though Chen Haining was in China at the time, as someone who followed the trends of scientific research closely, it was highly likely that he came across this report."

"I'm sure. Given the popularity of *The Globe Magazine* across all of China, Chen Haining could've easily gained access to every issue while working in Luokou."

"His 1910 paper is the perfect proof. The main thesis here is the burn rate of polonium. Chen Haining, after radically breaking with the use of fire for years, finally found a new way out. How did he even come up with these designs? Of course, there was no way that he could've conjured up the idea of nuclear fission, so he stuck to steam engines. You see what I'm talking about?"

I shake my head.

"He inserted polonium into a metal box. Polonium's radiation would ionize the air and the metal box would discharge, producing extremely high heat energy. With this design in mind, he attempted to replace the steam engine of an ornithopter with a polonium box. He never quite figured out how to calculate the burn rate of polonium, though, so his paper was nothing more than a hypothesis up in the air. Judging from his data, however, he must've conducted experiments too. I wonder how he got hold of the polonium."

"Wait, you said that he was using ionization to generate power? Which means . . . "

Shao Jing nods with a smug smile. "It was impossible to avoid electric sparks. Back in his time, he must've viewed electric sparks differently from fire. It was the sparks that eventually ignited the ammunition stored in the factory."

I am reminded once again of the strange jacket that Chen Haining had been wearing. "Did Chen Haining also learn how to shield himself from radiation? Thinking back, that jacket he was wearing when he died—the one with the metal accessories—was probably a customized protective suit. And the fact that the police found the protective suit on scene further proves that he was experimenting with nuclear engines!"

It seems like we have finally arrived at a logical conclusion. While relieved to find out that Chen Haining was neither a fool nor a murderer, I have an inkling that perhaps there are more alternative explanations to the case. "I have one last question. What really happened in Hanyang? How did Xu Jianyin die?"

"I would say it's a coincidence. It was common for accidents to happen to black powder factories at the time. Even the Shandong Bureau of Mechanics experienced a similar explosion in 1908, but luckily the casualty number wasn't high."

I know that I have no evidence to overturn Shao Jing's deduction, but for some reason, I can't get over my own version of the story—perhaps, an alternate history. In my story, Chen Haining harbored resentment toward Xu Jianyin for belittling him and deliberately hindering his research. As a result, the conservatives at court who wanted to eliminate the reform leaders used him as a weapon against Xu Jianyin and encouraged him to kill his mentor. After all, Chen Haining was also in Hanyang when Xu Jianyin died; surely, he would have the motive to commit the crime. Then, the conservatives plotted to wipe out Chen Haining as well, to stop him from leaking the truth. They didn't expect, however, that their leader Empress Dowager Cixi would die shortly after Xu Jianyin's death, which led to the direct downfall of the entire conservative party. It wasn't until 1910 that the remaining few conservatives managed to catch Chen Haining when he was least expecting, and they planned for him a death much like the one he inflicted upon his own mentor. They killed him out of fear, perhaps; or, simply out of a burning hatred for "modern" and thus foreign science, which eventually displaced the old Qing Empire that they had fought so relentlessly to preserve.

Though, I decide that I will keep my version of the story to myself.

• • •

About two weeks later, under the recommendation of Shao Jing, I draft an email to Professor Ding to explain our findings, attaching to the email the six articles that Chen Haining had written on the ornithopter.

After a nerve-racking wait that lasted about three days, Professor Ding responds. "Thank you both for uncovering someone so crucial to the study of modern Chinese science and technology history! I am not an expert in mechanics, so I need to ask my colleagues at the university to evaluate how probable Chen Haining's ornithopter design was. The good news is that a professor from the engineering school decided to take on our project the moment he read the papers, which means it must be worth further scientific examination." I can almost hear Professor Ding's warm chuckle and extraordinarily fast speaking speed.

Another month passes. Just when I am about to put the case of Chen Haining behind, Professor Ding follows up again with a short email and a few photos.

He is clearly excited about his findings. "The university established a special team on the research of Chen Haining. Half of the team is in charge of history, and half of the team is working on reproducing his ornithopter. Why, I couldn't have dreamed that a Chinese engineer who lived more than a century ago could single-handedly design such a cutting-edge ornithopter! Our team made minimal changes to his original design. The problem he faced back then was about the power source, but certainly power is no longer a problem. It looks like we can expect our ornithopter's launching party soon!"

Following the opening is a long paragraph about the ornithopter's economic and social significance in contemporary times, of how it could substantially reduce the length of aircraft runways and thus the size of airports. Finally, Professor Ding closes with a few short sentences that make me chuckle, "Please consider joining our research team! I don't want your talent to go to waste. Or, at the very least, you should submit a paper to our conference, which is taking place in a few months."

Responding to Professor Ding with a series of polite refusals, I click open the photos that he had attached to the email. Two older people who looked like professors and a handful of students are standing together on a field, holding various mechanical components that resemble wings, grinning at the camera. In every single photo there is an odd-looking chair—the replica of the one from a century ago that flew on kites.

Of course, the students would start their journey from building "The Kite of Jinan."

If Chen Haining could live to see this day, then perhaps after the strings of his kites were cut, he wouldn't have suffered the fall, I muse to myself. *At least his fall wouldn't have been as bad.*

Gold Award: Best Short Story of the 10th Xingyun Award for Global Chinese Science Fiction (a.k.a. Chinese Nebula Awards).

Originally published in Chinese in *Galaxy's Edge 001: Wonderland*, 2018.

貔貅

Pixiu

SHI HEIYAO

石黑曜

TRANSLATED BY ANDY DUDAK

Little locust, born in the dirt, forelegs treading, hind legs bent, long wings aflutter, alighting on a willow, asking Old Mister Cicada when he grows up, and when he gives birth; in January and February there is no you, in March and April you are born, in May and June giving birth, in July and August squandering time, and in September and October, you are returning to the underworld.
—Folk saying

Yandi the Flame Emperor wished to oppress the princes, so they turned to Xuanyuan, who practiced virtue, and built an army, who studied solar terms, and cultivated the five kinds of grain, and pacified nations, and nurtured the people, and measured the four directions. Who taught the Pixiu to be a valiant warrior, along with the tiger and the lynx and the bear, and with their aid he vied with Yandi in the Banquan Desert, and after three battles, he realized his aspiration.
—Records of the Grand Historian by Sima Qian,
   Royal Annals of the Five August Emperors, Huangdi Epoch

1

The first time I heard of the project was seven years ago.

By then I'd graduated. Even though my master's degree gave me some rallying power in the job marketplace, I was still part of a vast army waiting for work. After several months wasting time in my dorm, the move out date finally loomed.

I wasn't in this mire for lack of trying. My CV was all over the place. I was not surprised as an unemployed biology graduate, but after a few hundred CVs didn't yield even a bit of feedback, it was harder to convince myself the problem was only my field.

After my family learned of my situation, they advised me to return home and get a teaching job—that meant earn a living and find a wife as soon as possible. Their tone did nothing to ease my mood. I was running on empty when a company I'd never heard of came knocking. They wanted to meet with me and discuss something in detail. I immediately accepted.

They set up the meeting at a swanky, well-known wine café downtown. My contact called himself Xu Guang. He was dressed casually and seemed extraordinarily young for his rank. When he saw I'd overdressed in a suit, he was perhaps a bit surprised. Not long after we sat down, his boss showed up. After an exchange of pleasantries, they invited me to eat and chat. A few rounds of toasts later, I finally started feeling relaxed.

Then Xu Guang made his pitch:

They represented a medium-sized state-owned enterprise, Wuzhou Rare Earth Mining Industries Limited, under the jurisdiction of a mining group covering a southeast province. The company dabbled in investment—the wine café we sat in was one such outlay—but their core business was still mineral exploitation and smelting.

The boss, in his vaguely accented Mandarin, said: "Rare earth metals are more precious than gold. Do you understand? Explain it to him Little Xu."

Xu Guang held forth on rare earth elements, their valuable physical properties, how making alloys improved materials performance, and the fact that high-end electronics require rare earth metals for their very existence. "There are serious restrictions on exports. They're an important natural resource reserve in terms of national strategy."

I was pleased with my own natural resource reserve—of knowledge. At least something had come of all those chemistry classes. "Of course, and thank you so much for contacting me, but I'm afraid I wouldn't be of much use to you. In terms of mining, that is. I don't know much about it."

"We know that. On the mining side of things, maybe we could provide some training. But that's not what this is about. We've seen your dissertation. We felt maybe you could come and . . . give it a shot."

I felt I was missing something. "I'm a biologist. My research was on a strain of bacteria that, frankly, not many people care about. I tried to insert two gene segments, and I failed. So I don't understand . . . "

"Precisely. That strain that nobody cares about. That's just it. We need that little guy."

"For mining?"

"Yes. For extraction, or bioleaching. For metallurgy." He told me that in terms of salary I could rest assured. Although I wouldn't be part of the mainstream bioresearch establishment, I wouldn't be disappointed. I'd be able to arrange my own state-of-the-art lab, the company's best. "You'd be in charge of the whole project. Think about that."

Maybe it was the alcohol, but I felt I was groping for something in a haze. Some fixed but hidden future was looming in my mind. I couldn't quite make it out. I was pretty sure my biology education wasn't supposed to lead to this, but I couldn't find grounds to refuse.

Regardless, it was better than begging on the streets. So went my thinking.

"So, this project you mentioned . . . "

Xu Guang grinned. The boss picked up his glass to make a toast, and I hastily grabbed my own drink. After the round, Xu Guang began to speak, taking his time: "We're calling it 'Pixiu.' Do you know this word?"

2

I had in fact come across it, long before. It had to do with my grandmother, but I barely remembered.

Grandmother was a very traditional person. Her baking skills used to make me green with envy—from steamed buns and noodles to pastries and wontons, she could do it all. But her personality was difficult. She was crabby and tough, and once she'd made her mind up about something, a team of oxen couldn't move her. According to Mom, I was only a hundred days old when I first encountered Pixiu. Tradition demanded prognostication by straw-drawing on my Hundred Days Feast. My parents were college graduates who ran in science research circles. They were considered intellectuals and had little regard for traditions of this type, so they skipped it.

But in the end, Grandmother couldn't be talked out of it. Soon after my Hundred Days, she chose an auspicious day from her almanac and prepared a family gathering, complete with a ceremonial spread of food. After everyone had eaten their fill, Mom cleared the table. Then, with me in her arms, she approached.

The so-called drawing of straws was actually a red cloth on a table or bed for the display of various items. The infant was meant to choose one of these. Since the child had no discrimination, it would follow its inclinations and choose something at random. On the unseen, mystical side of things, the selection was supposed to predetermine the child's life. Grab a book, and you'd become a renowned author; grab a calculator, and you were doomed to keep the household books; snatch up a crayon, and you'd be a painter; a soccer ball meant a future in sports; a harmonica meant musician-hood; a mirror meant future fashion knowledge; and so on. A lot of nonsense.

I grabbed a sticker, a color image of a kind of talisman: broad wings sprouted from the shoulders of something like a panther, a beast of prey.

Mom says that when I grabbed it, Grandmother was overjoyed, clapping and cheering. She insisted I would grow up to earn a material fortune. Surely this was a good prospect. She had prepared the talisman with utmost care. Although there were other things on the red cloth representing money—a commemorative coin, a one-hundred-yuan banknote, copper coins from old dynasties—I had stumbled over those and snatched up the Pixiu without hesitation. Grandmother called it an image of wisdom. It didn't mean a future of small change or side doors, but abundant financial resources.

Everyone was happy to hear these words.

I caught pneumonia soon afterward and had to be taken to the hospital every few days. Mom and Dad were working and couldn't always do it, so Grandmother filled in. During this time, she would call me lowly names like Dog Head or Stupid Whelp. This was another of her old traditions: call a child a dog and grant it the tenacious vitality of a dog. This went on until I was over two years old and my trips to the hospital grew less frequent. Finally, she was able to go back to my original name. I don't remember much about this either.

But I do remember being very young and wearing a small pendant on red string. I remember the string seemed new, though perhaps it had been replaced several times. The pendant was a piece of resin lamination, the surface worn and scuffed and no longer transparent, though you could still dimly make out what was inside:

None other than that Pixiu sticker I'd grabbed when I was one hundred days old, according to Mom.

Grandmother had taken the sticker, and a lock of my hair, and she'd found a specialist to seal them in resin like man-made amber. She'd taken it up a mountain for blessing by a famous Taoist priest, rendering it safe and sound. It was meant to be worn and never removed, a safeguard of prosperity.

Perhaps because of this, Grandmother and I were very close. Later, I moved in with her because she lived close to my school. Every weekend she would make dumplings and pancakes and watch me contentedly eat.

She would tell me about the time Grandfather passed Peking University's entrance exam, then tested positive for TB. He was forced to go home and rest. He recovered but never went back to school.

Every time she brought this up, I would grip her hand and vow to someday pick up where Grandfather left off. I would attend that illustrious university. Grandmother would laugh heartily, and praise me and my good prospects, while caressing the safe and sound pendant.

"Do you know about Pixiu?" she asked after one of my declarations. I shook my head. She pointed to the pendant and said, "Originally, the Dragon King had nine sons, and the ninth was none other than Pixiu. Every day it ate riches and treasures, and then it got a sick belly and had diarrhea, making a big stink in Heaven. The Jade Emperor smelled it and covered his nose. 'Have you no sense of shame?' he cried and gave Pixiu an angry spanking. This sealed Pixiu's anus. It could no longer empty its bowels, just eat. So, its stomach soon filled to the brim with treasure. That is why Pixiu signifies accruing wealth and making profits."

This Jade Emperor tale made me laugh uncontrollably. I didn't really take its meaning to heart. Remembering this episode so much later, and the way Grandmother looked at Pixiu with single-minded devotion, it was like she fathomed my entire life. But maybe that's just my imagination.

After all, it was so long ago.

3

Wuzhou had become famous for its rare earth resources a few years before. Like other mineral products, rare earth minerals were under strictly enforced control in terms of exploitation. Thus, in name and fact, Wuzhou Rare Earth Mining Industries enjoyed seniority over all local mineral resources. Meanwhile, under the banners of wholly owned subsidiary companies, they'd achieved much in the field of investment. Nearly half the local economy was stimulated by the company, so it was quite famous too.

When I arrived in Wuzhou, the reception personnel wanted me to go directly to the R&D center and check in for duty, but I insisted on first visiting the mining site. I got directions and drove out of the city toward the nearest mine.

Several kilometers out, the air was already suffused with dust. Although the pit had already entered the last stage of exploitation, weeds growing on the perimeter aggregate, immense excavation facilities still roared and shook the earth. The roadway spiraled down the vast pit to the bottom.

I detected a faintly irritating scent.

"Sulfuric acid," Xu Guang said. I hadn't noticed him come and stand beside me. "After going through the primary filter to become refined ore, it's transported to a nearby processing plant to undergo sulfuric acid and high temperature treatment. This extracts the rare earths."

"It doesn't seem as bad as you said," I said, choosing my words cautiously.

"Oh really? The numbers are no cause for optimism. This is the third consecutive year showing negative profit growth. Most of the exploitable high-grade ore has been collected. We've lowered our standards to add new mines, but quality reduction means reduction in rare earth content. A ton of raw ore yields about half what it used to. Add manpower to that, and aging equipment . . . well, we need new ideas."

"So . . . "

He patted my shoulder. "So, let's see what you've got."

We went to the R&D center, but I didn't properly enter the lab for another six months. There was training in rare earth exploitation stages and workflow. During this time, I began to appreciate the scale of the task before me.

When it comes to copper, iron, and heavy metal oxide minerals, the primary refining method is high temperature dry metallurgy. For metal sulfide minerals and other types of minerals, hydrometallurgy is used, with acid or lye treatment coming first, then further extraction processes in the sequence, yielding useful metal elements, separated, and refined. Bacterial metallurgy, or bioleaching, is simply a branch of hydrometallurgy.

Bioleaching requires specific sulfur oxidizing bacilli, or rod-shaped bacteria. These microorganisms survive in relatively high-acidity environments. Their metabolism involves electron exchange with metal ions, oxidizing metal sulfides into soluble sulfates, and in some cases even generates sulfuric acid to accelerate the process. Ore thus treated by sulfur oxidizing bacilli, or *Thiobacillus oxidans,* can yield liquid soluble metal elements. At this point, as long as the bacterial solution is recovered, the required metals may also be obtained. When it comes to high-grade mineral resources, bioleaching costs a lot more than traditional industrial techniques, but regarding low-grade resources, it's the only viable option.

This was precisely what the company needed.

Project Pixiu was about finding a special bacterial strain that would target rare earth elements.

My predecessor had accomplished much. He'd taken bore samples at three different mines, a hundred samples at each site, and after lab cultivation, he'd conducted repeated screenings and independent cultivations. The remaining materials seemed to be the results of the last batch. He'd labored for five years.

Five years, and he'd never found an effective strain. No wonder he'd wanted to leave.

But I knew my predecessor had to have found something. Since Xu Guang wasn't telling me, I had to seek clues for myself.

After combing through all the data, I narrowed my search. There was a protein called Spi-213. Unlike copper and iron, rare earth elements are

SHI HEIYAO

not mineralized as sulfides, but as more stable phosphates, silicates, and fluorocarbonate salts—one of the reasons sulfur-digesting *Thiobacillus* was of no use here. However, ion exchange can occur between rare earth elements and other metal elements in mineral crystal lattices, and Spi-213, it turned out, could function as a kind of unidirectional catalyst, inducing replacement of rare earth ions in minerals with iron ions from the environment and combining them with polyhydroxy carboxylic acids.

The strange thing was, although all the relevant samples came from five sampling points in the same pit, no strain cultivated in the lab could produce this sort of organic acid, and there were no signs of the Spi-213 protein. My predecessor, after eliminating the possibility of exogenous contamination, had left an annotation: "ghost bacteria."

But when I saw Spi-213's spatial structure, I suddenly realized I'd seen it before. I hastily sought the old data, and there it was: a byproduct of metabolism in the S-fatty acid bacillus I'd researched. It bore a striking resemblance, topologically, to Spi-213.

That strain of bacteria I'd spent seven years studying was extremely anaerobic, and a participant in trophic mutualism.

Pixiu couldn't survive on its own.

Now I understood why Xu Guang had sought me out.

First, I had to take fresh samples. The original mining pit had been filled with waste by manual labor and was covered in vegetation. But with some effort, I found several of the bore holes.

After I had my samples, I did all I could to recreate the conditions of the original experiments. Unfortunately, there was no sign of the Spi-213 protein. This was what I'd feared. Too much time had passed between samplings. The physical and chemical environment had changed, and the bacteria had gone extinct.

Still, it didn't mean there was no hope. Embracing a can-do attitude, I decided to use the original sampling point as my ground zero and work outward from there seeking new possibilities. A few months later and several hundred meters outside the pit, I finally came across Spi-213 once again.

The newly discovered sampling point also happened to be a rare earth element peak value point. I tried to recreate the environment in a liquid substrate, and after many defeats, gradually began to find my way. It took several more months to obtain the Spi-213 protein, after numerous generations in culture.

That S-fatty acid bacillus of my former research was in the trophic mutualism category because of the unconventional way it kept its metabolism going. Most cellular life relies on oxidizing sugars to produce energy in the form of ATP. The S-fatty acid bacillus, however, in its anaerobic circumstances, could switch to breaking down fatty acids and benzoic acid sulfonate. This process consumed ATP, but this seemingly suicidal behavior didn't starve the bacteria to death. The product of its reducing, decomposing metabolism was useful to a strain of *Desulfovibrio*. In exchange, the S-fatty acid bacillus consumed some of *Desulfovibrio*'s ATP to maintain its life processes. In this interdependent relationship, both bacteria took what they needed.

My predecessor's failure made me realize that Pixiu's surviving form must be even more extreme than S-FAB's. It was completely novel in its maintenance of life. It could not, under any circumstances, survive independently. It had to rely on a cooperative partner. Since I couldn't find Pixiu directly, I determined to find its partner.

By adjusting the PH level of liquid culture media, and raising or lowering sulfide or sulfate content, I could selectively inhibit reproduction of certain bacteria, accomplishing my filtering goals. Of course, such adjustments might immediately kill Pixiu, but I rather expected to kill its partner and thus starve Pixiu to death. Under each targeting regime, and after several rounds of filtering, I expected to obtain the strain I sought, Pixiu's partner.

I don't remember how many times I repeated the process. One day I tracked down Xu Guang and showed him the genetic assay report.

"So, you found it?" After scanning the report, he lit a cigarette. When I didn't answer, he pointed to a DNA sequence and said, "What's this?"

"Pixiu's partner. A kind of *Desulfovibrio*. I hesitate to say 'host,' with the parasitic implications. It's really a symbiotic relationship."

"So why not get rid of it?"

"But they're—"

"Have you considered efficiency?" Xu Guang seemed uninterested in me repeating myself. "We need to simplify things. Just like crude ore becoming a concentrate. Have you tested these bacteria in terms of rare earth ore transformation efficiency?"

I shook my head, and Xu Guang nodded. "*Desulfovibrio* does not have the ability to displace rare earth ions. Taking the anaerobic environment into account, we would have to provide supplementary protein from the outside. This would waste almost half the resource."

"But if we separate them, Pixiu can't survive."

"I'm not denying that. Haven't you done gene recombination work before? I think it's time again."

"But I . . . failed last time."

"Since the bacteria would waste resources, we must remove it. You have more experience than last time, and you have our confidence. Please don't disappoint us." Xu Guang narrowed his eyes and got closer. "As for resources, we can, of course, provide. Just remember . . . we want results."

Insert gene fragments to make Pixiu independent?

I absently recalled that when I'd chosen biology, all those years before, I'd been eager to win the title of "life engineer." So why was I cowering from it now?

I had no answer.

4

"Why?" a boy once said.

Twelve years old and faced with this question, I had no answer for that either.

I wanted to flee, but there were others behind me. I knew I had no physical strength, so I didn't move.

The boy in front of me got closer and tore my safe and sound pendant from my neck. I tried to get it back but the others restrained me.

The boy held the red string and watched the pendant revolve. "What is it?"

"A safe and sound pendant. That's Pixiu inside."

"Pixiu? Ha! Hey Pixiu, you've got no anus, right? All you do is eat and never take a shit, right Pixiu? Ha!"

"Give it back! Grandma says Pixiu's gonna make me rich!"

"Rich? Really?" He tossed the pendant over his shoulder. "Hey, you still haven't answered my question. Why not lend me some cash? Are you deaf? Search him!"

I writhed and struggled, but my hands were secured by the gang. I couldn't move. The boy rummaged through my pockets and found what was left of my allowance. Unsatisfied, he glared into my eyes, grinning demonically.

He yanked down my trousers in a flash.

"Look! Red underwear! They're even decorated! Just like a girl's! Ha!"

That's when I discovered that closing your eyes only makes voices more distinct. I never told anyone about this incident, not my parents, not Grandmother.

I went looking for my pendant the next day, but it was gone. It didn't bother me so much. I hadn't planned on wearing it much anyway.

Grandmother asked after the pendant a few days later. I told her I didn't know what had happened to it, that I'd woken up one morning to find it gone. She said nothing about it. She just lit a few joss sticks in the home shrine and held forth on the animal zodiac.

Not long afterward, it was Lunar New Year, aka Spring Festival. Like others, I looked forward to a night of setting off fireworks—that, and the red envelopes full of cash that were distributed to children every year. But this year, to use my parents' words, I did not acquit myself well.

According to custom, the junior family member was to pay the senior members a formal New Year's visit. Then I would be entitled to the cash gift. But this was not simply keeping old folks company, not just chatting and eating with them. Grandmother and Grandfather were sitting erect in their chairs. Before them on the floor were two red cushions. I was to kneel in proper fashion, facing them, and touch my head to the floor three times while wishing them a happy new year. Thus would the old folks be appeased, and I would accept my red envelope.

So it had gone year after year, until this year.

This year, I refused to kneel. Grandmother beckoned me toward her, but I just hid behind Mom. Grandfather kept saying to forget about it, but Grandmother couldn't let it go. Dad pulled me into another room and quietly asked me why I was misbehaving. I sensed I was causing him to lose face, but I just kept shaking my head and insisting I wouldn't kneel. Even if it meant I wouldn't get my money.

After Dad left, Grandmother came in alone. I didn't dare meet her gaze.

She touched my forehead. "When you grow up, you'll understand. Whether or not they kowtow, you still have to give the children their red envelopes."

I cried, feeling somehow wronged.

We sat there in silence for a while, until Mom called for us to come eat.

"Your hair's a bit long," Grandmother said. "After the first month of the new year we'll have to get it trimmed properly."

5

There was no progress on Pixiu's transformation.

Not because I was hesitant to modify genetics. It was my work, after all, and I saw no fundamental difference between it and millions of years of natural selection. Of course, the opposition would say that natural selection is relatively smooth and steady, involving plenty of stasis, and therefor predictable.

But they'd be wrong.

Nobody can predict the future. The best you can do is limited inference or deduction.

This was, perhaps, why my research was stagnating.

Inserted gene fragments were expressing well in Pixiu, already quite an achievement considering my past failures. But like I said, nobody can predict the future.

Pixiu had been a carboxylic acid bacillus before forming its mutualistic relationship with *Desulfovibrio*. When I integrated a Desulfo gene excerpt into Pixiu, its organelles produced the necessary proteins to make it capable of oxidizing sulfides and carboxylic acid for energy. The latter was precisely the metabolite produced when Pixiu displaced elements in rare earth ores. However, my transformed Pixiu was still showing insufficient levels of Spi-213 protein.

At first, I thought the relevant section of the gene excerpt had been severed during insertion, compromising expression. I replaced several enzymes, but Pixiu still showed no signs of restoring Spi-213. I wondered if the whole plasmid was controlling the relevant gene expression. I tried to retain the original carboxylic acid bacillus genes, then insert the Desulfo gene as an independent fragment.

No change. The new bacteria could break down sulfides but couldn't displace rare earth elements. The inverse was also true.

Progress was stalled and time was dragging on. Xu Guang said nothing, though he did come more often to inquire about the work. Wuzhou Rare Earth seemed to be as well-regarded as ever, but within the company, the negative growth in metallurgy and exploitation was an undeniable fact. Over half of profits now depended on investment. Rumor had it workforce reduction would begin the following year. Several mines and companies were said to be slated for shutdown.

Although the R&D center was safe for the time being, pressure was mounting. After repeated consideration, I blended the purified carboxylic acid bacillus with Desulfo and delivered the liquid to Xu Guang for on-site testing.

And sure enough, it showed an effect. But analysis of reclamation from the liquid showed that transformation efficiency still wasn't up to standard. Without industrial value, its existence was worth no more than a joke.

I fell into prolonged, fretful idleness. I reviewed experiment notes unceasingly. I repeated experiments to no avail. I adjusted the liquid substrate composition, hoping to improve transformation efficiency. Ironically, what I'd already delivered to Xu Guang was the optimal proportion. To do better, I could only reduce PH while ensuring Spi-213 protein activity, but that would cause the bacteria to decompose. It would be killing the hen to get the eggs.

Pressure in the lab finally boiled over. I'd known this moment was coming, even before Xu Guang found me upgrading my online CV. He hurled my computer at the floor, smashing it to pieces, then harshly criticized me, ranting about my incompetence, all the money the company had wasted on me. I had yet to produce the slightest result. As far as he was concerned, I should pack my things and beat it.

I confessed I had no clear-cut plan. I begged for more time to think, to find a way forward.

"Find a way? You mean more time to polish that CV and flee like your predecessor? How about I give you a push? If there's no progress with the next field test, your ass is out of here!"

"Just wait a second."

"Fuck waiting!" Xu Guang slammed the door on his way out—and clear understanding suddenly dawned on me.

Spi-213's existence relied on the mutualism of two bacterial strains. Break that equilibrium either way and the protein vanished. Extremophile life must dispense with all useless or inefficient physiological functions. When a carboxylic acid bacillus can independently rely on an oxidizable resource for its energy, it may give up its partner's expensive, energy-consuming metabolism.

Instinctive choice.

It just needed a push.

There wasn't time to find another computer. I grabbed a marker and started scribbling on a window.

Since my objective was to improve Pixiu's transformation efficiency, I meant to increase the relative amount of Spi-213 while the bacteria were still alive. The protein was a sign of the two strains' mutualism. In other words, I needed to force them into truly dire straits and cause them to strengthen their interdependence.

It was subtraction, not addition.

I began planning new experiments and strategies, until the window-panes were covered in writing. Early the next day, the lab was forging ahead at full steam.

Results soon emerged.

After Desulfo had undergone some gene cutting, it could no longer use the nutrients in the liquid culture medium. For the carboxylic acid bacillus to survive, it had to first consume ATP for energy, then displace rare earth elements from ore with carboxylates, which would then get passed on to Desulfo for processing into sulfate. During this process, the energy Desulfo produced would be shared by both partners. In order to ensure its own sufficient energy consumption, the carboxylic acid bacillus had to increase its advantage, which meant substantially greater Spi-213 density.

Under an electron microscope, something I hadn't anticipated came to light: they didn't simply exchange carboxylates. The cell bodies of the carboxylic acid bacillus and Desulfo adhered together, became synthesized. They swapped cytoplasm, and even organelles, to directly exchange nutrients.

This was the true Pixiu.

I watched this intimate, miraculous scene until dusk, when the light outside began to dim. I turned on the lab lights and sat dumbfounded in my chair, becoming gradually aware of what had happened.

I'd created a brand new, independent life-form.

And its only reason for existence was to excavate rare earth elements from ore.

I suddenly felt an unprecedented dismay.

But its fate was already sealed.

Xu Guang read my Pixiu report and launched field tests immediately. When the first batch of liquid sample was poured into the experimental ore pond, I took my leave. I knew my creation would accomplish its mission. At the end of the test, the leached liquid would flow into a gathering pond, and there the blend of rare earth elements and Pixiu would be treated with a hydrochloric acid type reagent and further refined.

In my imagination, the resulting liquid was the color of blood.

I tendered my resignation the day after the test.

6

Because of my continuing higher education, I no longer lived at Grandmother's place. I didn't encounter Pixiu for quite a while.

In the new school, none of my classmates wore an eccentric safe and sound pendant. I was very happy to blend in.

Superficially, anyway.

It was just a normal fever at first. By that time the bird flu epidemic had passed, and my parents weren't too concerned. Unexpectedly, my common cold soon triggered inflammation, and my windpipe fell into the virus' hands. After I lost consciousness to my rising temperature, I was sent for an emergency hospital stay.

When I came to, Mom told me I was lucky to have gotten there in time. I might have developed acute pneumonia. I can't remember how I responded. My attention was drawn to a bedside plate of fruit.

"Grandmother came. She insisted on staying a while. She wouldn't leave until the doctors said you were in the clear."

Not long after leaving the hospital, I was summoned to Grandmother's place.

Passing through the front gate, an acrid smell found its way to the top of my nasal cavity: traditional Chinese medicine.

"Grandmother?"

I frowned, following the scent to the kitchen. Something had been stewing for a long time in the earthenware pot on the stovetop. A thick layer of stems and leaves—I didn't know what kind—covered the cutting board. Grandmother was chopping away with her thudding cleaver.

"Toad grass," she explained. "I asked around. This stuff cures inflammation of the windpipe, and alleviates fever, and detoxifies. You've had bad lungs since childhood. This stuff will work."

"But Grandmother, I've already recovered. You don't have to worry."

"Such a child! How can you not heed the lessons of your betters? If I say it's good, then it's good, so what's the harm in taking it? Do you know how much effort I put into finding and preparing it?" She turned off the stove flame and skimmed the upper layer of foam off the medicine, then ladled a bit of the thick medicine soup into a cup.

I explained I'd never taken traditional Chinese medicine before.

"What does that matter? You have to believe in this one. People have been drinking it for years and ended up completely cured of their illnesses. Drink."

I took the cup. A small piece of grass revolved in the liquid.

"Can't add sugar. That's no good. Hurry, drink it while it's hot."

Hence, Grandmother watched me choke down the noxious medicinal soup. Then she rubbed her hands on her apron and continued chopping toad grass.

I drank two more cups before I went home. They were no more pleasant than the first.

Late that night, I felt warm from head to toes. The cold air seemed to gnaw at my pores, and my body grew hypersensitive, particularly my skin. The slightest movement would produce a subtle, rejuvenating feeling. I could even ignore my gradually tightening throat.

Later, I was sent to the hospital for an acute allergic reaction that caused hives all over my body. I ended up telling Mom about drinking the Chinese medicine. I don't know if she requested it, or Grandmother decided on her own, but the next time I went to Grandmother's place, the toad grass was gone.

But the incense burner had been replaced by a new shrine, reportedly obtained from a fortune-telling master and capable of bringing fortune and warding off evil spirits.

An obsidian Pixiu had been placed within.

The next time I met Pixiu was after Xu Guang excavated me from a rural highland valley.

A small village temple on school property was being turned into a water boiling station, and many villagers bustled and protested around the construction site. My palms had grown rough and cracked over the past two years. Students had come and gone, but nothing had really changed.

"We'd like you to come back," he said.

"My work is here now."

"Two years . . . " Xu Guang studied me. "Even if you stay longer, what can you really hope to accomplish here?"

I had no good answer. I'd come up here to expiate my sins, to wield science and education against rural poverty. But it was an uphill battle, and we didn't seem to be getting anywhere.

Xu Guang swiped at his tablet computer, then handed it over. I browsed through a presentation, slower and slower, and last pausing on a photo.

"Pixiu needs you."

"You . . . what have you done?"

"A few small modifications. They're sexually reproducing now, but of course there are still problems. This time you don't even have to step foot in the lab. We want you as a consultant."

I handed back the tablet. "Would I have to meet that boss of yours again?"

"Boss? You're looking at the boss. Much has changed. And you know, with how we plan to reward you, you could rebuild here twenty times."

I knew he was telling the truth. He wouldn't joke about money.

While I was gone, the application of Pixiu had spread, allowing Wuzhou Rare Earth Mining Industries to not only become a model of innovation, but a leading minerals enterprise nationally. The government had approved the purchase of a special industrial zone, but following the launch of some new environmental policies that targeted mining industry standards, the cost of destructive exploitation had skyrocketed.

When Xu Guang found me, traditional mining was facing its second severe winter. On the road back to Wuzhou, I looked through the intro to the R&D center's lab. The biotech had evolved faster than I'd imagined. The success rate of inserted gene expression had gone up, and biological embedding tech had also improved, especially regarding invertebrates.

Despite knowing all this, when I saw the new prototype Pixius, I couldn't hide my surprise.

Ten or more organisms were slowly squirming in the breeding tank. Their unsegmented bodies moved via muscle contraction and expansion. Their backs and rears were encased in drill-bit-like spiral shells.

"The company wants Pixiu to be active and capable of movement," said the newly appointed R&D director. "The environmental taxes on mine restoration are too high."

"What you've done here . . . it certainly surpasses the old bacteria."

"It might seem so, but when it comes to the fundamental process of metabolizing rare earth ore, this new Pixiu is no different than your carboxylic acid bacillus and Desulfo. In fact, these new Pixius carry the genes of those old strains."

"And what are these shells?"

"Pixiu's abdomen secretes a sticky acidic liquid that erodes ore into edible grains. The Company wanted to find a way to consolidate rare earth elements for easier collection, so we altered Pixiu's internal carboxylic acid oxidizing process. Now the rare earth elements can be secreted. When they interact with atmospheric CO_2, a carbonate outer shell is generated."

I watched the breeding box attentively. A Pixiu's degree of liveliness seemed inversely proportional to its shell size. "Is there a growth limit?"

"This is precisely Chief Xu's point." The R&D director smiled faintly. "A shell grows until it blocks up the excretion passage. Waste material accumulates until finally causing organ failure."

"Just like Pixiu."

"Exactly like Pixiu."

"Such being the case," I said, watching him, "where is the problem?"

The R&D director brought me to a specimen cabinet. Inside were displayed a series of varying shells, the biggest around five centimeters. "Are you familiar with the Giant African snail? According to plan, Pixiu's shell should grow to fifteen centimeters."

"So why are they so small? What's the problem? Environmental?"

The R&D director nodded. "You hit the nail on the head. According to test reports, Pixiu is poisoning itself."

8

Grandfather committed suicide when I was in high school.

It was a boarding school, and I was in my third year. I only learned of the tragedy a week after it happened, from Dad's mouth. By then, Grandfather had already been cremated. Dad only called it suicide in passing, offering no details.

All I knew for sure was the death had thoroughly broken Mom.

Thinking back now, I was never close with Grandfather, but whenever I was confused, he was the one who could snap me out of it. There was a vast bookcase in his study. You could always find a variety of tomes there. To me, Grandfather seemed more like a friend. He was very important to others who loved him.

Mom shut herself in her room for several days, refusing to see anyone. I wanted to support her, console her, but all I could do was sit beside her and say nothing. Dad and I believed it was a short-term problem, that she'd be okay after passing through this period. It turned out we were right, though it was difficult.

Throughout the process, Grandmother didn't change. She lit incense every day, as always. Grandfather hadn't left a suicide note. I couldn't help wondering if this had something to do with Grandmother. She'd never learned to read, while Grandfather had completed half a college education. How had they met back then? I knew nothing of that era.

I knew nothing of their life.

About a month after Grandfather passed away, I requested my one and only leave from high school. That day was Grandfather's seventh and last Seven-Day ceremony.

In the house, a well-dressed Daoist priest brandished a sword and chanted scripture. Behind him, a younger priest rang a bell in harmony to an old cassette tape.

"Go on," Grandmother said, handing me a fold of yellow paper containing two joss sticks that stuck out half an inch. "Light them for Grandfather."

Stupefied, urged forward, I knelt before the memorial tablet and urn. The earthenware container was full of ashes. After Mom lit the fire, I threw in what Grandmother had given me.

Flame engulfed the paper. A unique sulfurous smell arose. The heat made my face sweat.

The ceremony lasted all afternoon.

Grandmother spoke with the younger Daoist priest at length. She never shed a tear.

Neither did I.

Eventually the ceremony ended, and I started cleaning the house. Grandfather had never liked the house in such a state. But when Grandmother saw me gripping the broom, she said, "No, stop. The priests said to wait at least a day, to let the Yin energy drain away before tidying up."

"Feudal superstition," I muttered.

"What was that?"

"I said you're full of feudal superstition!"

Grandmother recoiled, shocked.

"Come on," Mom urged, "be obedient. Don't be stubborn with your grandma. Have you forgotten basic manners?"

Glaring, I dropped the broom. I shouldered my backpack and headed for the door.

"Where do you think you're going?" Mom howled.

"Back to school!" I replied, matching her volume. Feigning a devil-may-care attitude, I bumped into the shrine on my way out.

The obsidian Pixiu fell to the floor and broke in half. The head rolled to the door. Behind the door, the hand-rolled dumplings lay in their cotton cloth, waiting for the boiling pot.

I didn't turn around.

9

A more detailed toxicology test report came out. The R&D director confirmed that Pixiu was indeed killing itself. While digesting ore powder, Spi-213 protein played a major role, but while displacing rare earth elements, the originally stable phosphate ions were affected by the acidic PH environment, and with other digestive fluid ingredients in play, an exotoxin was generated that destroyed Pixiu's immune system, thus triggering tissue failure.

No one, including the R&D director, understood why this exotoxin arose.

"Just like the shells," he said. "The spiral wasn't part of our plan, but we were just happy the shells worked."

This state of affairs seemed familiar.

Reading the data, I saw they'd completed many programs before my return. All were attempts to correct the exotoxin production process on the genetic level. The results had been lackluster. The experimental samples either couldn't ingest rare earth elements, or they quickly succumbed to the new toxin. In one case, the specimen even lacked an integrated digestive tract. It struggled for a few hours after birth, then starved to death.

Xu Guang had said that I was here for two reasons. First, I was familiar with most of Pixiu's underlying chemical processes, and the new prototype Pixius had been established on my previous work. Second, not having participated in specific work plans, I might see the problem from a new angle.

"What sort of angle?"

Xu Guang hadn't answered, but I gradually understood what he intended.

I had the lab suspend all gene-oriented work. We started from scratch observing Pixiu, objectively studying everything from physiological processes to behavior patterns. Meanwhile, I put together a small, special group, and we returned to the mining pit to gather new samples.

The research personnel didn't like these changes. Some even said it was a waste of time and refused to participate. When Xu Guang heard about this, he summoned me to his office. I explained my way of thinking, and he managed, with difficulty, to agree to my plan. He ordered everyone to do as I said or leave.

From then on, the lab became a quiet place. I had more alone time to observe Pixiu. I was amazed that a simple gene fragment could bring about complex and macroscopic behavior traits. For instance, Pixiu drew energy from transforming the rare earth elements in ore, but this wasn't enough to keep it going physiologically. It needed sources of carbon and nitrogen for replenishment.

The lab had intended to make Pixiu capable of eating a few simple plants, but Xu Guang opted for sealed feeding, or artificial, controlled feeding of proteins Pixiu could digest. During the planning stage, the R&D director implemented an idea to insert a new gene fragment in Pixiu's photoreceptor cells.

Pixiu didn't have vision as such, just a primitive light-sensing ability. But with expression of the new gene, it could be stimulated by specific frequencies of light. This stimulation feedback to the nerve center would produce a pleasant sensation in Pixiu. It would move toward the light source of its own accord.

Thus, all one had to do was put Pixiu's feed under the light source.

This new paradigm also led to elementary social behavior. Those Pixiu more sensitive to the food frequency discovered the food drops earlier. They were the first to take action, but at the same time they released a kind of pheromone to inform other Pixius. As compensation, Pixiu groups gave their food forerunners priority at concentrations of rare earth elements.

I sat before the cultivation tank longer and longer each day. I obtained new data, gradually coming to understand Pixiu.

At the same time, I began to have a strange, disconnected dream. I sat opposite Grandmother, facing her quietly.

Her face radiated an odd, serenity-inducing aura. I felt like I'd returned to childhood. Sometimes I'd wake, subconsciously trying to reckon how long it had been since I'd visited home.

After the objective review study came to an end, my little task force obtained the samples I required. At the next plenary session, I officially proposed my plan.

Genetic modification alone had been ineffective because of the vital connection between exotoxin formation and rare earth element transformation. The latter was, of course, the whole reason Pixiu existed.

The R&D director lodged a protest, firm in the belief there was nothing gene mods couldn't resolve. I retorted with Spi-213: as long as there was no way to replenish the protein, these discussions were meaningless.

"And what has your so-called 'special group' discovered?"

"Nothing," I admitted, but that hadn't been my original goal. I had the objective report distributed to everyone. "Everyone's work was consummate. On this point we should be confident. But now it's necessary to think of Pixiu as a new organism, one suffering from a serious disease. We need to think in terms of curing it."

I stood aside so the special group could explain their work:

There was a Clostridium strain subsisting in high phosphate density. It produced a protein called Nwa-019 that could, together with iron ions, fix phosphoric acid ions, and discharge macromolecular matter from its cytoplasm to the outside.

"So," the R&D director said, "we isolate the gene and put it in Pixiu?"

"No," the group leader said. "Think of it as a plan to cure a disease, not a protein processing factory. We want to alter the Clostridium to make it capable of living inside Pixiu. It would be a kind of . . . "

Symbiotic relationship.

Unprovoked, I suddenly recalled that safe and sound pendant I'd worn as a child.

10

After my college entrance exam, I quarreled with Mom about what I should major in. For my part, I wasn't loud. Mom persisted in her belief that I should go for something finance-related, or management perhaps, but I didn't want that. Not at all. The night before I was to fill out the form, we finally reached an understanding.

The next morning, I found something by my pillow: a resin-embedded gold pendant, a familiar-looking Pixiu.

"Grandma knows you're heading out to study," Dad explained, glancing at Mom. "She wants you to have it. If you don't want to wear it, hang it on your schoolbag or key chain. Or keep it in your dorm room."

I tossed it in my bag. In some corner of my psyche, I think I still reproached her, or myself, my own earlier helplessness.

Although we reconciled later, I didn't say a word to her for five years after Grandfather passed away.

During these five years, at Spring Festival and other holidays, I would follow my parents to Grandmother's. She changed a little. Chatting with my folks, she inquired after their health and nothing else.

Later on, Mom said Grandmother had taken up with traditional Chinese medicine again. She was obsessed with all kinds of healthcare products peddled on the street.

"We try to advise her, but she won't hear it," Mom said. Such reckless spending was not the way to go. She could end up in trouble if a real problem came along. I spent a week compiling research and science on what Grandmother had purchased, arming myself with numbers, charts, news reports.

I came and spread it all out before her. A pregnant glare reminded me that she couldn't read well, and even if she could, the charts and numbers would mean nothing to her. She frowned at one of the printouts. Her dry, withered finger shivered as it moved along a line of text. She had been deteriorating with age. I just hadn't been aware of it.

I sat by her side, trying to explain the basics. She said nothing. I couldn't guess what she was thinking.

"How about the pendant I gave you?" she asked about halfway through my lecture. I replied, and she launched upon her familiar explanation: "That is Pixiu. Old Folks have it from oral tradition that it brings wealth and fortune to your home."

"Pixiu's earliest official appearance was in *Records of the Grand Historian* by Sima Qian," I replied. "At that time, it was considered a wild beast like a tiger or leopard. It had nothing to do with bringing riches."

Grandmother quietly took this in. I continued my lecture on the unreliability of her healthcare products. Maybe it was just my imagination, but something seemed to diminish in her. Suddenly she was just a common, helpless old person.

"So," she said at last, "I shouldn't be buying these things, right?"

"That's right. Save your money. Exercise more. Go to the hospital for a checkup every six months. Much better than all that traditional nonsense."

"Okay." Pushing on her knees, she stood with great effort. "I'll heed your advice. You've grown up well, after all."

But I wasn't headed for Peking University, as I'd promised her. Not even close.

I said no more to her, or if I did, I can't remember what. I imagined the look of that long-lost safe and sound pendant. Pixiu, dim and lusterless under a layer of dust, stared at me and seemed to presage something.

11

I had no success.

My task force's Nwa-019-producing Clostridium was repellent to Pixiu. A long stay in Pixiu's digestive tract seemed out of the question. Nevertheless, I felt we were headed in the right direction.

The R&D director decided to alter the Clostridium's genes, rendering it capable of adapting to Pixiu's interior cell environment. I approved this decision, and it turned out to be right. On the night of the Clostridium's successful implantation, we had a party celebrating our heroic deed.

Xu Guang was surprised I didn't hole up in my room and update my resume. I joked that maybe I was getting too old for that.

Nine months later, the first batch of Clostridium-treated Pixiu reached the end of its life. Researchers extracted dark-skinned Pixius from the breeding tank and took the stiff bodies away for dissection. The shells were subjected to mass spectrometry and physical analysis.

Before all that, cursory examination had revealed an average shell length of about fourteen point five centimeters. The biggest was eighteen centimeters, an auspicious number.

Half a month later, the latest prototypes of Pixiu were put into practical production. Wuzhou Rare Earth's local media liaison convened a press conference. It was the public's first view of Pixiu's true colors. The anti-GMO crowd wasn't as vocal as we'd feared. I didn't even pretend to care about this.

I told my family about the broadcast time and Mom congratulated me. Later, when we talked on the phone, I didn't tell them that my dreams of Grandmother were growing less frequent, and that I was suffering from insomnia.

When I couldn't sleep, I would spend time alone in the lab. I would watch the slowly crawling Pixius in the breeding tank. I watched them drag their heavy shells and leave eroded trails on the ore surface until the sun rose. I told myself the experiment was a success. But I couldn't shake a sense of unease.

I started browsing the experiment records again, over and over, until one day I came across a draft of Pixiu publicity. The cover said, "Pixiu's recombinant genes are patent protected by Wuzhou Rare Earth Mining Industries Limited." But there was no mention of the breeding issue.

Something was nagging at me. I hastened to find the latest breeding batch number, then sought out the R&D director.

"Only three generations of Pixiu?" I said. "What happened to the fourth?"

"Fourth?" The R&D director raised a brow. "We never needed a fourth generation."

I soon found out that when Xu Guang mentioned sexual reproduction to me, it was indeed the tentative plan, but subsequent development revealed it had greater publicity value than real utility. Before I returned, most Pixius were unable to reproduce beyond a few generations. Xu Guang felt this was advantageous in terms of preventing unsanctioned breeding.

"If they want it," the R&D director said, "they'll have to buy it from us."

"And what about those control groups? Why is there no record of a fourth generation?"

"Because none were born." The director shrugged his shoulders. "As I think you know, mating frequency declines generation by generation. The third generation couldn't breed. As for the pre-Clostridium treatment samples, the exotoxin gradually accumulated. The third generation couldn't survive."

"You mean to tell me that the Pixius all become impotent?"

"It's either impotence or early death. But that's really ideal, isn't it? Benefit to the company is paramount. Frankly, I thought Chief Xu must have explained this to you already."

I hadn't talked to Xu Guang about it.

After the dissection report was released, I compared it with earlier records. Nwa-019 density seemed related to mating frequency. Why?

I couldn't figure this out alone, so I sought out my task force's leader and requested total confidentiality. He was silent after my pitch. I asked him what he needed.

"How about a month?"

I was very relieved I'd approached the right person. A month later, the research results showed up on my desk. Nwa-019 protein was effective, as we'd discovered, but as it eliminated exotoxin it also substantially reduced Pixiu's phosphorus content. This element was important in maintaining its original nervous system.

Nerve cells of low differentiation weakened during Pixiu's aging process, resulting in damage, and due to the reduced phosphorus content, this damage would be irreversible. This would trigger a continuous sensation of pain. The irritation would gradually strengthen, accompanying sexual maturity. By the time sexual behavior was possible, they would feel like their bodies were being ripped apart. It would bring their small brains to the brink of collapse. The nerve cells would have no choice but to shut down. This would leave them unable to distinguish other Pixius from the environment.

Thus, they couldn't reproduce.

Even worse, this reaction would get stronger by the generation—a complete deviation from natural selection, at first glance. But the previous, pain-insensitive strain of Pixiu was also the Nwa-019 rejector. It couldn't even reach sexual maturity, on average, and so couldn't even produce a third generation. As for the increasingly sexless strain, they lived longer and grew bigger. But the third generation couldn't differentiate mating partners from the environment, and thus couldn't produce descendants.

All of this was due to Nwa-019 ensuring survival.

"Is there a way to switch neuronal functioning back on?"

"I already tried," the group leader said. "You do that, and when they reach sexual maturity, they enter a condition like hunger strike. A few days later, they die."

They would rather starve themselves to death than live in pain.

"Mr. Xu and the R&D director came to the lab, by the way. They want data sorted by next month so other departments can get going on Pixiu commercial production, ASAP. You weren't here." The team leader wanted to say something but hesitated. "I thought you should know."

I had signed a contract with Xu Guang. I still had several years to go. But if I quit in advance, how much damage would it really cause? I guessed Xu Guang had probably done this calculation already.

The team leader and I stood there in silence.

"If you have something you want me to do," he finally said, "there's not much time."

12

Grandmother passed away in my last year of postgrad.

The omens began during Spring Festival: reduced appetite, yet no obvious weight change. Then, during her community plan check-up, her blood work came back with some abnormalities. The doctor exhorted her to go to a bigger hospital for more tests.

She didn't tell my parents. She continued going about her business for several weeks until something went wrong and forced her to get examined.

I learned of the results on the phone: intestinal cancer, late stage. Grandmother was sent to the hospital for acute abdominal pain. The doctors discovered a grave ascitic fluid buildup and were forced to take emergency measures. This was a matter of damage control, not a cure. Soon after, test results indicated her peritoneum had ruptured due to tumors of all sizes cramming her intestinal tract. She had lost her appetite because she couldn't digest or regularly defecate. A doctor told Mom they could carry out conservative treatment, forbid eating to clear the intestines, while supplementing with intravenous glucose, and wait for some restoration of health before following up with serious diagnosis and treatment. They drew up a treatment plan.

But we all knew it was too late.

During Grandmother's final days, she liked to sit in the hospital lounge looking out a window. One look lasted the whole day. I couldn't guess what she saw in the end. Pedestrians coming and going, maybe, or sunshine passing through leaves, or something else.

Later, she was taken home.

On the day before my dissertation defense, Mom sent me a photo. I hadn't seen how she looked in the end, until then. She was like a wasted candle, prematurely exhausted, life force drained, face withered, skin clinging to bone. A human skeleton.

I was in shock. I couldn't recognize that face. I couldn't see the person with whom I'd been so close as a kid. I had to suppress Mom's words from echoing in my mind: intestinal cancer, the tract crammed with tumors, no way to defecate. She had starved herself to death.

Just like Pixiu.

13

Outside my window was a shady field. There was no way to see that it had once been an abandoned mine pit, but I could foresee what it would soon become: the starting point of the future. As batches underwent testing, qualified Pixiu would set out from here, heading for places perhaps long forgotten, to accomplish their final mission. And all of this had, in some sense, originated in me.

How do we define life's purpose, after all? And who should provide the definition?

Back in those poverty-stricken rural highlands, I thought I'd found the answer. But I was wrong.

I wanted to find the answer in Grandmother's eyes. After all, she had believed in Pixiu more than anyone.

I didn't know why I was brooding on the sterility of Pixiu's fourth generation. Obviously, it had no real connection with the mythological animal Grandmother had always talked about. But I'd hoped it would become something completely new, a real, independent animal—even if it couldn't be depicted as a winged, feline chimera.

I couldn't conduct new experiments. The lab would be moved soon. Only the experimental records had been set aside for me. Records that could have been altered.

But I could still resolve this problem—perhaps. It was just that Xu Guang hadn't given me much time.

Spi-213 could bring about the exotoxin, which led to immune system destruction if left untreated. Nwa-019 led to chronic pain, the shutting down of neuronal function and perception, which made sexual reproduction impossible. This was the price Pixiu paid for existence.

I had thought of mining as Pixiu's reason for living. Now, looking through those piled experimental records, I realized mining was not its purpose, but its means of subsistence. We had designed it this way. We'd forced it to compromise between maintaining life and mining rare earths.

But this still wasn't enough.

I thought about Grandmother. Throughout her life, she resisted a world she understood less by the day, until both sides lost. But that was her foundation: simple and unremarkable justifications. She didn't understand compromise. She sought a way forward in the oral tradition of older generations. Hidden in those words, in Pixiu, was an instinct tens of thousands of years old—even if we were sufficiently clever these days to see it for a preposterous sham.

And even if life is hard, there's always the next generation.

This was just what Pixiu needed.

Its life was so painful. How could I give it the ability to love?

I charged into the lab and rummaged for the record I needed. I found it and inserted a new page. They would not be able to discover that the infant Pixiu's shell—no, it would start earlier, at ovum fertilization—would fluoresce faintly, invisible to human eyes, and this would last until the end of infancy. In every Pixiu, photosensitive cells attuned to this frequency would stimulate a reward sensation.

There would also be another change.

Pixius that could no longer shut down pain-producing nerve cells naturally starved themselves to death. They had to sense others of their kind, even if it was painful. At least they might know the joy brought about by new generations. A glimmer of light in the dark.

I wasn't totally sure about all this. I just had my hope.

I hoped, and I hope.

Perhaps, in time, there will be gene fragments to replace Spi-213 and Nwa-019, these that bring both pain and survival to generations.

But before that time comes, they will exhaust their strength, and raise their young, and for the glory of that moment, endure with patient restraint all the tribulations and evils of this world.

These insignificant Pixius will impart and inherit this conviction from generation to generation.

I just impulsively called Mom. I asked how Grandmother and Grandfather met. Mom burst into tears. She cried for a long time, then replied: "Those were hard times. They were introduced by a matchmaker hired by their parents. Back then, one family on its own might not survive, but two might have a chance."

I listened and found myself crying silently as a thought passed gently through my mind. It was a promise made long ago that can never be kept.

Originally published in Chinese in *Douban Read*, March 2017.

邮差

The Postman

LIAO SHUBO

廖舒波

TRANSLATED BY REBECCA KUANG

He called himself Jing[1], which was also what he named his ship.

To be honest, he didn't understand the full meaning of the word. All he knew was that a great creature by that name had once lived in the ancient oceans. His life was too boring, so he'd thought that a unique name might dilute the repetitive dullness of his days. That was the general idea.

Jing was a postman—an interstellar postman.

Radio signals could travel through empty space and light signals could travel through seemingly incalculable distances, but they could only transmit cold, hard information. Materials, warmth, and smells—these were more important to humans. It would have been a pity if there was no way to deliver these.

Interstellar postmen like Jing had thus risen to the occasion.

In other peoples' opinions, this line of work was very relaxing. If you wanted to, you could spend the whole trip in the cold storage chamber with the post and hibernate until you reached your destination. You

---

1 In Chinese, "Jing" (鲸) is the character for "whale."

could also go through the letters and read them using a see-through device. Although the matter of whether this violated privacy rights had been heavily debated in the Interstellar Tribunal, the practice was ultimately permitted. After all, not every postman wanted to hibernate. In any case, there were memory-wiping pills available at destination terminals. The postmen would swallow them in front of the mail recipients, and then it was like nothing had happened at all. Everyone was happy.

But Jing didn't enjoy either of these methods of killing time.

What he did on every voyage was collect messages from the boundless universe.

Jing's ship was fitted with additional antennae and signal receivers. They were extremely sensitive—he never missed a single message, even if it was only a short advertisement from a passing cruise ship.

As a result, the voyage records on Jing's ship always stored more messages than those of other ships. Even though most of the messages were from unknown origins—strange codes claiming to offer planets for sale, messy signal lines in snowflake patterns, or even high-pitched screams that sounded like they came from horror movies—Jing liked to listen to them all. He thought of these scattered signals as lonely creatures roaming the universe. Though it seemed as if he were searching for them, in truth they were the ones seeking him out.

Because Jing had discovered this unexpected hobby, he found his job fascinating. On the side of his ship, he'd painted what he imagined a whale looked like. That massive, mythical creature bore an expression of indolent satisfaction, opening its mouth wide to swallow a golden ray of lightning.

Jing also delighted in his everyday operations. While other postmen lazily delayed taking off, Jing spread his glider wings and rushed out of the port; his satisfied, slightly off-key singing echoing through the darkness of space.

Jing was, without question, the happiest interstellar postman of his time.

If only it weren't for what happened after . . .

The signal that changed his life appeared one afternoon. Jing was busy tidying up his storage, and he was unbearably tired.

He stretched, rubbed at his sore eyes, and prepared to turn off his receivers to go take a rest.

Suddenly, a signal broke through. Accompanied by red alarm colors and whining sirens, a line of text popped up on the receiver like an interrogation: "Reception confirmed? Yes or no?"

It was clear this signal had been sent deliberately—perhaps it was even a cry for help.

Jing didn't dare delay. He hastily shook himself awake and hit "receive."

The faint red display on the screen shuddered for a moment, then played a rather unfamiliar scene. Jing saw a house, though it didn't look like the solar-powered homes he was used to. Standing in front of the house was a girl wearing a blue dress, her hair braided in pigtails. She waved at him, smiling adorably, and shouted: "Hey! Dear Mister Postman, is there any mail for me?"

She recited an address: "We live at Rose Star City number 475, unit 901. My name is Lan Jing[2]."

As he watched her, Jing's confusion turned into astonishment.

He'd been delivering parcels across the stars for quite a long time. But he had never encountered someone sending a message directly to a postman.

This gave him a joy he'd never felt before. In the vast, boundless universe, someone had finally noticed his existence.

He rushed into the rear hold of the ship and looked through all of the parcels, then used the see-through device to examine their contents. Then he carefully checked a second time. But he saw nothing addressed to Rose Star City, not anything addressed to the signal origin location.

Disappointed, he sat down in front of the receiver. He deliberated for a while, and then switched on the camera.

He patted his cheeks and managed to squeeze out a smile. "Dear little girl, next time I'll definitely have a letter for you. Also, thank you for sending me a message."

The girl's smiling face really was too lovely. Jing couldn't forget it. When he reached the destination terminal, he even refused to swallow the memory-wiping pill. His client agreed with some difficulty, but he didn't seem very happy about it.

To tell the truth, if this had been the only time, then Jing could have only called it a rare and happy chance encounter in the universe.

2   In Chinese, "Lan Jing" (蓝鲸) means "blue whale."

Afterward Jing continued his life as a courier. But when he passed through that part of space again, he received another signal.

That little girl had grown up a bit. She still wore the same hairstyle and outfit, but she seemed to have left childhood behind. One thing that hadn't changed was her expectant smile.

"Hi, dear Mister Postman, do you have any mail for me?"

Her address was still the same. "We live at Rose Star City number 475, unit 901. My name is Lan Jing."

Jing realized that this signal was not a coincidence. That little girl was sincerely waiting for a message.

Just as before, he hurried to the storage hold, but after searching, he still found nothing for her.

And just as before, he recorded a video reply. This time, it occurred to him that the girl might be disappointed.

His spirits rarely fell like this. Before he reached his destination, he'd asked everyone he knew about Rose Star City.

Everyone seemed to have heard of it, but nobody knew for sure what it was. Some said that it was a city controlled by machines where humans didn't have to work. Others said it was a city of environmentalists whose habitants lived pastoral lives of farming and weaving. Some even said that it was a ghost city, where only one little girl lived.

This last speculation made Jing shudder. She must be so lonely.

"You should take the memory-wiping pill, Jing."

He heard a cacophony of noise around him; the voices of his delivery's many recipients.

"We understand that girl is very important to you, but you're an interstellar postman. You need to take responsibility for reading our mail."

"Would you mind waiting just for a moment?" Jing asked them. "I just want to figure something out."

He sat down. It felt like he'd realized only then that even though he'd put great effort into his collections, and even though he'd tried very hard to act as if his solitary travels were joyful and merry, the solitude of being an interstellar postman had still left a deep impression on him. That little girl's appearance had torn through his pretensions; now his longing, his worries, and his escapism had nowhere to hide.

If he didn't forget, how could he keep on being a postman? How could he keep on living?

This feeling was too awful. Jing swallowed a wad of saliva and gulped down the pill.

Afterward, Jing resumed life the same way he had lived it for so long before. He cheerfully redecorated the outside of his ship as the legendary whale took on new forms in his imagination. As always, he spread his glider wings and took off ahead of schedule, singing every time he took to the skies. His songs sounded just as cheerful as before, but those who knew him well thought that something about his voice had changed—either something had been added, or something had been taken away.

But what could it be? No one could say for sure.

Time flew past. In a blink, Jing the postman retired, and so did his ship.

He had never wanted to trade the ship away. But he had aged, and he didn't have the strength to fight for his old partner. He didn't even have the energy to decorate it anymore. He could only look on helplessly as the layers and layers of mystical creatures that he'd painted onto the ship's exterior were scrubbed away one by one. The customized antennae and receivers he'd installed were dismantled. Bit by bit, Jing's ship became a common vessel utterly lacking in personality.

He turned to leave. The maintenance worker called him back and told him that there were many materials still stored in the receiver. Did he want them? His aging mind, which had suffered the effects of too many memory-wiping pills, couldn't remember what he had stored there. He decided to have a look.

Jing borrowed a transmitter from the courier station and, hands trembling, plugged it into the receiver.

The screen flashed red in warning. Then the little, pigtailed girl appeared.

She stood in front of the house, waving cheerfully.

"Hi, dear Mister Postman, do you have any mail for me? We live at Rose Star City, number 475, unit 901. My name is Lan Jing!"

"Hi, dear Mister Postman, do you have any mail for me? We live at Rose Star City, number 475, unit 901. The recipient is Lan Jing."

"Hello, dear Mister Postman. You must be tired from your long journey. If you have any mail for me, please send it my way. I live in Rose Star City, number 475, unit 901. My name is Lan Jing. I'm the lady of the house now."

Those two sentences kept appearing in different variations. They became increasingly courteous; increasingly polite. The girl with pigtails gradually turned into a girl wearing sportswear; a college student wearing a graduation camp; a bride in a white dress; and then a young wife, who gradually became the mother of a young girl . . .

Jing's seeing and hearing had worsened with age. He had to turn the volume up as high as it would go, which attracted much attention from others.

The maintenance workers, the young new courier, and Jing's former colleagues all came over one by one, discussing the messages as they watched.

"After all these years, she still didn't receive any letters?"

"It looks like she wasn't just waiting for any letter, but something from a specific person? But it's hard to say . . . "

"She was pleading so sincerely, but Jing took a memory-wiping pill every time. Ah, how heartless."

They chattered loudly for a moment, airing every opinion under the sun.

Amidst the whirlwind of noise, Jing was silent. He didn't speak a word as he stared at the recordings that he'd long forgotten, yet had deliberately preserved.

Then he suddenly jumped up and set off at a run on his old limbs.

"Jing! What are you doing?"

The maintenance worker from earlier gave a shout and chased him as he ran. "You've already retired, you can't pilot the *Jing*. And if you use the ship for private, non-courier matters, you'll be sent to the Interstellar Tribunal!"

"I know, I know, but I don't have a choice." Jing's dentures had been shaken loose by the excitement, and they emitted a hissing sound as he spoke. He rushed into the station master's office.

The maintenance worker's words froze in his throat, and he fidgeted uneasily where he stood. He'd wanted to remind Jing that he was too old. Even if he found an interstellar travel company to take him to the girl right now, he might not survive the journey.

What happened next stunned everyone.

Jing didn't challenge the interstellar travel age limit. He also didn't risk breaking the law to pilot the *Jing* once again. In all seriousness, he made himself a "parcel" and handed himself over to the company, requesting that a courier send him to the minor planet where the signal had originated.

This indeed evaded all the possible risks and delays, but . . .

The voyage's outcome was not surprising.

Jing reached that little planet. But his body couldn't bear the heavy burden of space travel, and he passed away in the boundless universe.

As for the questions of whether that girl had received her precious message, and what exactly she was waiting for, the only witness in the affair—the courier who had delivered Jing—would only answer in vagaries.

More often, he chose to remain silent on the matter.

A long while passed. Then at last the young courier, after one too many drinks, told the whole story.

He'd felt uncomfortable about the trip from the start, so he'd accompanied Jing onto the minor planet.

What waited for them there was not the old house nor the smiling girl, but a sheet of vast, silent emptiness. That planet was an utterly lifeless world.

Jing dragged the courier along on a desperate search. They looked and looked, until they finally found it: sunken in the thick stardust was a tiny video recorder and signal transmitter.

A red light indicated the transmitter was still on. But it was now very faint, flickering on and off.

When he saw this, Jing gave a loud, hearty chuckle. He laughed and laughed; and then he didn't move again.

Rose Star City was a place on a planet that had existed three hundred years ago.

This planet had been home to a civilization spanning a thousand years, but in the end, the ancient land had been destroyed by the impact of a giant meteorite.

The interstellar communication systems of that era weren't that advanced, so the people of Rose Star City could only record their images along with distress signals and send them out to every small planet, hoping by some chance encounter, someone might come save them.

But the couriers now knew that their plan had ultimately failed.

"Too much time had passed," said the young courier. "That thing had already eroded, so it only sent out half of the message . . . Jing only saw that girl growing up, but not her cry for help."

The courier took a sip of his drink and shook his head helplessly. "In other words, the thing that engrossed Jing all his life was at best a message in a bottle . . . and was written three hundred years ago, so it's practically an antique."

Everyone fell into a silence that could have been for the girl, for Jing, for the destroyed planet, or for something else—loneliness. Couriers could never escape the loneliness that pervaded their lives every hour and every second.

Then the young courier began to toss back shots, as if deliberately fleeing from the subject.

The maintenance worker from before was now also an old man. He stood up, excused himself from the table, and slowly strolled out of the ship's cabin. The ship once named the *Jing* was parked outside. He couldn't see any traces of the creatures that once decorated the ship. But the *Jing*, sitting quietly, seemed ready to spread its glider wings and take off at the slightest sound.

The maintenance worker remembered the night Jing had decided to become a postman. He had looked at Jing, who was leaning against his ship, so excited that he'd started coughing. He couldn't help but shake his head and ask, "Is it worth it?"

Jing had only given a slight smile and confidently signed his name on the death waiver.

The maintenance worker then thought to the night when the young new courier's ship had first set sail. Everyone had heard Jing's singing again that night—that gleeful voice resounding toward the universe. Though it was a bit raspy, it was just as pleasant as always.

Something had returned to that voice. Now it lacked nothing.

In that moment, the maintenance worker thought, Jing had been an interstellar postman who no longer feared anything.

Whatever it was that had returned, it contained truth, loneliness, and death.

It also contained love.

Originally published in Chinese at
www.wcsfa.com (*Kehuan Xingyun Wang*), August 2016.

About the Authors

(in order of appearance)

Shuang Chimu (双翅目) is a science fiction and speculative fiction writer. Their books include *The Rooster Prince* (2018), *Academy of the Lynx* (2020), and *The Mask of Intelligence* (2022).

Liu Xiao (刘啸) is a programmer, science fiction fan, and member of the China Science Writers Association. He has won the Light Year, Future Sci-Fi Master, Len Hu and Dun Huang Awards for his stories and currently lives in Shanghai, China.

Yang Wanqing (杨晚晴) is a science fiction author. He has won many awards, including the Galaxy Award for Chinese Science Fiction, and his works have been selected as among the Best Science Fiction Works in China many times. His short story collections include *The Returned Man* and *Double Helix*.

Hui Hu (灰狐) is a retired military official and science fiction writer. His novel *Solid Ocean* won the Gold Award at the 10th Chinese Science Fiction Nebula Award. He has written more than 1.8 million words of science fiction.

Congyun (a.k.a Mu Ming) Gu (慕明) is a Chinese speculative fiction writer and a programmer from Beijing, currently living in New York, US. She was born in 1988 in Chengdu, China, and has published short stories and novellas in Chinese since 2016. Her stories can be found in *Science Fiction World, Non-Exist Daily, Flower City, Chinese Literature Selection,* and various writing contests and anthologies.

She has won multiple awards since 2017, including three Douban Read's Novella Writing Contest Awards, Masters of Future SF Writing Contest, the Best Short Story at the 31st Galaxy Awards, and the Best New Writer Award in the 11th Global Chinese Sci-Fi Nebula Award. Her first collection, *Colora il Mondo,* was published in January 2021 in Italian and will be followed by her first Chinese collection, *The Serpentine Band,* in 2022 Fall. Her website is metamin.me.

Liang Qingsan (梁清散) is a science fiction writer, researcher, and multiple winner of the Chinese Nebula Awards, including the Gold Award for Best Short Story. His academic paper, "The Edition Research on Wu Jianren's 'New Story of the Stone'", was published in Japanese in *Fiction Since the Late Qing.* He has published several novels including *Silent Winged Wheel, The New New News: Dark Shadow of the Magic City, Shanghai Girls in the Kitchen, The New News: Rise of Machinery,* and *Literary Girl Detective.*

Shi Heiyao (石黑曜) was born in 1990 in Qingdao and graduated from Beijing Normal University with a master's degree in children's literature. He won the first prize in the fantasy category of the 5th Douban Read Writing Contest, first prize in the 6th Future Science Fiction Master Award, and a silver award as "Rising Star of the Year" in the 10th Xingyun Awards for Chinese Science Fiction (a.k.a. Chinese Nebulas.) His books include *Lilia, My Star* (short story collection), *Exotic Surprise* (young adult science fiction adventure novel), and *The Wandering Earth: To the Dungeon* (an adaptation picture book).

Liao Shubo (廖舒波) has won the Galaxy Award for Science Fiction and the Starfire Award for detective fiction, and has published more than three million words. She is currently writing science fiction and thriller stories set in the Tang Dynasty.

About the Translators

(in order of appearance)

Born in China and raised in the United States, **Carmen Yiling Yan** (言一零) was first driven to translation in high school by the pain of reading really good stories and being unable to share them. Since then, her translations of Chinese science fiction have been published in *Clarkesworld, Lightspeed,* and *Galaxy's Edge,* as well as numerous anthologies. She graduated from UCLA with a degree in Computer Science, but writes more fiction than code these days. She currently lives in the Midwest.

Andy Dudak is a writer and translator of science fiction. His original stories have appeared in *Analog, Apex, Clarkesworld, Daily Science Fiction, Interzone, The Magazine of Fantasy and Science Fiction,* Rich Horton's Year's Best, and elsewhere. He's translated many stories for *Clarkesworld,* and a novel by Liu Cixin, among other things. In his spare time he likes to binge-watch peak television and eat Hui Muslim style cold sesame noodles.

Rebecca F. Kuang (匡灵秀) is a Marshall Scholar, Chinese-English translator, and the Astounding Award-winning and the Hugo, Nebula, Locus, and World Fantasy Award nominated author of the Poppy War trilogy and the forthcoming Babel. Her work has won the Crawford Award and the Compton Crook Award for Best First Novel. She has an MPhil in Chinese Studies from Cambridge and an MSc in Contemporary Chinese

Studies from Oxford; she is now pursuing a PhD in East Asian Languages and Literatures at Yale, where she studies diaspora, contemporary Chinese literature, and Asian American literature.

Judith Huang (錫影) is an Australian-based Singaporean multimedia creator, author, Rosetta Award-winning translator, musician, serial-arts-collective-founder, Web 1.0 entrepreneur and aspiring-VR-creator.

Her first novel, *Sofia and the Utopia Machine*, was shortlisted for the 2017 EBFP and 2019 Singapore Book Awards. You can find out more about Judith's work at www.judithhuang.com.

Emily Xueni Jin (金雪妮)(she/her) is a science fiction and fantasy translator, translating both from Chinese to English and the other way around. She graduated from Wellesley College in 2017, and she is currently pursuing a PhD in East Asian Languages and Literature at Yale University. As one of the core members of the *Clarkesworld*-Storycom collaborative project on publishing English translations of Chinese science fiction, she has worked with various prominent Chinese SFF writers. Her most recent Chinese to English translations can be found in *AI2041: Ten Visions For Our Future*, a collection of science fiction and essays co-written by Dr. Kaifu Lee and Chen Qiufan (scheduled to publish September 2021) and *The Way Spring Arrives,* co-published by Tor and Storycom, the first translated female and non-binary Chinese speculative fiction anthology (scheduled to publish April 2022). Her essays can be found in publications such as *Vector* and *Field Guide to Contemporary Chinese Literature.*

About the Editors

Neil Clarke (neil-clarke.com) is the editor of the Hugo and World Fantasy Award-winning *Clarkesworld Magazine* and several anthologies, including the Best Science Fiction of the Year series. He has been a finalist for the Hugo Award for Best Editor (Short Form) ten times, won the Chesley Award for Best Art Director three times, and received the Solstice Award from SFWA in 2019. He has been editing and publishing works in translation since 2011, which is how he came to know his co-editors. He currently lives in NJ with his wife and two sons.

Xia Jia (夏笳, aka Wang Yao) is Associate Professor of Chinese Literature at Xi'an Jiaotong University and has been publishing speculative fiction since college. She is a seven-time winner of the Galaxy Award, China's most prestigious science fiction award. Her science fiction collections include *The Demon-Enslaving Flask* (2012), *A Time Beyond Your Reach* (2017), and *Xi'an City Is Falling Down* (2018), and *A Summer Beyond Your Reach* (2020), the latter of which is published in English. She's also engaged in other science fiction related works, including academic research, translation, screenwriting, and teaching creative writing.

Regina Kanyu Wang (王侃瑜) is a writer, researcher, and editor, currently pursuing her PhD under the CoFUTURES project at the University of Oslo. She writes science fiction, nonfiction, and academic essays in both Chinese and English. She has won multiple Xingyun Awards for Global Chinese SF (Chinese Nebula), SF Comet International SF Writing

213

Competition, Annual Best Works of Shanghai Writers' Association, and more. Her stories can be found in her collections *Of Cloud and Mist 2.2* and *The Seafood Restaurant*, various magazines, and anthologies. She is co-editor of the Chinese SF special issue of *Vector,* the critical journal of BSFA, *The Way Spring Arrives and Other Stories,* an all-women-and-non-binary anthology of Chinese speculative fiction, and the English version of *The Making of The Wandering Earth: A Film Production Handbook.* When she is not working on science fiction related projects, you can find her practicing krav maga, kali, boxing and yoga, or cooking various dishes and baking her favorite desserts.

Made in the USA
Las Vegas, NV
22 November 2023